I MARRIED AN INCUBUS

Prime Mating Agency

REGINE ABEL

CONTENTS

A match made in Hell…

When investigative reporter Malaya Velasco accidentally uncovers the corruption of one of the highest judges of the Obosian justice system, she is framed and condemned to a life sentence on the deadly prison planet Molvi. In her despair, she begs the Prime Mating Agency for an arranged marriage with one of the Wardens of the prison. Her match? A sinfully handsome Obosian Hell Lord with a sharp tongue, intriguing piercings, and icy-blue eyes cold enough to freeze hell over.

After recently regaining freedom from enslavement, the last thing Kronos needs is more off-worlder drama, let alone a so-called human soulmate—who happens to be a criminal no less! But justice must be served, and a soul as pure and mesmerizing as Malaya's must be protected, whatever the cost to himself.

With their enemy always two steps ahead, both the life of his mate and the future of his House are on the line. Will Kronos be the protector Malaya so desperately needs while she proves her innocence, or are they both doomed to fail?

DEDICATION

To those who fight for justice, who speak for those without a voice, and who fight for the weak and the helpless.

Do not be eager to condemn a stranger purely based on hearsay or the harsh words of another. Judge them on their verifiable actions instead of letting yourself be used as a tool to realize someone else's agenda.

Evil hides in many places. A righteous face can hide the darkest soul...

CHAPTER 1
MALAYA

Standing in the Obosian courtroom before the foulest judge in the universe, I listened with seething rage at my sentence. Perched atop his high seat a few meters in front of me, Judge Wuras smirked with undisguised malice as he spoke the words of my condemnation.

"Malaya Velasco, you have been found guilty of murder in the first degree against Roman Pavel. For this crime, for your continued refusal to admit your guilt, and for your obvious lack of remorse, you are hereby condemned to a life sentence to be served on Molvi with no possibility of parole. May your punishment be an example for any other who shows such blatant disrespect for life as you do. May the gods have mercy on you for you shall find none here. Do you have any last words, Condemned?"

I lifted my chin defiantly, refusing to let that worm see how devastated I felt. Granted, I had known my fate before the trial even started—if that farce could even be called that. It still crushed me to hear the verdict that equated to a death sentence. In truth, death would be kinder than what awaited me on Molvi.

"All I have to say is that you may have won this battle, but you have not won the war. Your corruption will end sooner than later. And the world will know you for what you truly are," I hissed.

"Silence!" Judge Wuras shouted, jumping to his feet.

He leaned over his pulpit, his claws digging into the wooden surface, and his broad wings spreading wide behind him. Under the glaring light overhead, his four black horns shone with an almost mythical glow, just like his silver white eyes. Their pitch-black sclera made the irises stand out even more, as was always the case with this species. If not for the ashy-gray color of his skin, his cheeks would undoubtedly be flushed with anger.

"You are lucky that you've already received a life sentence, and that the death penalty isn't an option. But then, for a criminal such as you, and an unrepentant liar, death will find you soon enough once you mingle with those of your ilk on Molvi. Guards take this vermin away," Wuras said.

I didn't need to look over my shoulder to know my lawyer Torgal was shaking his head in discouragement. Alienating the one who held my life in his hands didn't exactly qualify as smart. But I had nothing left to lose, and I wanted him to know that I wasn't going down quietly. Even if I didn't make it out of this alive, I hoped his other victims would make enough similar outbursts to raise the suspicion of the guards and of the court-room staff.

Two such guards walked up to me. One attached the hook of his leash to the ring of my cuffs, then tugged for me to follow. With my ankles also chained, I wouldn't be able to walk with long strides. But all Obosians were naturally quite tall, and he didn't seem to care much that I literally had to fast walk behind him in baby steps to keep up. The second guard shadowed me, as if I could possibly do anything against them.

Sure, I'd taken self-defense lessons like most women. But at 5'10, and one hundred and sixty-five pounds, I looked scrawny next to those Obosians. They were easily at least 6'5 and two hundred and forty pounds of pure muscle. More even if you counted the weight of their massive leathery wings and just as imposing double set of horns. Under different circumstances, I probably would have found them attractive. After all, they looked like a cross between a demon and Drow elves, with their charcoal gray skin, pointy ears, and very pale hair with shades varying from snowy white to silver gray. And only on very rare occasions had I seen any of them with actual black hair.

But one thing they all had in common was their hard and unyielding obsession with obeying the letter of the law. Too bad the motherfucker at the top happened to be the only known corrupt Obosian in existence.

Torgal immediately followed, hurrying to walk by my side. He was the only person allowed to enter past the secured location down to the cells. I gave him a sideways glance, guilt instantly washing over me. He didn't deserve me making things more challenging than they'd already been. The Temern had fought tooth and nail for me. His bird-like species possessed empathic abilities that had allowed him to recognize my innocence right away. Unfortunately, while judges and local authorities often took their evaluation into account, their word could not be used as evidence of absence of guilt. After all, you couldn't prove they hadn't been bribed to say just that.

In his early fifties, Torgal had served as legal counsel in this court for the past twenty years. The Odiom sector handled many of the most serious crimes of all genres. As he loved a great challenge, and especially defending victims, he had faced many nearly impossible odds and won. He had been my only hope, and remained the one person that could help me get out of this mess before it was too late.

To my surprise, we walked past the endless rows of cells where I had previously been held pending my hearing. The other prisoners showered the guards with insults while hurling taunts and catcalls at me. A few of them tried to call out to Torgal to take on their cases. As much as I had hated being one of the only females in this cell block for all the harassment it subjected me to, I worried even more about where they were now taking me. There definitely was safety in numbers. I preferred to be exposed to the constant lurid comments of the other inmates than to be isolated somewhere with no witnesses as to what might be happening to me. There was no question in my mind that Wuras would want nothing more than for me to be permanently silenced as soon as possible.

We crossed another cell block before taking a secure lift down to an even lower floor. Once the doors of the lift parted, my heart dropped. I'd been sent to solitary confinement. I opened my mouth to express my outrage, but one stern look from Torgal silenced me. Why in the world would he want me this isolated? This was the perfect setting for an assassination.

However, I implicitly trusted the Temern and therefore forced myself to follow his lead. Halfway through the long hallway, barely lit with spread out recessed ceiling lights, the guard in front of me stopped next to one of the countless windowless reinforced doors which lined both sides of the wide corridor. He slapped his hand on the biometric lock and spoke his name. The door immediately unlocked, sliding open with that barely audible hum. Tugging once more on the chain, he drew me inside the tiny room.

I clamped down on the panic trying to take over me. Four thick stone walls enclosed the rectangular space, which couldn't be more than three meters wide and five meters long. A narrow flat surface with a thin cushion served as bed. Frankly, a stretcher offered more space than that. A toilet in the opposite corner with a sink completed the furniture. Despite the small grid way out of reach on the ceiling providing ventilation, I could already picture myself suffocating in the room. Worse still, there didn't appear to be any switches for the single light stone embedded in the wall. The guards more than likely fully controlled the lights. When they decided it was time to sleep, you wouldn't have a say in it.

While Torgal stood quietly inside the room, just next to the entrance, the guard unhooked the chain leashing me, then freed me of my cuffs.

"Sit," he ordered, pointing at the joke that would be my bed.

I complied, and he walked towards the door, his attention shifting to Torgal, while the second guard kept watch.

"You have twenty minutes," the guard told my lawyer before exiting the room and closing the door behind him.

A deafening silence followed the beeping sound of the door locking.

"Solitary confinement?" I said in disbelief to Torgal.

He approached and sat at an angle at the foot of the bed so that his dark green wings—the same color as the down feathers covering his body—could hang comfortably behind him.

"Wuras doesn't want to risk you repeating to others what you said in court. It wasn't wise to provoke him further," Torgal said in a slightly chastising tone. "But it actually works in your favor."

"In my favor?" I asked, baffled.

"In public, it would have been more complicated for us to freely discuss," he explained. "But this is also the safest place for you. Accidents happen in the cells above. Some species have long-range abilities that are not always easily restrained, or that the guards may not even be aware of. By the time they do, the damage is done. Solitary confinement has an extra layer of security, cameras, and strict records of everyone coming and going from the cell. If anything unfortunate were to happen to you, there would be no way for them to cover it up. You will be safe here."

"Okay, fine," I conceded. "But how do we get me out of here? Did Kayog agree to help me?"

My heart sank when Torgal averted his pale brown eyes and nervously rubbed the side of his beak.

"It is complicated. Linsea, his wife, is fiercely negotiating with the UPO's Intergalactic Affairs Bureau for permission to intervene," he said in an apologetic tone.

"Why does she need permission? What do they have to do with Kayog's mating agency? He saved Rihanna. Why can't he save me?" I asked, feeling both confused and outraged.

"Kayog is bound by the UPO in many ways," Torgal explained. "They had a vested interest in rallying the Yurus in establishing a peaceful relationship with the other inhabitants of their homeworld. Their Chieftain's marriage to Rihanna allowed the UPO to provide the Yurus with some of the tools they needed to achieve that goal."

"Then marry me off to some other primitive species who has something that the UPO covets!" I said in a tone making it obvious this should be self-evident.

Torgal heaved a sigh. "Unfortunately, that's not how it works."

"This judge is corrupt! You know it! He got me jailed because I got too close to exposing all the shady dealings and wrongful incarcerations he's been involved in," I exclaimed, vainly repeating what he already knew in my distress.

"You do not have to convince me, Malaya. I have felt your honesty from the beginning. Unfortunately, you no longer have any proof or evidence to hold against him. When it comes to lawfulness, Obosians are untouchable. Their entire society is built on their obsession with following rules and the letter of the law. Even though I know you're speaking the truth, proving that Judge Wuras is corrupt is an almost impossible feat."

"Which is exactly why he needs to be exposed! Based on my research, Obosians have very few criminals," I conceded. "However, the few that I did find have tentacles that spread far and deep. Surely the UPO wants to put a stop to that?"

Torgal nodded. "They do. The problem is that Wuras is extremely powerful. He did not take kindly to Kayog getting Rihanna off the hook. Right after that, he tightened the laws so that we can no longer use the same loophole. You will *have* to go to Molvi."

His words and the sorrow on his face crushed me. This was a death sentence. I doubted I would last a week.

"But do not despair yet, Malaya," Torgal added quickly when two loud bangs sounded on the door, letting us know our time was already up. "We continue to fight for you. I promise that we'll talk again before your transfer."

The door opening put an end to our conversation. The guard's icy-blue eyes sent a chill down my spine as he sternly looked at my lawyer. Torgal patted my shoulder in a gesture of encouragement then, rising to his bird feet, he walked out of the room, his long fluffy white tail trailing behind him. The guard didn't spare me a glance, content to walk out and shut the door behind him, sealing me in what felt like a tomb.

Over the next five days, my panic and paranoia steadily grew as I didn't get any word from the Temern. The only way I kept track of time was through my meals being served, and lights out in the evening, then on in the morning. The guards never spoke to me except the one time on the first day to tell me I'd be transferred in a week. That would be in two more days.

I had started making my peace with the fact that I wouldn't make it out of this one when a loud bang on my door nearly had me jumping out of my skin. It was too early for the next meal. Surely they had not moved up my transfer? I hurried to sit on my bed, as was expected whenever the guard entered my cell.

Heart pounding, I saw the red light of the lock turn blue, then the door swished open. A choked sound escaped me at the blessed sight of Kayog and the stunning female by his side, who I recognized as his wife, Linsea Voln. She was a high-ranking ambassador for the UPO. With her pristine white feathers, and the few dark specs on her chest, she shared the same color palette as a snow owl. But to me, she looked like an angel descended from above. The UPO didn't send her anywhere unless serious business needed to be handled.

Kayog, with his maroon wings, golden down feathers adorning his chest and the tip of his long and fluffy white tail, was also my knight in shining armor. Together, they formed a striking couple.

"You have visitors," the guard said in his usual clipped tone. To him, I was just another lowlife criminal, and he made sure I knew how he felt about people like me.

With infinite tenderness, Kayog gestured for his wife to enter first. He followed her in and nodded at the guard to let him know his services were no longer required. To my surprise, the second guard who had escorted us on the first day walked in with two stools that he placed in front of my bed. Kayog thanked him, and once again gestured for Linsea to sit before he settled on the other stool next to her. Seconds later, the guards closed the door behind them, the light on the lock turning back red.

"Oh, my God!" I exclaimed, my voice shaky with emotion. "I could hug the both of you right now. I thought you'd forgotten about me."

This wasn't even an exaggeration. Solitude didn't work well for me. Although I would not describe myself as a hardcore extrovert, I definitely did not qualify as an introvert. I needed to see people, to talk and interact with others. The past five days with nothing but four gray walls and my troubled thoughts to keep me company had nearly driven me insane.

"No, my dear. We had not forgotten you," Linsea said in a warm voice, while removing a small sphere from a pouch hanging on the discreet belt around her waist.

Temerns didn't wear clothes, their feathers and tails hiding all their naughty bits. They occasionally wore accessories like bracers, belts, or bags. While the Obosian guards had undoubtedly thoroughly searched them first, it surprised me they would have allowed her to bring in this device. It hovered a meter over our heads and a cone shaped beam of light surrounded us, indicating the area included in the cone of silence.

"A scrambler?" I asked, stunned.

"To make sure no one is eavesdropping," Linsea said, her gentle face slightly hardening. "You have made a powerful enemy who is highly displeased to see us getting involved."

"But you *are* getting involved," I echoed, the hope in my voice thick even to my ears. "Your presence here means good news, right? You found a workaround?"

My chest constricted when Linsea hesitated before answering.

"Not exactly. As Torgal informed you, there is no way around your going to Molvi. Our only hope is to pair you with someone on that planet."

I recoiled as I stared at her then at Kayog in horror. "Paired with a prisoner?! How the hell is that going to help me?"

"Not a prisoner," Kayog corrected in a gentle, almost paternal tone. "The goal is to match you with an Obosian or one of the employees on Molvi. But ideally, it would be with an Obosian."

"Are you serious?" I asked, flabbergasted. "No Obosian will ever take me. They're all walking around with a massive self-righteous stick up their asses. They don't care that I might be innocent. If Judge Wuras said I'm guilty, that's it. They can't make mistakes or be corrupt, even if the crime was committed right under their noses by one of them."

"Obosians can indeed be self-righteous in their belief that one of theirs couldn't possibly break the law," Linsea said in an appeasing tone. "To be fair, it is accurate for the most part. However, as one of their spouses, you would live safely with them in their fortress rather than in one of their playgrounds. You do not want to be stuck down there."

"Fuck Obosians," I said stubbornly. "Give me an employee."

"An Obosian would be wisest," Kayog countered. "They

have a lot more power. If you are paired with an employee—the majority of whom only perform repair tasks, restock supplies, and dispose of those who didn't make it in their respective Sectors—you will be quite limited in what you can do to prove your innocence. Chances are, you will remain stuck there for the rest of your life."

"Whereas an Obosian is the complete opposite," Linsea added. "With a Hell Lord, he chooses where you serve your sentence, which will obviously be by his side in his fortress. As his mate, you will have the ability to mingle with others."

"And travel off-world?" I asked, hoping against hope.

Linsea snorted and gave me a 'don't be silly look.'

"Obviously not. But you'll be safe. You may even convince him to call in favors to allow you to visit other Sectors and speak with the prisoners," she said. "The UPO is determined to see Wuras go down. But we need irrefutable proof of his wrongdoings. All your evidence was destroyed, so we need new proof. Right in the heart of Molvi, you'll be in the ideal position to get all the dirt on him."

I shifted on the bed, chewing my bottom lip while reflecting on their words. As much as the thought of being married to an Obosian didn't appeal to me—not to mention the fact that I couldn't picture a single one of them agreeing to this—I also recognized the validity of their arguments. I didn't just want to be safe, I wanted to take down Wuras and regain my freedom. To achieve this, I would need someone in a position of power able to give me access to my former contacts and, even better yet, to the other inmates wrongfully incarcerated by that piece of shit.

"Okay. I see your point. Does that mean you already have someone in mind?" I asked.

Linsea turned to look at her husband. He shook his head.

"I have spoken with a few potential candidates to assess their willingness to consider such an unusual pairing," Kayog said carefully. "I have not found your soulmate, although I'm getting a bit of a hunch. My presence here was merely to assess your personality to have a better sense of who could make a successful pairing for you."

I waved a dismissive hand. "He doesn't have to be a soulmate match. After six months, we can just divorce, and I'll be free."

My heart sank when both of them simultaneously shook their heads.

"You got a life sentence," Linsea reminded me in a gentle but firm tone. "The only thing that can overturn your sentence and give you back your freedom is Wuras's demise."

"This also means that it is imperative that you find a way to please whoever you are paired with," Kayog cautioned me.

"What does that mean?" I asked, my stomach knotting with an unpleasant suspicion.

"It means that your mate is the only one who can terminate your union after the six-month trial, if he is displeased with you," Kayog explained. "Should that happen, you will be sent to one of the prison Sectors below to serve the rest of your sentence. Therefore, my priority is to find your soulmate. But failing that, I want someone who you can have a good life with for the long term."

I stared at him in shock. "You think I will fail in my efforts to find proof," I whispered, crestfallen.

Once more, the Temern shook his head. "We think taking down Wuras will be hard and will take a long time. Chances are, it will take longer than those six months. For this reason, I'd rather you spent this long time with someone who makes you happy and who won't divorce you as soon as the trial period has ended."

"We just need you to continue to have faith," Linsea added in a reassuring tone. "We are fighting for you. On the day of your transfer, we promise it will be for you to meet your chosen mate."

CHAPTER 2
KRONOS

I glared balefully at the transport shuttle approaching my landing pad. What in Tharmok's name could an ambassador of the United Planets Organization possibly want with me? Surely this wasn't still about that monumental mess on Shimli? That shameful part of my past only deserved to be forgotten. I, an Obosian of the Warrior caste, firstborn son of the noble House Aramon, captured as a slave by a wretched Nazhral. If not for the treacherous way in which they had drugged my drink during an official off-world reception, Saydi and her goons never would have gotten the best of me. I could reduce them all to ashes by merely lifting my hand.

Could Saydi be the reason for their presence?

As was my due, I had demanded she serve her sentence in my playground. The stupid female had thought to try and impose her law on the inmates. She'd found out the hard way the true meaning of survival of the fittest. The males and females alike in the Quadrant I'd placed her had gone out of their way to make an example out of her. Finding out the horrible experiments she'd performed on young Edocits—a dryad-like species—to create a new, highly addictive drug she intended to flood the market with didn't endear her to the others.

For all their faults, even the most vicious of my prisoners—all rounded up in Quadrant Four—held no love for those who harmed juveniles. As my people fed on emotions, I had gorged more than once on Saydi's pain and terror in the days following her arrival as the prisoners put her in her place. As with most of my new toys, I'd quickly lost interest and hadn't paid attention to what kind of treatment she continued to receive. The last time I'd flown over her Quadrant, she'd seemed fairly broken, her former beauty defaced by many nasty scars.

If they're here to get Saydi back, will I grant them their request?

By law, no one could remove a prisoner from Molvi unless that inmate had died, had completed their sentence, or had received a pardon—which never happened. The only other option would be if a High Judge granted a temporary extradition ruling for the purpose of an off-world investigation or hearing. And even then, the Warden of his Sector would need to consent.

I could refuse and only allow her to testify remotely.

While I didn't consider myself as particularly cruel, the thought of granting Saydi any kind of reprieve and comfort while on an off-world trip to go testify in another case rubbed me the wrong way. She deserved constant and endless pain, like she had inflicted on those young Edocits for years.

But I would wait and see what arguments the Ambassador would lay down before passing judgment.

Once the shuttle completed its landing, I slowly approached as the ramp lowered, and the doors parted. To my shock, it wasn't just Ambassador Linsea Voln who disembarked, but her husband Kayog as well. What in Tharmok's name was the matchmaker possibly doing here?

My spine stiffened, and I narrowed my eyes at him with suspicion as they closed the distance.

"If you're here to ask me to release a prisoner for one of your matchmakings, the answer is no," I said preemptively in an imperative tone. "Whoever you want to pair with one of my wards will have to come and settle on Molvi with their match."

"That's exactly the goal!" Master Voln said with enthusiasm, taking me aback. "And hello, Lord Aramon. As you've apparently guessed, I am Kayog Voln—though I would prefer you simply call me Kayog. And this is my lovely wife, Linsea Voln, whom I understand you've met before."

I scrunched my face for the not-so-subtle way he'd pointed out my rudeness in not properly greeting them upon their arrival before launching into my diatribe.

"I have indeed," I said begrudgingly. "Welcome to Molvi, Linsea, Kayog," I said, nodding at each of them in turn, before staring at Kayog. "You may call me Kronos."

"Excellent!" Kayog said with the same enthusiasm that had me instantly annoyed—which only seemed to amuse him.

His behavior screamed that they had something to say that would highly displease me, but he felt confident he'd get his way.

"We have much to discuss," Kayog said, giving me a pointed look. "Serious matters."

Once again, I felt irritated for my continued failure to show myself hospitable at this even less subtle hint that I should invite them in and provide them with some basic comforts.

"Then let's go to my office. This way," I said in a grumpy tone.

I wasn't trying to be rude, but I also didn't have much time to grant them. Furthermore, I really didn't particularly care about whatever had brought them here. I enjoyed keeping to myself and minding my own affairs. Off-worlder issues were of little consequence to me.

As I led them to my office, they ogled my domain with

appreciative glances. No doubt realizing—or sensing through their empathic abilities—that I wouldn't welcome small talk, they spared me the usual polite flattery one makes under similar circumstances. I opened the door, stepping into my office first, then waving them in. For a split second, I considered pulling a couple of chairs in front of my desk then thought better of it. Despite my annoyance, I'd been rude enough for one day. They did not deserve me being such an ungracious host. But reminders of my time as a slave—brief though it had been—always brought out the most unpleasant side of me.

"Have a seat," I said in a slightly less grumpy tone while gesturing at the comfortable set of couches in the seating area next to the patio door onto one of the many terraces of my domain.

"Thank you," Linsea said with a grateful smile that further fanned my blossoming guilt.

She had been extremely kind and considerate to me and the other prisoners after the Enforcers had freed us from captivity.

They settled in the large couch across from the chair I headed towards. I couldn't repress an amused smile at their contented expressions at finding the back support at a convenient enough height to accommodate their rather beautiful sets of feathery wings. Obviously, Obosian furniture sought to accommodate our own leathery wings.

"Do you wish for beverages or other refreshments?" I asked, finally remembering my manners.

Relief flooded through me when they simultaneously shook their heads.

"Thank you but that will not be necessary," Kayog replied. "We do not intend to abuse too much of your time."

By the subtle spark of amusement in their eyes, their empathic abilities had no doubt betrayed my uncharitable thoughts.

I grunted in response and settled down in the chair facing them.

"So what important matter do we need to discuss?" I asked, going straight to the point.

"We are here on a mission to stop major criminal activities and protect innocents who have been seriously wronged," Linsea said.

I perked up upon hearing those words. "You have my attention."

Linsea smiled. When it came to upholding the law, we Obosian could be amusingly predictable. However, the quickness with which her smile faded set all my senses on high alert.

"What we are about to share with you will be shocking. Please hear us out with an open mind," Linsea said carefully, her words making me even more suspicious. "A very important member of your society, Judge Wuras, has become corrupt and needs to be stopped."

I jumped to my feet, my *lumiak* surging from my fingertips, the electrical tendrils crawling around my hands as I glared at the couple in outraged anger at such slander.

"You dare?" I exclaimed.

"Peace, Kronos," Kayog said in a soothing voice, his palm raised in an appeasing gesture.

"You can see souls. Do you see any deception in ours?" Linsea asked in a similar tone.

Like her husband, she had remained seated, their bodies relaxed, unthreatening, and unafraid. I shifted my vision. The glowing lights of their souls shone bright... and pure.

"Please, sit," Linsea said in a soft voice, gesturing at my chair.

Teeth clenched, I doused my *lumiak* and reluctantly resumed my seat. "There must be a mistake. Wuras is the highest-ranking and most powerful Obosian judge of our times," I argued.

"He is," Linsea concurred. "But as you're probably aware, great power has a tendency to corrupt those who wield it."

"Even if this was true—not that I believe it—why bring this to me?" I demanded.

Linsea shifted her pristine white wings and clasped her hands on her thighs with graceful movements.

"A reporter was investigating him," she said, choosing her words carefully. "She had gathered irrefutable evidence against him, and she had scheduled a meeting with the Enforcers to hand what she found over to them. That very day, the Obosian police force conveniently arrested her for murder."

"The person with the so-called proof is a criminal?!" I exclaimed, wondering how they could be so gullible.

"No," Linsea said forcefully. "Wuras set her up in order to silence her. As proven by your reaction just now, who would believe a convicted murderer over a highly respected judge? She's innocent."

Once more, I peered at their souls. Whatever the truth of the matter turned out to be, they genuinely believed what they were telling me. But this couldn't possibly be real.

"We have three Temerns working at the Obosian courthouse and defending cases before him. Over the past few years, he has convicted at least eight people whose innocence we're one hundred percent convinced of. Wuras didn't care. According to their empathic assessment of the judge, those people were condemned before their trial even began. I know this is difficult for you to accept or contemplate as being in the realm of possible, but we are being honest."

"I know," I said in a dejected tone before leaning back in my seat, my wheels spinning. "I can see that you believe everything you are saying. However, Wuras is Obosian. I do not need to tell you that my people uphold the law to a fault. It defines not only our society but who we are as individuals. I cannot accept what you are saying as factual, no matter how much *you* believe it to be."

"The guards and the clerks at the courthouse both fear and despise him," Linsea added in a passionate tone, leaning forward in an unconscious effort to convince me. "He has something on them or is blackmailing them."

"Are you saying that the guards are corrupt, too?" I asked, rolling my eyes, and making it clear they had now lost what sliver of credibility they held with me.

She shook her head, unfazed by my reaction. "No. The vast majority of them are not. But we suspect that Wuras has issued threats of framing them or their loved ones if any of them dared to expose him. If that were to occur, we both know who would be believed over who."

I hated this, all of it. I ground my teeth for a few seconds while reflecting on their words.

"Even assuming this fantastic tale of yours was true, why bring this to me? What do you expect me to do about it?" I asked.

"As you accurately guessed based on my presence, we are here to match Malaya," Kayog said. "We want a match that will allow her to pursue her investigation and nail Wuras. At least one of his victims is actually your ward and imprisoned in your Sector."

I pursed my lips and slowly nodded. "While I fail to see how that will help her investigation, and although we do not normally perform weddings for the inmates, I can have it arranged, if it will help you."

Despite the stiffness of his beak, Kayog gave me a mocking smile in response to my words.

"We're not looking to match her with a prisoner, Lord Kronos," Kayog said. "We want to match her with you."

I abruptly straightened in my chair, barely stopping myself

from jumping to my feet upon hearing such an outrageous suggestion.

"Me? Have you lost your minds? Why in Tharmok's name would I marry a murderer?!"

"She's innocent," Linsea interjected.

"She's been convicted," I said in a tone that brooked no argument. "Therefore, by law, she's a criminal. You may be sincere in your belief that Wuras is corrupt, but I'll need far more than your *belief* to be swayed."

"We came to you first because Malaya is your soulmate," Kayog said in a factual manner.

"WHAT?! You truly are insane."

Kayog scoffed. "Not to brag, but I'm sure you've heard of my reputation when it comes to matchmaking. I have never been wrong, and I'm not this time either. Under the circumstances, I couldn't have hoped for a greater blessing than for the two of you to be a perfect match."

While I stared at him, too shocked to speak, he placed a small disc on the low table between us and activated its holographic projector. The 3D image of a woman appeared, slowly pivoting on itself.

"A human?!" I exclaimed, wondering what other mind-boggling revelations he still intended to slap me with.

Humans were weak, temperamental, undisciplined, and with a disturbingly high propensity to commit crimes of every type. To make matters worse, they couldn't even fly.

"I'm sorry. I cannot marry a murderer," I said, leaning back in my chair, ready for this entire farce to be done.

"For the billionth time, she's not a murderer," Kayog said, a mix of anger and frustration seeping into his voice. "Clearly, if she was, she couldn't possibly be your soulmate."

If this had been his attempt at an indirect compliment as to the fact someone this strict about upholding the law couldn't possibly fall in love with someone able to break it, it failed miserably to move me. When I failed to respond—seeing no point in repeating arguments I had already stated—the Temern lost what shreds of patience he still possessed. It took me aback, considering I was indeed well aware of his reputation as an infallible matchmaker, but also for his sweet and amiable—if not paternal—disposition.

"Fine. If you cannot be bothered to save the life of your soulmate or assist in righting the terrible wrongs committed against innocents, another will show more courage," Kayog said in an icy tone that had even his mate stiffening.

"Excuse me?" I said, in just as cold a voice.

"You may be fine with letting an innocent be thrown in with the foulest criminals in the galaxy, but we're not going to let Malaya die. Thankfully, Lord Amreth will take her," Kayog said in a disdainful tone.

That struck me like a boulder in the chest. "Amreth?! Amreth has consented to such a union?"

"We approached him and a few others we knew could potentially be more... flexible before meeting with Malaya," Linsea said, trying to remain diplomatic. "We wanted to be certain that we could provide her with a few options. But once we met her, my husband got a hunch that she was yours. So naturally, we came to you first after that discussion."

"But since you cannot be bothered—" Kayog added.

"Do not test me, Temern," I growled.

"I'm not testing you, Obosian," Kayog replied in just as stern a tone. "We do not have time for you to sort out your inner conflicts. In two days, Malaya will be sent to Dakon's playground. You know perfectly well that she will not survive there a week. So if *you* won't, *I* will save her."

I flinched upon hearing which Sector they intended for her to serve her time. Of all the Hell Lords—as humans had labeled us —Dakon was the most inflexible... though some would say the cruelest. Contrary to all other Wardens, he hadn't divided his

Sector into Quadrants. He didn't need to. He only accepted the foulest miscreants of the galaxy. Life expectancy of his prisoners rarely exceeded a few days, or a few weeks. Only the most vicious managed to establish a stronghold, which they fiercely defended.

I cast another look at the female's hologram. By human standards, she was attractive. It could save her life in that cesspool. But considering how she would be used, a quick death would likely be preferable. And if she truly was innocent, allowing her to be sent there would be an even greater crime than the one she had been sentenced for.

I glared balefully at the Temern, barely repressing the urge to growl angrily at him. "What's the point of giving her to Amreth if they are not soulmates?" I challenged. "I thought you only performed perfect matches."

"So far, I have. But if breaking my perfect streak is the price to save this sweet woman, then I'll gladly pay it," Kayog said, lifting his beak defiantly. "Malaya and Amreth may not be soulmates, but their personalities are well-aligned and compatible. They will have a happy enough life together. Compared to the others, he is the best alternative match."

"Tharmok take you and your threats," I grumbled.

"They are not threats, Lord Kronos," Linsea said in a gentle voice while reaching for her husband's feather-covered hand and giving it a gentle squeeze. "This is our only other option to save Malaya."

Unable to continue looking at them, I got up on my feet and walked to the tall glass doors leading to my office's private terrace. I didn't need to examine their soul again to recognize the sincerity of their endeavor. The disappointed outrage Kayog felt towards me stung. I couldn't read minds, but I knew at a visceral level that he had started thinking Malaya deserved someone better than me—assuming she truly was my soulmate.

But a murderer?

I had met Wuras on a few occasions during official gatherings Obosian nobles loved to attend so much to impress each other with their wealth, status, and piercings. I absent-mindedly fiddled with one of the rings adorning the outer edge of my right pointy ear. A rare algarium ring given to me for intercepting a group of inmates who were attempting to escape the prison where I was performing my Warden training on Grubrya. Each of my piercings attested to moral standards and my achievements in upholding the peace, enforcing the laws, and protecting the innocents.

And if that human is as innocent as they believe…

"Would it help if I told you that all Prime Mating Agency unions come with a six-month trial period," Linsea said in a soothing voice.

I glanced at her over my shoulder. "Six months?"

She nodded, a glimmer of hope shining in her eyes. "Six months during which you would get to see for yourself that she is indeed innocent and truly your soulmate."

"But six months during which you must make an honest commitment to try and make the relationship work," Kayog cautioned.

"Hmmm… And what if that union doesn't work for me by the end of those six months?" I challenged.

"Then you will divorce her and be free to resume your life as you see fit," Kayog replied.

"And what of her?" I asked.

"We will try to find her someone else," Kayog said matter-of-factly.

"And if you fail?" I insisted.

"Then she will have no choice but to serve the rest of her sentence in Dakon's playground," Linsea answered in her husband's stead. "But tell me, Lord Kronos, what is six months if it can help prove whether the highest judge in your court is corrupt or not? Wouldn't arresting him—or alternatively proving his innocence—be the greatest act of justice you could perform on behalf of your people?"

I scrunched my face as if I'd bitten into something foul. "Fine. She has six months to prove you right. But may the gods protect her if she proves false."

"She won't," Kayog said with triumphant confidence.

"We shall see," I replied.

CHAPTER 3
MALAYA

I had never been the crying type. In fact I took great pride in my strength of character in the face of adversity. But when Torgal came to give me the news from Kayog confirming a match with the Hell Lord, I bawled my eyes out from relief. It had arrived less than an hour before lights out on the eve of my transfer. The stress of the past few days had undoubtedly shaved a couple of decades from my life.

But I was not out of the woods just yet. According to the message Torgal had relayed to me, my soon-to-be husband was fairly reluctant. Big shocker there. Frankly, I couldn't imagine what kind of arguments Kayog and Linsea had to throw at Lord Kronos to sway him in my favor. Still, the Temern's warning didn't fall on deaf ears. I would have to be extra sweet to ingratiate myself to my husband.

I instantly chastised myself for my instinctive inner groan at that thought. My tongue could be my own worst enemy. Submissive and pushover didn't belong in my vocabulary. As an investigative reporter, I tended to speak my mind, had a quick repartee, and didn't suffer fools. Considering how stuck up and self-righteous those Obosians usually acted, it would take every shred of my willpower not to make him want to strangle me within the first couple of days.

Like Kronos, I struggled with the idea that he could possibly be my soulmate. Granted, based on his holographic portrait, which Torgal had shown me, that Obosian was far from being hard on the eyes. If nothing else, it should make performing my marital duties not too horrendous of a chore. In truth, I didn't really care if we weren't truly the perfect match. All that mattered is that I would live. If something good came out of our union, great. And if not, so long as I nailed Wuras's criminal ass to the wall, all of this would have been worth it.

The guard barking orders at one of the noisy inmates snapped me out of my musings. I peered around the cabin where over one hundred prisoners and I were both shackled and strapped to our passenger seats. Since our journey to Molvi had begun, I'd gone out of my way to avoid eye contact or draw any attention to myself. The convicts, male and female alike, terrified the fuck out of me. Although I knew better than to judge a book by its cover, I didn't doubt all of these guys had committed whatever crime they'd been sentenced for. A few faces I recognized from the extensive coverage of either their trial or the galactic manhunt that had eventually led to their arrest.

As our ship prepared for landing on Molvi, all my fears resurfaced with a vengeance. What if Wuras had somehow managed to bribe or intimidate one of the guards taking me to the prison planet, and I somehow got 'lost' in the administrative process? What if an unfortunate 'accident' happened to me as I climbed down a set of stairs? What if…?

Our straps—which also served as safety belts—unlocking forced my mind away from the paranoia that threatened to take over me. Following the guard's instructions, my group—the left half of the passengers' cabin—remained seated while the inmates from the right side stood up and filed out in a disciplined fashion. The electric tendrils swirling around the guard's hands undoubtedly played a non-negligible role in their good behavior. From all accounts, a single zap from them put to shame even the most powerful taser. Rumor had it that they could literally turn you into ashes with their power.

There was a reason Obosians were the most feared wardens of the galaxy. With their ability to see and feel nearby souls, even the most high-tech stealth shield wouldn't save you from detection. The flight speed of mature Obosian Warriors broke every possible record, and their electric touch was strong enough to power the electrical cores that provided energy to the various Quadrants of their Sectors.

No one escaped from Molvi.

When our turn came, I kept my head down and followed quietly. We descended the shuttle's ramp onto a dark gray platform. Large circular spots marked the position where we needed to stand. We all picked a spot, lined up in ten rows of ten, which formed a perfect square. The guard's order for us to remain still and not stray from our position—especially those at the edges— took on a darker meaning once the platform started moving. The damn thing served as a giant lift, lowering us to the triage level, a good fifty meters below.

Naturally, just my luck, I happened to be in the front row. A single shove from one of the psychos behind me would send me plummeting to my death. Then again, a few Obosian guards could be seen flying around the wide space, although I didn't know how much effort they'd put in catching one of us should we fall.

Thankfully, everyone behaved, and our platform settled with a clang on the lower floor. All around us, at least a dozen other similar platforms held their one hundred inmates, each platform separated on all sides by a five-meter-wide pathway. Its pristine white color sharply contrasted with our platforms.

A humongous screen ahead indicated the name of the Sector inmates were assigned to. Once the name of your Sector appeared, a soothing feminine voice also called it out through the com system. The shock collar of the people assigned there vibrated—thankfully, not in a painful fashion… at first. Those people would then follow the arrows appearing on the pathway, indicating where they had to report for processing. Failure to comply within seconds of the first collar vibration would shift said vibration to steadily increasing pain until the inmate got their butt moving on the path.

My heart skipped a beat when the third Sector displayed on the screen turned out to be Dakon's. I held my breath, dreading my collar would vibrate. I nearly wept with relief when it didn't. The far-too-famous serial killers, drug lords, and flesh traders who filed out for that Sector confirmed my greatest fear. I would have been destroyed there.

After two more Sectors being called, and a third of the people having already been processed, the Aramon Sector was called at last. I nearly squealed with delight when my collar vibrated as further confirmation. I followed the blue lights on the floor to one of five rooms, where more guards performed the final triage. Each Sector being divided into four Quadrants, they split us according to the severity of our crimes. To my dismay, I was sent with the Quadrant Four group—the foulest criminals.

My paranoia came crashing back like a tsunami as the people from my group lining up ahead of me got their inmate number tattooed on their foreheads. Visually—at least to my human eyes —the number was invisible. But on the giant screen of the surveillance monitors, a huge number starting with the letters AS —for Aramon Sector—followed by a series of numbers was clearly visible.

Angry tears pricked my eyes at the thought of being branded like a fucking animal for a crime I didn't commit. I didn't care that it was invisible to the naked eye.

As I reached the desk, a blue light scanned my face and pulled up my file on the guard's monitor. He stared at his screen for a while before looking back at me, his gaze assessing. I tried not to panic when his eyes slightly went out of focus. Their pale, icy-blue irises glowed a little against their dark-gray sclera, making me even more nervous. He was looking at my soul.

Whatever he saw appeared to confuse him. He glanced at my file again then back at me, before standing from the stool he'd been sitting on. I took an involuntary step back, intimidated by his impressive height and mass. The stern look he gave me had me holding still. He called out a single word. I couldn't say if it had been a name, a command, or an Obosian word foreign to me. But seconds later, another massive Obosian guard came into view and made a 'come here' gesture.

I hesitated, glancing over my shoulder then back at him, before pointing at myself to make sure he was gesturing at me. The guard who had scanned me made an annoyed sound that had me jerking my head towards him, panic ready to settle in again. He waved his hand in an exasperated fashion, indicating that I should get moving. I didn't let him do it twice, too relieved not to have been branded.

Fuck my life… I'd never been such a mess. But why couldn't those assholes just use their fucking words and give clear instructions?

The second guard, who had gestured for me to come, glared at me as if I was deliberately being difficult. It took all my willpower not to tell him to open his damn mouth next time instead of assuming I could read minds. But I wisely kept my thoughts to myself.

To my shock, although we proceeded to the shuttle hangar where all the other inmates were being loaded into large passenger shuttles clearly labeled with their respective Sectors, we went a different way. The guard—who turned out to be the pilot—took me to a luxury personal shuttle in the far-left corner of the hangar.

When he lowered the ramp to allow me in, for the first time

in the three weeks since my arrest and the beginning of this entire nightmare, I finally truly got a sense that everything would be all right. I made it.

But as I settled in the plush leather passenger seat and remained still as the guard secured my seatbelt, my thoughts shifted to the fact that shackles still circled my wrists and ankles, a shock collar hugged my neck, and a baggy, camouflage-style prisoner uniform 'adorned' my body. Even if I had tried, I certainly couldn't have made a bigger fashion statement on my way to my wedding.

It was all the more depressing that, growing up on Earth, I had always pictured myself having a fairy tale ceremony, dressed in a modern baro't saya gown made of the finest piña fabric. It would have the exaggerated butterfly sleeves typical of my Filipino heritage, with intricate embroidery.

Generally speaking, I'd never been too big on traditions. But that dress had been a childhood dream of mine. Made by weaving the fibers of the leaves of the pineapple plant, piña fabric was light and airy, perfect for our tropical climate. Considering how hot Molvi got during the day, it would have been ideal here, too.

But nope… I'd be strutting my convicted self in the least sexy outfit anyone could have conjured up.

His task completed, the guard sat in the pilot's chair and took off. The smooth and silent way our shuttle cut through the air further screamed luxury. It was nothing like the little dinghies I often found myself traveling in while on an investigative mission. It gave me hope that, despite my future husband's apparent reluctance, he would still choose to have me travel in comfort.

My gaze wandered over the breathtaking landscape of Molvi.

At first glance, you'd think we'd traveled back to the prehistoric era. Insanely giant trees blanketed the ground for miles and miles. The foliage was so thick, some of the leaves so wide, you couldn't get even the slightest glimpse of what kind of life scurried below. It struck me then that the greenish-blue and midnight-blue shades of the leaves matched the pattern of my camouflage prisoner outfit.

Most species gave their prisoners brightly colored outfits that made them easy to spot wherever they went, and especially if they were trying to escape. But then, most species didn't have the ability to see and feel nearby souls. The Obosians would detect their presence even if the prisoners hid behind a wall. That could only mean those uniforms meant to protect the prisoners from whatever horrors lurked in the forest surrounding them. A shudder coursed through me at the thought I should have been on my way down there.

In the distance, the occasional clearing could be spotted. We were too far for me to see exactly what was happening there, but some had visible buildings, which I presumed to be the prisoners' shelters.

Bordering those forests and clearings, extremely long mountain chains and wide bodies of water divided the territory. According to rumors, the Obosians artificially created those mountains to delineate their respective Sectors. While it sounded almost impossible, the sharpness of their edges, the abrupt way they rose from the ground, without the slow rising slope of a natural landscape gave those rumors credence. No life thrived on the dark gray stones of those cliff-like mountains. At their summit, I spotted the occasional massive fortress, which constituted the dwelling of one of the Hell Lords.

And soon, one such impregnable castle would become my new home.

The shuttle beginning its descent reclaimed my attention. I looked ahead through the front window. The mansion rising before us took my breath away. Multi-level terraces jutted out of the mountain near the summit. The entire dwelling appeared to have been carved directly in the stone over three stories. Despite the dark stones, the building was angled in a way that plenty of sunlight would flood every room through the tall floor-to-ceiling windows pretty much throughout the day.

From up here, I counted at least two large inner gardens, a tall waterfall that ran into a massive pool, at least twenty rooms, a huge landing pad, and what I presumed to be a ship hangar. The abrupt cliff below the fortress ended in a large river snaking along the mountain range. I didn't doubt for a minute that nasty critters dwelled in its depths, adding an extra layer of security against any prisoner who could have crossed the forest and made it to the shore across from the house.

My stomach fluttered as the three silhouettes near the landing grew bigger. Another shuttle was already parked there. My pulse picked up as I stared at the imposing Obosian next to Kayog and a human female. The Temern measured at least 6'2" but looked borderline tiny next to Kronos. The Obosian's large and muscular body undoubtedly reinforced that illusion—especially since Kayog was himself amazingly fit, though a lot more lithe.

My eyes remained glued to Kronos's face while the guard performed an exceptionally smooth landing. I hated that I couldn't read his thoughts. That male took poker face to a whole new level.

Poker face with a heavy dose of grumpy.

The guard removed my seatbelt and helped me up, forcing me to look away from my soon-to-be husband. My self-consciousness came back with a vengeance as I made my way to the exit. The ramp finished lowering with a soft whining sound and the doors parted before me. I swallowed hard, shame and humiliation burning my cheeks as the metallic sound of the chains linking my ankle shackles marked each of my steps down the ramp.

The guard stopped me at the bottom of the ramp and cast an inquisitive look at Kronos, who gave him a single sharp nod.

That apparently was his cue to rid me of those damn shackles. It couldn't have happened soon enough.

Kronos's icy-blue eyes seemed to grow even colder as he observed us. He gave me a critical look, no doubt comparing my real-life appearance versus the hologram he'd seen. By human standards, I qualified as a fairly attractive woman. But how did I rate in the eyes of an Obosian? Then again, my less-than-sexy outfit did nothing to flatter my figure.

My gaze flicked nervously towards Kayog. He peered at me with his usual warmth. I gave him a stiff smile before glancing back at Kronos. If I could read minds, I'd bet all my possessions that he was asking himself why the fuck he had agreed to this. I wanted to say hello or anything to break the uncomfortable silence, but I wasn't allowed to speak until given leave to do so.

As soon as he was done, the guard simply turned around, climbed back inside the shuttle. To my dismay, he didn't take off and merely stayed watching us through the windshield.

"My dear Malaya, here you are at last!" Kayog exclaimed in a warm and enthusiastic tone, as soon as the doors of the shuttle had closed.

He gestured for me to approach. I complied, relieved that I managed to walk straight despite my knees feeling wobbly and my growing panic that the pilot still wouldn't leave.

"I hope you had a safe trip," Kayog continued, seemingly oblivious to Kronos's frosty demeanor.

"The trip to Molvi was uneventful. But the one from the spaceport to here was extremely comfortable and the view was breathtaking," I added, casting a grateful smile at Kronos as a thank you for that fancy shuttle.

He didn't respond or otherwise react, content to stare at me with those icy-blue eyes of his, made even more intimidating by the black sclera surrounding them.

"I'm glad to hear it," Kayog said, still ignoring Kronos's

rather rude behavior. "Malaya, please meet Priestess Isobel Biondi, who will officiate your union today."

He waved at the slender, human woman next to him. She appeared to be in her late fifties, early sixties. Based on my research, she'd traipsed throughout the galaxy, accompanying Kayog on many of his arranged marriages to preside over them. The sympathy in her eyes—not to say pity—hit me hard. Yeah, in her shoes, I'd also feel sorry for the bride marrying a guy who clearly wanted nothing to do with her.

How the hell had Kayog gotten Kronos to say yes, if he was this unhappy about it?

I gave her a stiff smile, then turned towards Kronos when Kayog gestured at him.

"And this is Kronos Aramon, your betrothed. Kronos, meet Malaya Velasco, your bride."

"Hello, Kronos," I said, relieved that my voice didn't shake as much as I was inside. "It is an honor to meet you."

I almost extended a hand for him to shake but thankfully didn't. Judging by the slow once over he gave me, punctuated by a single grunt in acknowledgement of my words, he undoubtedly would have left my hand hanging.

Anger flared within me.

Okay, fine, his people were super stuck up when it came to law and order. But I didn't twist his arm into marrying me. Kayog had alternative candidates willing to save my ass. Why did he agree if it was only for him to stand there with a fucking tree trunk up his ass and glare at me with his holier than thou expression? My tongue burned with the urge to let him have it. Lucky for his ass, I was the underdog in this mess, or he'd find out how vicious I, too, could be... verbally.

Kayog must have made a mistake. There's no way that jerk and I are soulmates.

Still pretending to be oblivious to the obvious malaise between us, Kayog turned to pick up a large, ornate box on a small hovercart behind him. The wide span of his wings, even folded, had kept it hidden from view.

"My beloved Linsea sends you her regards, as well as this little wedding present," Kayog said, showing me the fancy box. "Under the circumstances, she figured you would like something a bit more fitting to wear for the ceremony."

My jaw dropped, and my eyes nearly popped out of my head as I stared in turn at the box then at Kayog. How incredibly thoughtful! I probably would have hugged and smooshed his adorable bird face if Kronos hadn't ruined the surprise with a disbelieving scoff.

"Whatever for?" Kronos grumbled, his voice laced with outrage.

Kayog gave him a stern look. "Surely, you cannot want your bride dressed in a convict's uniform for your wedding?"

Kronos shrugged, an air of pure annoyance settling on his features. "What does it matter? This is merely a five-minute formality to make the agreement binding. There is no need for dresses or any other such nonsense."

Saying I felt crushed would be the understatement of the century. Of course, this had no meaning for him or his culture. He also had no particular reason to want to please me by going out of his way to accommodate me. And his assessment of the ceremony itself couldn't be more accurate. The Prime Mating Agency weddings gave 'expedited' a whole new meaning. We would be done in less than five minutes. So why waste twenty minutes getting dressed for it?

Because this was supposed to be the happiest, most memorable day of my life.

"It's okay," I said with a stiff smile. "He's right. While I'm deeply touched by the gesture, a dress isn't important under the circumstances. I don't mind getting married like this."

To my shock, Kronos took a menacing step towards me. He

glared, teeth—and fangs—bared, his icy-blue eyes glowing. Startled, I took a step back and pressed a palm to my chest.

"You've been here less than five minutes and already you lie?" he hissed.

I bristled at that. Dropping my hand pressing against my chest, I fisted both hands by my sides to rein in the anger surging back within me with a vengeance.

"It's not a lie. It's called being diplomatic and considerate," I snapped back. "You've made it abundantly clear that my presence here inconveniences you. I'm trying to lessen the burden I'm imposing on you, and sided with your argument so that you wouldn't be the bad guy in this situation."

He advanced by another step, getting in my face. This time, I stood my ground and lifted my chin defiantly.

"You assume that I care whether people deem me the 'bad guy' or that I can't handle contradictions," he replied, his voice just as stern.

"I'm not assuming anything. I'm merely trying to be nice," I said, refusing to be cowed.

"I don't need you to be nice. I need you to be *honest*. Can you be honest, little human?" Kronos asked in a condescending tone.

"My name is Malaya," I said in a clipped tone.

The corner of his full lips slightly quirked up with the shadow of a smile.

"Well then, little *Malaya*, can you be honest?"

Despite my burning urge to tell him to go fuck himself, I took a deep breath to keep my cool. After all, the shuttle was still here, and I had no intention whatsoever of sitting my ass in it a second time, comfy or not.

"No woman wants to get married dressed like a criminal, especially when she's innocent and has been framed," I said in a controlled voice. "Kayog doesn't need to tell me that you are reluctant to have me as a wife. The coldness of your 'welcome' has made your feelings abundantly clear. But whether you want me or not doesn't change the fact that marrying you is my only chance to survive this mess and hopefully get justice. So if that means I have to bend over backward to make my presence tolerable to you, I will do it. And that includes casting aside my childhood dream of marrying in the traditional gown of my people."

He studied my features for a few seconds, his smirk returning, this time a bit more pronounced.

"Well, that wasn't so hard, was it?" he asked in a taunting voice.

Something snapped inside me upon hearing the provocation in the way he pronounced those words. Instead of punching him in the throat as I ached to do, I threw all caution to the wind and just gave him the fucking honesty he wanted.

"Actually yes, it was," I snarled, tears of anger pricking my eyes. "It was extremely hard, and it's fucking humiliating. I may not be a saint, but I'm not a goddamn criminal. Yet here I am, having to choose between getting slaughtered by actual criminals inside Dakon's Sector, or marrying a man who clearly has nothing but contempt for me. And I have no choice but to take the abuse with a fucking smile if I want to live. All this because a corrupt Obosian judge is empowered to pursue his life of crime with all impunity. Is that an honest enough answer for you?"

Kronos recoiled and stared at me with a stunned expression throughout my diatribe. When I finally shut up, I flinched and lowered my eyes, berating myself for letting my emotions get the best of me. The past few weeks had been such hell, his dreadful welcome and attitude had simply been the final straw.

And now my stupid mouth will get my ass right back on that fancy shuttle with a one-way ticket to true Hell.

I warily glanced back up at Kronos, who towered over me by a good head and a half. He appeared to be studying my face, but his gaze was slightly out of focus, hinting he was instead peering at my soul with a troubled expression. He cast a sideways glance at Kayog, as if he'd just been hit with traumatic news. The Temern lifted his chin with a smug expression, which had Kronos looking like he'd just bitten into something foul.

He studied my face again, this time as if he was seeing me for the first time, leaving me completely baffled. Just when I thought he was going to speak he looked over my shoulder at the guard piloting the shuttle. My heart lurched when he gave him a sharp nod. Was he telling him to come get me?

Instead, the shuttle took off with a soft humming sound. I jerked my head over my shoulder to have visual confirmation and could have wept with relief when I saw it quickly flying away. While nerves still painfully knotted my stomach, his departure lifted a heavy weight off my shoulders.

I turned back to see Kronos taking the ornate box from Kayog's hands.

"This way, then," Kronos said in a grumpy tone, gesturing with his head for me to follow.

I gaped at his receding back before casting a confused look at Kayog. He was staring at me with his silver eyes filled with something akin to paternal pride and approval. He clapped his feathery hands together in a silent applause and jerked his head towards Kronos to tell me to get a move on.

That snapped me out of my shocked daze, and I hastened after Kronos. He was already walking down the incline from the landing pad terrace to a lower humongous balcony that spanned nearly half of the sprawling mansion. I wanted to feast my eyes on the stunning layout clearly divided into distinct entertainment sections, but there would be time for that later. He headed for one of the imposing sets of glass doors between the floor-to-ceiling reflective windows that lined the entire façade.

The doors parted upon his approach. Kronos slowed down ever-so-slightly to give me a chance to catch up. The interior of the mansion took my breath away. Despite the monochromatic color palette—consisting of off-white, light beige, and dark grays—the décor was anything but boring. For some reason, I had expected hard lines and sharp angles everywhere to match Kronos's stiff and unyielding personality. Instead, beautiful organic patterns carved directly into the stone gave the house a warm and inviting atmosphere. Every piece of furniture had rounded edges and gentle curves. The clever lighting illuminated paler elements of the house, giving them a dreamy glow.

We walked past an absurdly huge living area to our right, which faced the terrace we'd just arrived from. Instead of going down the large corridor, at the other end of which there appeared to be one of the two interior gardens I'd spotted during my flight here, Kronos headed towards another swirling sculpture carved into the light gray stone of the wall.

To my surprise, he waved a hand in front of a luminous stone embedded in the pattern. I gasped with awe when the sculpture seemed to turn into some kind of thick liquid, swiftly unraveling its pattern to open the path into the hygiene room beyond.

"Wow!" I whispered to myself.

This place was fucking gorgeous! With a will of their own, my feet carried me inside the room as I gaped at its elegant yet muted beauty. The sink sat in the center of a wide counter made of a similar swirling motif. It occupied a third of the right wall from the entrance, with a mirror that ran up to the four-meter-high ceiling. To my surprise, it wasn't just a water closet but a complete hygiene room with the largest shower I'd ever seen. Two dozen discreet body-massager showerheads lined three sides of the shower. Then again, it made sense to help wash the back and long wingspan of the Obosians. It also explained why the toilet seat sat at a noticeable distance from the wall to provide space for their wings behind it.

The sound of Kronos gently putting the box down on the counter reclaimed my attention. He was observing me with undisguised curiosity, devoid of any of the previous coldness and disdain.

Something had changed after I'd lost my shit. Based on Kayog's silent applause and Kronos's sudden change of attitude, I'd done the right thing. How the fuck was getting angry the solution?

He looked at my soul.

Was that the reason? Did looking at my soul reveal something that mollified him? Did it convince him I was telling the truth? I had no clue how their power worked. Obosians kept it secret for understandable reasons. The only thing they made public was that they could see and sense any soul within a certain range, regardless of stealth or other camouflage methods.

Whatever had caused this shift in attitude, I welcomed it.

"You may change here," Kronos said in a soft and polite voice. "There are towels, soap, and any other toiletry you may require here," he added, gesturing at a tall, standard cupboard door on the wall opposite the sink. "I'll wait for you outside. Simply wave the back of your hand in front of this light to lock the door and wave your palm in front of it to unlock and open. The door can only be locked and unlocked from inside," he added, the taunting glimmer returning in his eyes.

This time, however, it didn't sting me like the previous ones.

"Thank you. I really appreciate it," I said, sincerely.

He stared at me with that odd intensity of his. Once more, his eyes went out of focus. It was subtle, but enough for me to know he was looking at my aura again. To my surprise, he gave me a half smile when he refocused on me. With a slight nod, he walked out of the room.

On instinct, I approached the door to lock it, then decided against it. It was silly, but locking it felt like it would be an insult, like I didn't trust him to respect my privacy. Despite our rough first start, I believed a good man hid behind that cold and stern exterior. Even though I totally couldn't see it right now,

Kayog believed we were soulmates. He'd never been wrong. Considering he had not let me astray so far, I would continue to put my faith in him.

Not wanting to test Kronos's patience any longer than necessary, I swiftly opened the box, ornate with golden embossed patterns. Feeling like a child on her birthday, I frantically pulled out the white silk paper inside. I froze, my jaw dropping at the sight of the most exquisite baro't saya gown. Reaching inside the box with shaky hands, I picked up the baro't, which was the top of the dress. It was definitely a modern take on the outfit. A gorgeous floral lace had been embroidered on the most luxurious piña fabric I'd ever touched. It formed a rather sexy bustier that didn't cover my pierced belly button. The same flowery dentelle adorned the edges of the oversized butterfly shoulders of my baro't.

I reverently placed the top on the counter before reaching for the saya—the skirt. Full length with the same lacework in strategic places, the skirt actually had an insane slit up to the middle of the thigh. It was scandalously sexy, and I couldn't love it more. I quickly stripped out of my baggy camouflage prisoner suit and slipped on the stunning dress. It fit so perfectly, you'd think it had been custom made for me.

The front of the skirt dipped into a little V-shape. The way the baro't and saya sat on my body convinced me that Linsea had known about my navel piercing. For this reason, and as Kronos possessed quite a few of his own, she'd undoubtedly chosen an outfit that would draw his attention to one of the things we had in common. Truth be told, I loved flaunting that piercing, which I didn't get to do all that much in my line of work.

Peering back inside the box, I retrieved the elegant pair of high heel shoes. The same pristine white as the dress, they also boasted some floral embroidery. Like the dress, they were my exact size. Last but not least, a single barrette with pearls laid out like flowers sat on a cushion at the bottom of the box, with a pair of pearl earrings. I quickly put them on and fixed my hair. Taking a step back to admire the final result in the mirror, I could have wept with happiness.

I looked stunning.

A dab of makeup—eyeliner and lipstick—would have made this picture perfect. But considering I'd just narrowly avoided getting married in a camouflage potato sack, I wouldn't complain. My heart filled with love and gratitude for Kayog and Linsea. It was silly to be this moved that I should look pretty for whatever this marriage was. But I couldn't help it.

I closed the box and neatly folded the prisoner suit to leave the room as neat as I'd found it. Taking a deep breath I waved my palm in front of the light, and the door opened. Kronos had been standing slightly to the left, his back to me. He turned around upon hearing the swishing sound of the door unraveling. He froze the moment he laid eyes on me.

His icy-blue irises seemed to expand, filling even more of the dark sea of his sclera as his gaze roamed over me. When it stopped at my exposed belly button, and the dangling navel barbell ring adorning it, Kronos's face took on a lascivious expression that struck me like a boulder. The way the tip of his dark-gray tongue poked out to lick his upper lip—as if he was imagining it was my navel he was licking—resonated directly between my thighs. Such a powerful reaction left me reeling.

For the first time, I gave Kronos a really good look. I'd been so focused on not pissing him off that I'd not really taken the time to evaluate the man I'd have to lie with for the next six months. He was crazy tall—at least 6'7", maybe more, which I totally dug. His face was quite attractive, with high cheekbones, a noble nose, and plump lips that begged to be kissed and devoured. He wore some kind of breastplate made of the strangest mix of black leather and scales, expertly stitched with silver threads, and secured to his body by magnetic clasps on the sides. Elegant matching black pants hugged his muscular thighs, and shiny black boots completed the outfit. The size of the biceps on his bare arms hinted at how well-defined his pecs and abs would likely be.

Judging by the number of piercings in his eyebrows and pointy elf ears, I couldn't help but wonder how many more of them he possessed. Apparently, the same thought was crossing his mind.

"This outfit is indeed better," Kronos said at last, his voice deep and pleasantly rumbly—another fact I'd been too frazzled to notice earlier. "Come."

Without another word, he turned on his heel and headed back out.

Better?! That's it? Sheesh, pile on the compliments, why don't you?

I immediately chastised myself for my silly reaction. That dress made me feel gorgeous, and the needy part of me wanted it acknowledged. The way he'd looked at me when I came out, I'd expected him to either gush over how hot I looked or tear it right off my back to have his unbridled way with me… which would have been quite awkward.

Still, his cold and distant façade had slipped, granting me a glimpse of a hot and dirty side of my future husband that I'd never be able to erase from my mind. As I followed him out of the house, hypnotized by the gentle swaying of his long tail, I couldn't say if that freaked me out more than it turned me on.

CHAPTER 4
KRONOS

Leading Malaya back to the terrace, I still couldn't believe I had agreed to marry a convicted criminal. And yet, her soul was clean… more than clean. In fact, I'd rarely gazed upon a soul half as beautiful as hers. It shone with the strength of a thousand suns, its glow mesmerizing... enthralling.

Her earlier speech also held no deception. Whether she was guilty or not, Malaya genuinely believed in her innocence and in Judge Wuras's corruption.

This was a problem.

If proven true, Malaya's accusations would cause the biggest scandal to rock my people in generations. The political and societal fallout from this would be monumental. I didn't want to have to deal with this mess. But I couldn't overlook it or turn a blind eye without betraying everything I stood for and believed in. Worse, it would make me a coward.

I cast a sideways glance at the human. She constituted my most immediate problem to handle. The gods knew I was in no hurry to wed. However, if she truly was my soulmate as the Temern claimed, then I couldn't let her slip through my fingers.

Malaya couldn't have been more different than everything

I'd imagined when Kayog first mentioned her to me. She was smaller and more fragile-looking than I expected, but also much prettier. That prisoner outfit had hidden the beautiful curves of her body, and especially that mouthwatering piercing in her navel. I shouldn't be focusing on such superficial traits, but I couldn't help myself. When she had stepped out of the hygiene room, the wave of lust that had surged through me had left me reeling. It almost felt like when our juveniles entered their first heat. I couldn't wait to find out if she had other piercings elsewhere.

Her emotions also proved to be a feast I intended to shamelessly indulge in. Her anger tasted good. But her happiness tasted divine. What would her pleasure taste like? That said, it disturbed me how murky and icky her pain and humiliation had felt. I regularly fed on the pain and despair of the prisoners, which always constituted an agreeable and satisfying meal. Why should her distress taste so unpleasant?

But such musings would have to wait until later. Kayog and Priestess Biondi had moved down from the landing pad to the main entertainment terrace. I barely refrained from rolling my eyes to see them standing by the pool. With the pretty plants and the breathtaking view of Molvi's landscape as backdrop, it made for a respectable setting to hold a wedding.

It baffled me why they would go to such an extreme to make this feel like a traditional union between two people in love. I had heard of the countless unusual places Kayog had held similar expedited marriages. A part of me suspected he was doing it for Malaya. For some reason, this whole deal appeared to be of importance to her. The emotions radiating from him whenever he looked at or interacted with her had a strongly paternal and protective edge to them. Another part of me believed he was playing a game to either shame or mollify me.

While I wasn't an empath in the traditional sense like his species was, I could nonetheless feel other people's emotions—

or rather taste them if I so choose. As he had rightly guessed, the moment Malaya arrived, I carefully examined her soul and sampled her emotions in response to my intentionally less-than-friendly welcome to test her true nature.

Every last one of her responses had shattered my preconceptions as to who and what she would be like. To my shock—and surprisingly to my delight—she was turning out to be rather attractive, both inside and out. To be honest, I'd also felt relieved when I told Zolran he could leave. As cold and inflexible as I often came across, I would have taken no pleasure in sending her back to triage to be picked up by Dakon's guards. But I would not have married a criminal had she failed my test.

"Malaya, my dear, you are breathtaking!" Kayog exclaimed with that paternal pride and affection he always projected whenever he addressed my soon-to-be-mate.

It baffled me. As far as I knew, he'd only met her once or twice before when this whole ordeal began. What could have forged such a strong bond? There was nothing inappropriate between them. Anyway, a single meeting with Kayog and Linsea sufficed for even the slowest person to see those two were madly in love with each other. But my curiosity was now piqued. I'd have to find out how she had gained such devotion from him.

"You're too kind," Malaya said, her pretty face glowing with a heartfelt gratitude as she beamed at the Temern. "I can never thank you and Linsea enough for such a thoughtful and wonderful present."

Unable to resist, I absorbed a sliver of the emotional energy she thus emitted. Tharmok take me! It tasted sweet and tangy, with a sprinkle of heat. It took every bit of my willpower not to start gorging on her. I almost projected my *bakaan*, the aura every Obosian possessed that physiologically affected people from merely making them feel appeased and relaxed, to making them mad with lust.

The knowing smile the wretched Temern cast my way

slapped me back to the present moment. What doubt I might still have about the fact part of this was orchestrated to force me to see Malaya's appeal completely vanished.

"If you are both ready to proceed, please approach," the priestess said. We complied, stopping a meter from her. "Great! Now please stand side by side and hold each other's hand."

Once more, we did as requested. Malaya's hand felt tiny in mine, instantly stirring my protective instincts. The warmth and softness of her skin had me itching to caress the back of her hand, which I obviously didn't do.

"We will begin with the Veil and the Cord," Isobel said, giving a discreet nod to Kayog.

I frowned, confused as to what that meant. But Malaya's gasp drew my attention. The air of disbelief and wonder on her face only increased my confusion. I followed her gaze and noticed Kayog had yet another box hidden by the span of his wings. He retrieved a white fabric from it. Malaya's breath hitched when he unfolded it as he approached us. Another powerful wave of joy and gratitude radiated from her, making me feel dizzy by its potency.

As stated by the Priestess, it turned out to be a very long veil, sheer with floral embroidery at the edges. Since I recalled the brides in human weddings were often veiled, I didn't think much of it when Kayog began pinning it on her hair, other than finding it strange they hadn't included it in the box before she went to change. As far as I knew, the bride walked down the aisle with her face already covered by it.

However, not only did Kayog not cover her face with it, only her hair, but then he placed the other half of the veil across *my* shoulders, keeping it in place by a magnetic clasp on my breastplate. Whatever expression my face displayed seemed to amuse him as he wrapped his right hand around his beak in a typical gesture for bird folk to express shame or repress laughter.

In his case, it was definitely laughter.

"The veil is the symbol of the purity of the love that can only be found between a married couple," Priestess Biondi said in a solemn voice, reclaiming our attention. "It symbolizes the shield that will protect your union from negative external forces, and the shelter under which you may find comfort, strength, and solace in your times of need."

While she spoke, Kayog went to retrieve a second item from the box. This time, it appeared to be a long rope made of strings of white pearl-like beads. As he placed it over Malaya's head, the three strings of the rope resting on her shoulders, I realized the very long cord had been bound in an infinity symbol. The first circle bound Malaya, and the second circle he placed over my head to rest on my shoulders.

"This cord is the symbol of unity and of the eternal bond of love and fidelity," Priestess Biondi continued. "One can be over-powered, but two can stand strong against adversity. A cord of three strands is not easily broken. The first strand represents you, Malaya. The second represents you, Kronos. And the third is the love that will bind your future in an unbreakable thread, what-ever storm, whatever challenge strains it."

Malaya's hand tightened around mine as the priestess spoke those words. To my shock, I found myself instinctively returning the gesture. Now that I no longer believed her to be a criminal, that wretched need to protect and reassure her once more came to the fore.

Not to mention the burning urge to taste the torrent of emotions pouring out of her.

"We are gathered here to celebrate the union of this woman, Malaya Velasco, and this Obosian male, Kronos Aramon, in the sacred bond of marriage. Such union must be entered into freely, with honest intentions, a genuine commitment, and not for finan-cial gains or deceptive purposes," the priestess said. "Malaya Velasco, do you freely and willingly take this Obosian male, Kronos Aramon, to be your lawfully wedded husband, for better or for worse, through good times and hardships, in sickness and in health, until death do you part?"

"I do," Malaya said, her voice a little shaky from emotion.

"Kronos Aramon, do you freely take this woman, Malaya Velasco, to be your lawfully wedded wife, for better or for worse, through good times and hardships, in sickness and in health, until death do you part?"

"I do," I replied, stunned by the sense of peace—almost rightness—that descended over me as I spoke those words.

"Kayog Voln, do you confirm that you stand here as both witness and Ninong to this human female, Malaya Velasco, and this Obosian male, Kronos Aramon, as they freely committed to be legally married to each other in accordance with human and galactic laws?"

"I do," Kayog said.

I had no idea what a Ninong was, but I figured it was linked to whatever that veil and cord ritual had been.

"By the power vested in me by the Clerical College of Earth and the United Planets Organization, I declare you husband and wife. Kronos Aramon, you may kiss the bride," Priestess Biondi said.

I turned to face Malaya... my wife. The cord and veil binding us didn't afford us much room for wide movements. My eyes locked with hers. They were an unusual and stunning shade of dark green and brown, framed by infinite natural eyelashes. To my delight, they held no fear, just an understandable nervousness laced with something akin to shyness. Her fingers tightened a bit more around mine. This time, I caressed the back of her hand with my thumb in a soothing gesture. Her eyes widened ever so slightly in response.

I cupped the side of her neck with my free palm, my thumb gently lifting her chin as I leaned forward. Malaya's lips slightly parted as nervous energy radiated in droves from her. The moment our lips touched, a bolt of lust exploded in the pit of my stomach. I barely managed to rein in my *bakaan*, but I couldn't help tasting her emotions again.

Big mistake.

Blood rushed to my groin, and my abdominal muscles constricted painfully in response to the throbbing between my thighs. Tharmok's blood! If her blossoming arousal from this chaste kiss tasted this good, feasting on her emotions once I had her writhing beneath me in the throes of passion would drive me insane.

Fearing I might lose control to the irrational desire this little human awakened in me, I ended the kiss with far more reluctance than I'd ever admit to. My gaze locked with my mate's. Shock, awe, and confusion flitted in quick succession on her face. I couldn't read emotions the way the Temern did, but in that instant, I knew beyond any doubt our brief kiss had affected her the same way it had me.

"Congratulations!" Kayog exclaimed, breaking the magic.

"Thank you," I grumbled, turning back to face him.

As I did so, the movement tugged at the veil and cord binding me to Malaya. She emitted a nervous laugh and cast a sideways glance at Kayog.

"Oh, right!" the Temern exclaimed, while approaching to remove the cord and veil from us. "I make a poor Ninong, it seems."

"Ninong?" I repeated.

"It's the name we give the godfather of a couple's wedding," Malaya explained in his stead. "Usually, the Ninong and Ninang are a couple chosen for the great strength of their own marriage and who can help guide the newlyweds with whatever hurdles they may encounter in their union."

I nodded slowly. While I suspected Kayog and Linsea had not so much been chosen but rather volunteered for the role, the undeniable love and harmony in their couple would make them the perfect candidates for this.

The Temern respectfully folded the veil and cord and placed them with much care back inside the box that the Priestess held open for him. He then closed the box and returned to us before carefully handing it to Malaya.

"You have gone through some truly difficult and frightening times. But those hardships had a purpose, and it was to bring you here to this male," Kayog said once more in that paternal tone he always used with my mate. "There is absolutely no question in my mind that you two are soulmates. He's a good male. And together, you will accomplish great things, and save many innocents."

"Thank you. Thank you for everything," Malaya said, her voice full of emotion.

To my shock—reflected on Kayog's face—Malaya threw herself into his arms. His surprise gave way to that paternal look again, and he returned her embrace, closing his wings around her before rubbing the side of his beak on her temple. He released her a brief moment after. She gave him a sheepish grin while mumbling an apology.

He chuckled. "It's all right, Malaya. Everyone needs a hug from time to time, myself included. But before I leave you to better make each other's acquaintances, I must remind you of the terms of the agreement," he continued, in a more serious tone. "Normally, a second wedding should take place before the day's end according to the groom's culture. However, as Obosian weddings involve a permanent, unbreakable bond, that requirement is lifted until you have completed the trial period. For the six months of that trial period, you both commit to make every genuine effort required to give this relationship a chance to succeed. You also pledge to consummate your union tonight. If at the end of the trial period, either one of you wants out, the marriage will be dissolved, and Malaya will be sent to Lord Dakon's Sector to serve the remainder of her sentence. Otherwise, you will remain together here to formalize your union according to local customs. Any questions?"

We both shook our heads. While Malaya had merely blushed at the mention of performing our marital duties, I didn't miss the tension stiffening her back when he broached the possibility of her being sent to Dakon's Sector should our union fail. I couldn't tell how things would evolve between Malaya and me over the upcoming months, but I wouldn't let her end up in such a dreadful place. Despite the many questions I had about what exactly had transpired with her case, I no longer questioned her innocence. No criminal could possess so beautiful and pure a soul as she did.

"Excellent! Isobel and I must be on our way. We have many more happy couples to bind on their new journey together. But before I go, I brought you a few wedding presents, Malaya," Kayog said enthusiastically.

He looked left towards the elevated terrace of the landing platform where his shuttle still waited for him and the Priestess. We followed his gaze only to see his pilot coming down the incline connecting the two terraces, a hovercart laden with a series of crates shadowing him.

"What's all that?" Malaya asked, echoing my thoughts.

"All your non-confiscated personal belongings I managed to recover," Kayog said smugly. "You will find your clothes, shoes, holographic albums, as well as the journalism awards you earned over the years."

"Oh, my God! Kayog, you're freaking amazing!" Malaya exclaimed. "You're not just a Ninong. You are my fairy godfather!"

The Temern chuckled, looking pleased. It had been thoughtful of him, but I couldn't help feeling a little annoyed that he had cheated me out of providing for the needs of my new mate.

"Linsea and I have also added a few personal gifts. Nothing

fancy. The two most expensive ones are a new computer and a datapad," Kayog explained. He turned to me when he noticed my frown. "Naturally, under the circumstances, you will need to authorize the use of certain features."

Mollified, I grunted my assent. Thankfully, Malaya didn't make a fuss about it, having apparently understood that strict rules were applied to convicts when it came to access to technology, and especially communication systems that allowed them to contact people outside of their Warden's control.

After a few more words, we bid the Temern and Priestess goodbye and watched their shuttle take off. As soon as their shuttle began fading on the horizon, I turned to look at my mate only to find her already staring at me with an unreadable expression.

"Are you afraid of me?" I surprised myself by asking. Nothing in her demeanor expressed fear, and yet I needed to know.

"No, I'm not," Malaya said with a confidence that took me aback.

"You're not?" I insisted, raising an amused brow.

She shook her head, the same unreadable expression on her face. "Kayog wouldn't have married me to you if he thought you were evil or would do me harm."

I tilted my head to the side as I studied her features. "You trust him *that* much?"

My mate nodded without hesitation. "Completely. I've seen all the good he has done over the years. He's a good, trustworthy male who goes out of his way to spread happiness around him, and justice in the process when he can."

I pursed my lips while weighing her words. While he was mainly a matchmaking agent, Kayog had indeed meddled in political, diplomatic, and economic matters for quite a few of the couples he paired. Although always indirect, his interference in favor of the primitive species involved couldn't be denied.

"Does that mean you believe his affirmation that you and I are soulmates?" I asked.

"Kayog says so," she replied, matter-of-factly.

"That's not what I asked. What do *you* think?" I insisted.

This time, she paused, taking a moment to ponder on her response and choose her words. For a reason I couldn't explain, it stung me that she didn't reply to that question with the same speed and assurance she had with the others.

"I have no reason to doubt Kayog," Malaya said at last. "Personally, I won't lie, I don't see it. Don't get me wrong, I think you're very attractive. But if we had randomly met in the street, I doubt either of us would have sought to exchange a word with the other. We would have just walked past without acknowledging each other."

"Right…" I said in a non-committal fashion.

It seemed to pique her curiosity. "You don't feel we're soulmates either, right?" Malaya asked, a sliver of uncertainty seeping into her voice.

"The Temern believes we are," I replied with a shrug.

I chuckled when she gave me a 'Are you serious?' look for my evasive answer only moments after I called her out for doing the same. I bowed my head in concession.

"Yes. I believe we are soulmates," I said. Her shocked expression upon hearing my response only made me smile further. "Like you, I do not feel it and probably wouldn't have spared you a second glance had we met under different circumstances. But now that fate has forced that communication, I have given you a second glance. Beyond the fact that Kayog has never been wrong, you are an attractive woman, your soul is unexpectedly quite beautiful, and your emotions are… delicious."

She gaped at me, having clearly not expected that response from me.

"Delicious?" she echoed, looking baffled.

By the way she flinched, that had not been the question she'd meant to ask. But her mind had likely been too confused still when she blurted out the question.

"Mmhmm," I replied in a teasing fashion. "Come, let's get inside."

Without waiting for her response, I set the hovercart to follow, turned on my heel, and headed back inside the house. I heard the discreet clicking sound of her heels as she hastened after me. Not wanting to drag the cart behind me throughout the imposing mansion, I made a left turn in the first wide corridor we encountered and kept walking past the first two rooms, stopping at the one on the left before the end. I opened it, and entered with the cart, which I led to a corner of the room.

Although she didn't gasp as I had expected, the radical shift in Malaya's emotions when she realized where I had taken her made me chuckle. I faced her with a mocking smile while she tried to keep a neutral expression on her face.

"Relax, little human. We are not going to couple… just yet. This is your bedroom," I said teasingly while gesturing at our surroundings.

"*My* bedroom?" she repeated with a questioning look. "Not ours?"

I shook my head. "No. You have your own room. However, as required by our contract, we *will* couple tonight. After that, well… that will be up to you."

Malaya blinked rapidly, visibly taken aback by my words. For the first time, I wished I possessed the Temern's empathic abilities. I would have loved to know if the flurry of emotions fleeting over her pretty features expressed relief or disappointment. Through my own powers, I could only perceive that they were conflicted.

"Our rooms are connecting," I added, pointing at the connecting door. "We have a larger communal hygiene room, although there are also private ones," I continued, pointing to each in turn.

"I see," Malaya replied in a tone that seemed to indicate either the exact opposite or the fact that she didn't quite know how to feel about it.

I smiled, suddenly intrigued by the prospect of learning all her emotional nuances and how she responded to the various situations her new life here would confront her to.

"Are you hungry?" I asked.

She blinked once more. This time, Malaya seemed more surprised than shocked. "Actually, now that you mention it, I am getting hungry."

"Good. Dinner will be ready by the time I finish giving you the tour of the house," I said in an approving tone. "Come."

CHAPTER 5
MALAYA

Relief flooded through me when Kronos simply turned around and walked out of the room without waiting for my response. When I first entered the room and realized I'd stepped inside one of the most gorgeous bedrooms I had ever laid eyes on, I had indeed thought he meant for us to do the deed right away. Saying that freaked me out would have been quite an understatement.

I didn't actually dread sleeping with him. Any way you cut it, it was happening tonight. Beyond the fact that I wanted to secure my position here for the next six months, as the hardcore Obosian that he was, Kronos would make sure we honored the terms of the contract. At least, he looked rather hot. And that kiss earlier, brief though it had been, had my toes curling something fierce. At a visceral level, I suspected that sex with my brand-new husband would be wild and dirty.

A part of me was looking forward to it, but not right this minute.

I was only grateful for the radical change in his attitude from the moment he had agreed to let me change into this stunning wedding gown. He'd gone from being a total stuck up douchebag to someone reasonably pleasant. He'd even chuckled and smiled a few times. I really liked it when he did that. It softened his face in the most wondrous way. Kronos naturally had a noble presence, which could be perceived as him having an air of superiority. I was starting to think it was a misleading impression.

My mother was like that. She was a very classy lady. People often wrongly assumed that she was snob, distant, and thought herself better than others. She was merely reserved and introverted. But for those who knew her, she was the sweetest and most loving person in the world.

I could only hope the same would apply to my Obosian.

As I reentered the hallway through which we had come to my room, my eyes flicked this way and that, taking in the refined beauty of my surroundings. Everything here was bigger than life. The hallways were so wide you'd think each room was a classroom instead of a bedroom in a private residence. The vaulted ceilings all had to be at least four-meters high, and higher still in the central area of the house. They'd all been carved directly into the stone of the mountain then polished.

The entire domain had just the right level of elegant furniture. I wouldn't qualify it as Zen, or minimalist, but it certainly wasn't cluttered. As Kronos gave me the tour, his large leathery wings shifting from time to time, I realized the wide spaces both in the various corridors and in between furniture was to allow room for him to spread his wings without knocking stuff over. I could imagine the mess he would cause in the cramped apartment I used to live in if he suddenly decided to stretch with those massive wings of his.

As I had accurately guessed during my flight here, the mansion—not to say castle—was spread over three tiers, with more guest rooms than I could count, three humongous living areas, each with their own imposing terraces, an industrial size kitchen with a banquet dining room big enough to seat forty people, and two smaller dining rooms in a more reasonable size for a family, or in this instance a couple. An entire wing of the castle was actually reserved for Kronos. It contained his office, a training room, and then an entire surveillance room with countless monitors, computers, and other machinery. I couldn't even begin to imagine what purpose they served in securing the prisoners.

But my favorite parts were undoubtedly the inner courtyards with the most amazing gardens overflowing with fragrant, colorful, exotic plants like I'd never beheld before. The largest one of the two actually had a waterfall which fell into a large basin on the main floor—which happened to be the middle one—that turned into the longest pool in the galaxy.

It would take me days with a map to find my way around this place without systematically getting lost.

"Your home is beautiful," I said in all sincerity. "But isn't this way too big for a single male?"

He snorted and gave me an amused sideways glance. "This is now *our* home, and I'm no longer *single*."

I scrunched my face at him, which made his smile broaden. Yeah, I really like how he looked when he smiled, especially the way it stretched those plump lips of his.

"You are correct, it is a huge dwelling, but standard for a Warden," Kronos explained as we made our way back to the smaller dining room on the main floor. "Most Wardens belong to a noble family on Vargos, the Obosian homeworld. So a large mansion is expected to reflect their status. We also entertain often. They are lavish and extravagant affairs that require this kind of space."

I couldn't help a snort at the way he rolled his eyes while describing those events. "You do not like to entertain or go out?" I asked with genuine curiosity.

He shrugged. "I do not feel any particular need to socialize. But I do not mind partaking in those events, or even organizing them for that matter. It's just that after a while it gets tiresome to see the same braggarts trying to one up each other or impress the rest of us with the same tired old things. For all that, it is nice to catch up with some of the people I actually care about."

"When you say organize, surely you have some kind of catering service, right?" I asked, feeling daunted merely by the thought of trying to keep this place clean.

Kronos laughed, his icy-blue eyes gleaming with mischief. "If you wonder if I would cook for the hundreds of people who would descend on my house, absolutely not. We all have Nundars to maintain our homes and handle domestic chores such as cleaning and cooking."

"Nundars?" I repeated, staring at him questioningly as we were entering the small dining room.

He gestured at something inside the room with a teasing smile. I glanced in that direction, and my jaw dropped at the site of the lavish meal that had been laid out on the table. Not even twenty minutes prior, the table had been bare.

"What? When? How?" I exclaimed, looking left and right for who might have set up the table during our brief tour of the house.

Kronos chuckled. "The Nundars are extremely discreet. They are what humans would call our familiars. They're not animals, but intelligent and independent people in their own right."

"So why are they familiars?" I asked, sitting down in the chair Kronos had pulled for me.

"In many ways, their survival depends on us. They are extremely sensitive to the energy people emit. The wrong type will negatively affect them, especially violent emotions," Kronos explained.

I frowned at that comment. "Then isn't living on the prison planet housing the foulest prisoners the worst possible location for them?"

Kronos smiled. "Technically, that is correct. In practice, as you can see, our dwellings are way out of reach of the prisoners. Should our homes be unwelcoming to the Nundars, they would leave and find a new patron."

He gestured with his chin for me to start digging into the food. Although I didn't know what any of this was, it all looked appetizing. I reached for a mix of the various cuts of meat and vegetables, taking only a small amount of each to sample them.

"You will meet them sooner than later," Kronos continued while serving himself as well. "Their appearance might be a little strange to you, but they are extremely peaceful and spiritual. Do not be surprised by the fact that they do not speak."

"Why? Is it a physical impairment or spiritual choice?" I asked with genuine curiosity.

"A mix of both," Kronos said, visibly amused by my baffled reaction to that response. "They used to speak but gradually stopped using physical speech. They communicate with a form of telepathy. It's not an actual language. In truth, I wouldn't even know how to define it, if it's even possible. It's like a thought transfer. You just know what they said."

"Wow! That sounds amazing. But why did they stop speaking?"

"Because thought transfer was clearer and more honest. Words can be misinterpreted or deliberately deceptive," Kronos said matter-of-factly.

"Ah! Honesty again," I said teasingly.

He smiled, but this time it didn't reach his fascinating eyes. "Honesty is everything here. Although you'll have few interactions with the Nundars, never try to deceive them."

"I have no intention to do so," I said, suddenly feeling uneasy about the implied threat, should I do so. "But now I'm curious as to why I've never seen or heard of Nundars before."

"They exclusively dwell with Obosians," Kronos replied after swallowing his mouthful. "Like them, my people feed on emotions, and they in turn feed on ours."

"Wait, what?" I asked, my gaze flicking to his full plate before looking back up at him.

He grinned, his fangs peeking beneath his generous lips. "While we do eat regular food, it represents less than a quarter of our diet. Obosians mainly feed off emotions. We would be close to what you humans call Incubi."

"You're a sex demon?" I blurted out, immediately kicking myself for it.

Kronos burst out laughing before studying my features with the strangest expression. "You sound horrified. Would that be so bad?"

I shifted in my seat, unsure if shock or arousal had prompted the conflicted emotions swirling through me.

"Truth be told, I'm not quite sure how to respond to that," I said honestly. "From what little I remember of the lore, the victim of an incubus or a succubus will have the best sex of their lives during their sleep, but the demon will suck their life force in the process. Over time, the human will wither away and eventually die from it."

Kronos's grin broadened. "The part about having the best sex of their lives is accurate. There will indeed be energy being sucked out of you, but it is not your life force. Merely the energy generated by your emotions. It will not drain you in any way, shape, or form. And I can assure you that you will *not* be sleeping through *any* of it."

My cheeks felt on the verge of bursting into flames while my mind took a deep dive into the gutter. With my wretched vivid imagination, I pictured myself writhing beneath him while he pounded into me with his wings deployed. He'd be snarling at me, his eyes glowing with an otherworldly light, his fangs descended, while he sucked in my very soul in an endless beam through our open mouths.

Good God! I could almost feel him inside me, filling me to bursting with his humongous cock. To my horror, my inner walls began constricting, and the dull throbbing between my thighs made me want to squirm.

Kronos did that thing again where his face took on a lascivious expression, and he only poked out the tip of his tongue to lick his upper lip. It made me instantly wet. There was no question in my mind that he enjoyed using his tongue, and that this was an unconscious tick that triggered whenever such naughty thoughts crossed his mind. That first time, too, when he'd done it after seeing my navel piercing, I'd instantly felt hot and bothered. It was as if…

No way?!

"Oh, my God! Are you doing something to me?! Are you…?"

I abruptly stopped talking, although I continued looking at him with outrage. How was I supposed to ask if he was using his incubus powers to turn me on? Surely that had to be the reason for such a strong reaction to his mere words?

"Something to you like what, my mate? Turning you on?" Kronos asked, his eyes darkening, and his voice dropping an octave. "No, my dear. Your current arousal is entirely on you. Well, maybe my words helped. But it's still all you. When I use my *bakaan*, there will be no question who is doing what to you."

The way he spoke those words contained an undeniable dare. Kronos wanted me to ask him to show me the difference between what I was feeling right now and him using his *bakaan*—whatever that was. My tongue burned with the urge to tell him to proceed. But I was already mortified enough that he knew I was aroused.

I scrunched my face, chastising myself for bringing up the embarrassing topic to begin with. Although, to be fair, he was the one who had compared his people to incubi.

"So what's *bakaan*, anyway?" I asked in a slightly grumpy tone.

My cheeks heated a bit more at the look he gave me. If a

look could speak, his would be calling me a coward. Yeah, fine, on that front, I was. But hell, I'd just met the man barely an hour ago. I wasn't ready to have him doing his sex demon magic on me, least of all at the dining table.

"If *that's* the question you want to ask, I will gladly enlighten you, my mate," Kronos said in a provoking fashion that had me itching with the urge of tossing some food at his face. "*Bakaan* is a special energy that Obosian constantly emit passively at degrees so subtle most sentient beings won't perceive it. But we can control the intensity and amount we expend. It's like an aura that will affect everyone in range."

"Are you saying you can turn on a bunch of people with it just by standing in their midst and… expending?" I asked, my eyes bulging.

Kronos burst out laughing. "Technically, yes, I can. But in practice, no, I don't. I do release my *bakaan* on a wide radius to feed my Nundars. But it is a low intensity emission. If I was to actively use it at that level on you, it would simply make you feel calm and relaxed, as if you'd just received a full-body massage. The more I increase its intensity, the stronger the emotions you will feel, from well-being, to arousal, to full-blown pleasure, and even to climax."

"Your aura can give someone an orgasm?" I blurted out, my damn mouth running away with me again.

"Mmhmm," Kronos said with a provocative glimmer in his eyes.

I shifted again in my seat, the throbbing between my thighs only growing stronger. I needed to shift this conversation to a safer territory, but I still had tons of questions left for him.

"But how do they actually feed from you?" I asked, still picturing people with their mouths open, sucking in some beam of light out of him.

"Mostly through the skin, but you can also breathe it in," he explained. "For Nundars, it is passive. They have no control over it. Whenever they're in the presence of this type of energy, their bodies will automatically absorb it, which is why they need to carefully choose the surroundings they will live in."

"But not for Obosians?" I asked, before taking another bite of my food.

"Correct. For us, it is active. We choose whether we want to taste someone's emotions, and how much of it we want to consume," he replied, in a serious tone before the glimmer of mischief returned in his icy-blue eyes. "Some emotions we want to gorge on. But others are absolutely foul."

"I'm guessing anger and violence must be unpleasant," I said, actually fascinated by this.

Kronos snorted. "No, not at all. Violent emotions can be quite tasty."

I recoiled, taken aback by that response.

"There are many causes for anger and violence. Even sorrow can be delicious," Kronos replied with a serious expression again. "It's the reason people love to attend sport events in auditoriums, especially those involving combat like in gladiator arenas. And why people love movies with gut-wrenching emotional scenes. You will bawl your eyes out, and still say it was the best movie ever. The tears of someone mourning the loss of a loved one are especially delectable."

"Excuse me?" I exclaimed, this time flat out shocked, not to say outraged. "How can you take pleasure in someone's pain?"

"We do not take pleasure in their pain. The devastating loss and sorrow are all that most people see when they bear witness to someone falling apart during a funeral or in the moments following the passing of their loved one. But what *we* perceive is the endless and undying love they shared with that person. It shines with the glow of a thousand suns and permeates every single particle of the emotional energy the mourner expends. It's like being wrapped in the light of the gods themselves. The only emotion tastier than that is the birth of a child."

I nodded slowly. "Wow, okay. I never thought of it in those terms. So… if violence and extreme sorrow are tasty to you, what the heck do you find unpleasant?"

"Deception," he said without hesitation.

"Riiight. I seem to recall you mentioning something about dishonesty," I said in a mocking tone.

He chuckled. "Yes. I hate lies. Give me a painful truth any day over a pretty lie. I may balk at it, especially if it's something I will struggle to reconcile with. But I still want the truth."

In that instant, I knew beyond any doubt that he was referring to my situation with Judge Wuras.

"Malice and cruelty are the other emotions that taste foul to me depending on the circumstances," he continued.

"Under what circumstances would malice and cruelty ever be okay?" I exclaimed, flabbergasted.

"When an evil person gets their comeuppance," he said, matter-of-factly. "You're an investigative journalist. I'm sure you've seen cases where a victim finally got revenge on their abuser and gave them a taste of their own medicine—as you humans like to say. While their actions may be questionable under the law, tell me you didn't take some measure of pleasure in that retribution."

That gave me pause. Yes, I had seen some horrible cases where the victim or relative of the victim had taken revenge on the perpetrator. As much as I didn't support vigilantes, in some cases, I silently rejoiced at the cruelty and savagery with which they wrecked the perpetrator. In truth, despite my strong belief in karma, I would lie by saying I wouldn't take extreme pleasure in seeing Judge Wuras suffer every single one of the worst pains a prisoner could endure on Molvi.

By the mysterious smile Kronos gave me, I suspected he'd guessed what thoughts were crossing my mind.

"Does that mean that you mostly feed from your prisoners?" I asked, feeling a little uneasy about it.

"Of course," Kronos replied, leaning back in his chair, apparently sated. "Pain and fear are my main source of emotional energy from my prisoners. And before you ask, no, I do not torture them or deliberately put them in dangerous situations. That would be illegal."

"But then how do you get a regular dose of pain and fear from them?" I asked, baffled, picturing myself surrounded by rabid prisoners. "I mean, wouldn't it all be the type of unpleasant fear from people being mistreated by the evil top dog in the prison?"

"No. I fly over my Dark Quadrants and feed from the emotions rising from them," he explained. "Every Warden—except Dakon—has divided their Sector into Quadrants. The prisoners are split among them based on the gravity of their crime and how dangerous they are to other inmates. The most unredeemable ones are placed in Quadrant Four—the Dark Quadrant. There, it's a constant battle for survival, with many of the prisoners battling for dominance. There are no innocent victims there, nor do they perceive themselves as such."

"Wait, so you mean that, had I been sent to Dakon's Sector, as Wuras had initially intended for me, I would have been placed with the foulest murderers?" I exclaimed.

He nodded, a subtle frown marring his forehead. "Dakon only takes the worst criminals in the galaxy. Everyone is aware of this. That Wuras would have assigned you there is very... troubling."

My heart leapt in my chest. While I wouldn't press him just yet, his words confirmed he was starting to believe me. Or at least, he didn't believe I deserved to be with such criminals. His entire demeanor had significantly changed to the point he'd even gotten a little flirty with me. I didn't doubt that examining my soul had convinced him of my honesty. This boded well for the future.

"Then I'm even more grateful you spared me from that fate," I said in a soft voice.

He grunted in a non-committal fashion.

"Does that mean that you have a guard post in each Quadrant?" I asked, genuinely curious to understand better how their system worked.

He huffed, as if I'd said something outrageous. "Not at all. The prisoners discipline themselves. I provide them with electrical power, and once a week, they get basic tools, materials, and resources to fend for themselves. They must manage them on their own."

"But what if someone or a subgroup tries to appropriate it all?" I argued, stunned.

He laughed. "Someone *always* does, usually newcomers. It never takes long before the other inmates set them straight. If you piss off the others enough, they will cast you out. The forest isn't friendly, especially at night. You do not want to be alone down there."

"Wow! But doesn't that automatically put newcomers in a tough spot? I mean, if they have limited resources to begin with, why would the current inmates welcome a new mouth to feed?" I asked, putting my utensils down.

"To the contrary, the smart ones welcome new additions," he countered. "Prisoners must earn their keep. Each Quadrant has specific resources that can be exploited. They have no obligation to harvest them. But if they do, I buy it from them. And with the credits they earn, they buy additional resources and tools on top of the basic ones they would naturally get."

"So their comfort level is entirely in their own hands!" I exclaimed, impressed.

"Exactly. The Quadrants One and Two live quite comfortably."

I frowned, struck by a sudden thought. "But couldn't they use those tools and materials you bring them to build weapons?"

He smiled and flicked a strand of his long, silver-white hair over his shoulder. "They do, to protect themselves against potential raids from Quadrants Three and Four. Those are rare as there are separations between Quadrants that are quite dangerous to cross. But inmates also build weapons to hunt in the forest or fish."

"Which means they could also use them against you!" I exclaimed.

Kronos chuckled as if I'd said something cute. "First, they would need to get to me, which is no easy feat. There are three kilometers of forest between their Quadrant and this fortress. Both wild and trained beasts patrol the forest—and I don't mean cute ones. Beyond the forest, the river, which circles the perimeter, teems with the most voracious aquatic creatures in the galaxy. And then there's the cliff that is impossible to climb all the way up here."

"Okay, that does sound like quite the gauntlet," I conceded, feeling reassured I wouldn't wake up in the middle of the night to some fugitive having snuck his way in here.

"And second, I can see souls. This allows me to perceive ill-intentions from afar," Kronos explained. "I fly over my Sector twice a day, always at completely different times to catch my prisoners unaware. While their camouflage suit allows them to blend somewhat in the forest when they want to hunt or forage for extra food, it cannot fool me or the guardian beasts deeper in the forest. And third, you saw my surveillance room below. There are plenty of sensors to inform me if anyone is trying to cross the forest to come here or to reach a different Sector."

"Well, it looks like you have everything under control," I said with a certain dose of admiration.

"I do," he said smugly.

I chewed my bottom lip, wondering if I should ask the question burning my tongue.

"Speak," he said in a commanding voice, noticing my hesitation.

"I was just wondering if you think someone like me would survive in any of those Quadrants," I confessed sheepishly.

To my surprise, he seemed to seriously weigh the question instead of mockingly telling me I didn't stand a chance.

"In my Light Quadrant One, yes. It wouldn't be easy, but you would survive. In Quadrant Two and Three, maybe. Not sure." He tilted his head to the side and gave me the strangest look as he studied my face. "You are wondering what will happen to you if I divorce you in six months."

My face heated, and I shifted uncomfortably in my seat. "Kayog already said I'd be sent to Dakon's Sector to serve the remainder of my sentence," I said with a shrug. "But I was wondering if I could be sent to a Light Quadrant like yours instead, if it came to that."

"Why waste energy on such musings?" he asked, looking seriously baffled. "We have six months to prove to each other that we are soulmates. *That's* where you should be focusing your efforts. Give me reasons to want to keep you forever instead of drawing negative energy onto us with grim thoughts."

"But do I even stand a chance of making you want that?" I blurted out, flinching inwardly as soon as the words came out.

"I married you, didn't I? If we didn't stand a chance, I would have let Kayog take you to Amreth."

For a stupid reason, my chest warmed at that response. I hadn't been fishing for reassurance—at least not consciously—but it certainly accomplished that.

His armband beeped, and he pushed his chair back before rising to his feet. "I must leave for now. It is time for me to fly over my Sector."

"Oh, okay," I said, standing up as well. I cast a look at his plate. It was still half-full. "You didn't eat much for someone your height and with your muscle mass. Sorry I made you talk so much."

Kronos snorted, his eyes taking on that mischievous glimmer I was starting to recognize. "I'm leaving room to feast on you tonight."

My jaw dropped, and my cheeks all but burst into flames from embarrassment.

Kronos's smile broadened, and he waved at the table. "You can leave all this. The Nundars will take care of it. I'll be back later."

With this, he turned around and walked away, his tail swaying in a hypnotic fashion.

CHAPTER 6
MALAYA

Feeling a little guilty for leaving the mess on the table, I found my way back to my room to deal with a different type of mess. My thoughts and emotions were all over the place, thanks to Kronos giving me a whiplash.

I didn't know what to make of the male I'd just married. He'd gone from utterly rude, cold, and borderline disdainful, to playful and flirty. Who was the real Kronos? At first, beyond the fact that he believed me a criminal, he hadn't seemed too pleased by my appearance. Granted, the camouflage convict outfit hadn't helped, but still… Although I really noticed his change in behavior towards me after I came out of the hygiene room in my wedding gown, I believe my outburst had prompted him to revise his opinion of me.

Whatever the cause, I welcomed it. And above all, that he believed we were indeed soulmates—despite not feeling the bond any more than I did—gave me hope. He was right. Instead of worrying about plan B in case he ditched my ass at the end of the trial period, I needed to make him fall in love with me.

But can I fall in love with him?

I reflected on the matter as I entered my room. It truly was a breathtaking house, and this room in particular. Floor-to-ceiling reflective windows made up the entire front wall of the room with direct view of one of the countless private terraces of the house and of the stunning landscape beyond. The king-sized bed sat on the right side. Behind it, the same type of gorgeous sculpture, like draped liquid metal—but actually carved out of stone— swirled up the wall to half of the ceiling. A clever mix of dark and pale grays, white, light beige, and pale gold gave the room an understated luxurious feel.

It didn't have a breakfast table, but a desk could serve that purpose, not to mention the plush seating area, with a fireplace and giant screen. This bedroom alone was bigger than my entire old apartment. I strolled over to the standing mirror next to the vanity near the bed and gave myself an assessing once over.

I couldn't recall the last time I found myself this good-looking, thanks in great part to this gorgeous dress. My gaze dropped to my exposed navel, the clever lighting in the room making the silver piercing almost sparkle. I flicked it with my index finger. Memories of the way Kronos had licked his upper lip with the tip of his tongue when he first saw it flashed back before me. The flame of arousal instantly sparked low in my belly.

Good God! How could he affect me this much? Less than a couple of hours ago, I'd been tempted to tell Kayog to take me to the other guy because Kronos was too much of a douche. And now, I was standing here fantasizing about the things he would do to me tonight.

I didn't know if I could fall in love with Kronos. Hopefully, I would. But I could certainly fall in lust with him. Heck, I was already there. Once I'd stopped hating on his cold and haughty ass, I'd really enjoyed our conversation during dinner and getting to know a bit more about what he does here. There seemed to be a playful side to him behind that high-and-mighty façade. And above all, a really sexy and kinky male lurked beneath that strong alpha exterior.

Obviously, I'd known about the Obosians' ability to see souls. But that they fed on emotions took me by surprise. I couldn't recall ever seeing it mentioned anywhere. Were they deliberately hiding that fact? It would creep out some people and be flat out problematic for certain primitive species who would deem it not only offensive but also sacrilegious. Did it make me a freak that I found being married to an incubus to be exciting as hell? No pun intended…

I gave my dangling navel piercing one last flick and proceeded to empty the containers Kayog had recovered. I'd been so frazzled by this whole mess that what I would wear once here had been the last thing on my mind. Was there even a shopping mall on a prison planet? Aside from hosting parties in their respective castles, did the Wardens have some entertainment center for their spouses and families? Did their families even live here with them?

Realizing I knew so little about my new home both poked my naturally inquisitive mind and depressed me. Nobody knew about life on Molvi aside from the fact it was the worst prison planet for a criminal. Assuming there was some form of entertainment here, I likely wouldn't be allowed to go hang out there. Kronos marrying me didn't change my convict status. Did that mean I was under house arrest until such a day I managed to prove my innocence? With the Obosians being such sticklers for law and order, would they shun me if Kronos decided to take me to one of their parties? Would they shun *him* for marrying a criminal?

My shoulders slumped, and I heaved a sigh as I began pulling out my clothes from the containers. Despite the somber thoughts traipsing through my head, I couldn't help the smile settling on my face as I pulled some of my favorite outfits from the crates. Kayog and Linsea were truly fairy godparents to me.

I started hanging them in the ridiculously large walk-in closet entirely dedicated to yours truly. I couldn't even fill a third of it with my belongings. However, the container filled with my unmentionables had me dying with embarrassment… and excitement.

After pulling out my collection of very comfy—but also very not sexy—cotton nightgowns, I found a pile of something wrapped in ivory white silk paper and tied with a golden ribbon. My gut instantly told me Linsea had slipped in some sexy lingerie to replace the granny panties they undoubtedly found in my undies drawer—since I'd not found any of them so far in the containers. The thought that some stranger had raided my underwear drawer was beyond mortifying. Linsea must have facepalmed hard at what she found.

Obviously, I wanted to believe she had handled it, and not Kayog. That would make it even more mortifying.

Eager to see what it contained, I carefully placed the rather big bundle on the bed and untied the bow. My jaw dropped at the sight of the beyond sexy lingerie sets it contained. Most of them were a combo of a babydoll with a G-string in red, blue, black, white, and gold. All the babydolls parted in the middle to reveal my navel. I also found a few teddies, once again with either a cleavage so plunging it exposed my navel, or cut-outs did. Last but not least, a few sheer robes completed the sets.

I felt on the verge of combusting from embarrassment. It wasn't the thought of wearing such exquisitely sexy lingerie for the man I needed to fall head over heels in love with me that bothered me. But the fact that people who I considered almost like mother and father figures had acquired for me the naughty outfits I'd use to seduce said man with.

Fuck me sideways…

Finding another bundle in silk paper confirmed my initial thought that Linsea had found my granny panties and discarded them. In exchange, she sent me a sexy collection of undies, from thongs, boy shorts, and bikini briefs, to a variety of bras, including sport bras and strapless ones. A large box at the bottom contained all the toiletries a woman could possibly need. I could kiss her for this.

Although Linsea had to be in her late sixties—even though she barely looked forty—she had exquisite tastes... a little on the raunchy side. Then again, considering she'd acquired them for me to seduce an incubus, her choices made sense.

Once done unpacking my clothes, I glanced at the two remaining containers, which would be the computer and other similar things Kayog said he'd brought me, before peering outside. We had arrived here fairly late in the afternoon, and the sun was already halfway down on the horizon. I didn't know what time it was, but Kronos had been gone for at least a couple of hours. He'd likely return soon. I didn't want to scramble to make myself presentable once he came knocking for us to complete our contractual duties.

That thought had my nerves acting up again.

The computer could wait. Seducing my husband couldn't. I looked through my brand-new set of sexy outfits and settled on a white, see-through babydoll that contrasted beautifully with my coppery skin. It had flowery embroidery reminiscent of the ones on my wedding dress. A split front conveniently opened and closed with a magnetic clasp between the breasts.

Not wanting to dally any longer, I hurried to my private hygiene room. I would have used the joint one but didn't want to risk Kronos walking in on me if I wasn't done yet. That, too, was ridiculously big and fancy. The layout matched the one from the hygiene room near the entrance where I'd changed into my wedding gown. I hopped into the shower and quickly washed myself, more grateful than ever I'd gotten laser hair removal done years ago.

As soon as I finished, I nearly jumped out of my skin when a fan system I hadn't even noticed started blowing on my back to dry me. Of course, it made sense for the Obosians to have such a system to take care of their humongous wings. It worked wonders to dry my hair.

The whole time I was showering, and then dressing, I kept straining my ears for any sound that would indicate Kronos had returned. When I finally came out of the hygiene room, all dolled up, I'd convinced myself that he had indeed returned, but I hadn't heard him. In my paranoia, I almost went out to check his room, then berated myself for acting like a fool. If I kept this up, Kronos would think me some kind of sex-starved maniac.

While he had undeniably turned me on a couple of times today, and although I had to admit that the whole incubus business had me extremely curious, I wasn't impatient to get down and dirty with him. I'd never been the type to go all the way on a first date. Under different circumstances, I would want us to wait and get to know each other better before taking it to the next step. But this was literally a matter of life and death, and I wouldn't give Kronos any ground to be displeased with me.

When he's ready, he'll know where to find me.

I turned back to the couple of remaining containers and opened the biggest one first. As suspected, it contained a top-of-the-line personal computer with dual holographic monitors, a printer, and a fancy datapad with integrated 3D projector. At the bottom, I found a card with an access code to the UPO network. If I was ever to rebuild my file against Wuras, I would need online access. As a prisoner, it was a huge ask. In most cases, it would be deemed an unrealistic one. Inmates only had access to closed networks to keep them from plotting their escape. If that meant Kronos babysitting me whenever I got online, so be it. I would nail Wuras's scheming ass to the wall, even if it took the rest of my life.

I glanced outside the giant windows. The sun had fully set. A clever mix of glowstones and luminous plants fully lit the terraces outside. Kronos was still nowhere to be seen. I realized then what had me so on edge. It reminded me of when I had surgery for a ruptured Achilles tendon. I fully trusted the surgeon for whom this was a routine procedure, he'd performed so many of them. But he'd been held up by an emergency surgery, which delayed my own operation. The wait had driven me insane. My fertile imagination just went on conjuring all kinds of nightmare scenarios, all the ways things could go wrong, from an impromptu power outage, including power generator failure, to me falling in the 0.000001% of cases with the worst complications.

The minute a nurse was finally able to give me a firm time my surgery would take place, it immediately appeased me. It anchored me. Then I was able to focus on other things without feeling so anxious. As dumb as it sounded, I would be freaking out a lot less if Kronos had simply said "Be ready at ten for us to cross that chore off our list."

Heaving a sigh, I turned back to the smallest container left and opened it. My eyes nearly popped out of my head, and a happy squeal escaped me when the wondrous scent of spices wafted to me. I rifled through the large bags inside: bay leaf, garlic, ginger, pandan, lemongrass, tamarin, chili pepper, annatto seed… all the Filipino spices I would likely never find here. Kayog had even included jars of patis, bagoong, shoyu, and anchovy paste. I loooooved cooking, which I didn't get to do as often as I'd like with all my traveling for my journalism work.

Will the Nundars allow me to cook?

Those thoughts were cut short by movement at the edge of my vision. My heart skipped a beat when I spotted Kronos flapping his massive wings as he flew over the stone railing of the main terrace to make a smooth landing. With a will of their own, my feet took me to the tall glass walls to observe him. My stomach fluttered when he unlatched the clasps of his breastplate to remove it as he continued walking towards the house. Unfortunately, he soon vanished from view.

Heart pounding into my throat, I listened for the sound of his footsteps, but I could barely hear anything. First, because of the roaring of my blood rushing through my ears. Second, because this freaking house was too damn well soundproofed. And third because, despite his great size and muscle mass, Kronos looked like he was gliding when he walked.

A choked gasp escaped me when a brushing sound resonated near my door. I couldn't say if it had been directly on my door or on the wall next to it. But it definitely wasn't a knock—maybe just Kronos's wings rasping against the wall when he shifted them.

Or maybe he's perceiving your freaked out emotions, and he's giving you a heads up.

To my shock—or was it relief?—Kronos kept walking past my room to his own. After maybe a couple of minutes that felt like hours, I distinctly heard the sound of the door in our joint hygiene room open. The small light stone by the door turned red, indicating it was in use. Moments later, the muffled sound of raining water reached me.

Feeling wobbly on my feet, I went to sit at the edge of my bed. This was the point where I should calm down. No more uncertainties remained. And yet, I couldn't recall the last time I'd been this freaked out. It made no sense. After all, it was just sex with a literal sex demon, who happened to be quite hot *and* my soulmate.

I closed my eyes and inhaled deeply. Dusting off my old meditation techniques, I tried to control my breathing to calm myself down and to bring my pulse back to a steadier rhythm. I struggled at first to quiet the panicked little voice at the back of my head, but I gradually got there. By the time my blood stopped roaring in my ears, the eerie silence around me became deafening. I stiffened, realizing the water had stopped raining in the adjoining room.

Moments later, I heard a soft knock on my door. I jumped to my feet and nervously clasped my hands before me.

"Come in," I said, stunned to even be able to form words or that they should come out so clearly without the terrified trembling I expected.

The door parted open in that almost magical unraveling fashion they all did here. My heart skipped a beat when I saw Kronos leaning his left shoulder against the door frame. He was naked and barefoot, except for a short, gold-embroidered black scarf wrapped around his waist like a sarong. It wasn't uncommon for Obosian males to be seen wearing these types of sarongs or short leather skirts like ancient Romans and Egyptians.

It looked fantastic on him.

My gaze roamed over the perfection of his body, previously hidden by his pants and breastplate. Besides his scrumptiously well-defined abdominal muscles, it was the golden barbell piercings in his nipples that caught my attention. I suspected he would have more of those elsewhere on his body, based on the number of piercings in his eyebrows, septum, and ears.

And I bet he has at least one more further south.

I looked back up at his face to find him also examining me. My sheer babydoll didn't leave anything to the imagination. To my relief, despite the neutral expression on his face, Kronos didn't seem disappointed by what he saw.

"You look beautiful," he said in a hushed voice.

"Thanks," I whispered back before giving him a quivering smile and nervously tucking a lock of hair behind my ear.

Without another word, he straightened from his leaning position and extended a hand towards me, his palm up. A throng of butterflies took flight in the pit of my stomach as I willed my feet to move forward. I stopped directly in front of him and placed my hand in his. Our gazes still locked, he gently caressed the back of my hand with his thumb in a soothing fashion.

Seconds later, an immense sense of peace washed over me.

The tension knotting my back, and the butterflies swarming in my stomach in a frenzy suddenly vanished.

He's using his bakaan! He's appeasing me.

It was an odd sensation, but in a very pleasant way. I smiled with gratitude. The gentle, almost tender way in which he returned that smile messed with my head. This time, whatever lingering fear I still harbored vanished. His Obosian aura had nothing to do with that one. Something about Kronos, the way he looked at me, didn't rush me, and tried to soothe me made me feel safe.

Remaining quiet, Kronos led me by the hand to his room. It was located five meters down—the length of our shared hygiene room—at the end of the hallway. He hadn't closed his door. His room took my breath away. As elegant as mine, but in much darker tones, everything about it screamed masculinity and discipline. It didn't make it somber and rigid, but it gave the room a sense of peace and order.

Where my room had light beige organic patterns swirling up the walls and over half the ceiling, Kronos's had straight exposed beams made of black wood against dark brown wood panels covering the wall. The symmetrical lines made the high ceiling look even taller. The layout of his room otherwise mimicked mine but rotated in a mirror image, even down to the entire section of wall made of floor-to-ceiling windows overlooking a huge terrace.

The soft swishing sound of the door closing behind us reclaimed my attention.

I realized then that he was still holding my hand. He gently tugged on it, drawing me closer to him without actually pulling me into his embrace. At the same time, the pleasant feeling—like a warm and fluffy blanket wrapped around me—vanished as he stopped using his *bakaan* on me.

I almost whimpered and asked him to keep doing it but reined in that instinctive reaction. Sure, it felt good. But I loved that Kronos only used his power to douse my initial panic, but not to alter my responses now that we were about to get down to business. I wanted to be in control of my own reactions and responses to what would happen between us, not be enthralled by some external power.

"Are you afraid?" he asked in a gentle voice, that rolled over my skin like a soft summer breeze.

"No," I whispered, shaking my head. "I'm nervous, but... I trust you. I know you won't hurt me."

"I'll *never* hurt you, Malaya. However this union came to be, you are my mate now. It is my duty to protect you and keep you safe from anything that could cause you harm... be it me, or anyone else."

My eyes widened upon hearing those words.

Is he saying...?

"Anything?" I asked in a hesitant voice.

"Anything and anyone," he reiterated with a firmness that sounded almost like a pledge.

My heart fluttered. Although he hadn't clearly spelled it out, I believed at a visceral level that he'd just promised he would see me through this mess and protect me from Wuras. Under different circumstances, with a different man, I might have wondered if he was just buttering me up to get in my panties. But Kronos didn't need to play mind games for that. I'd given him a golden pass to dive right in.

He cupped my cheek with his free hand and caressed it with his thumb.

"If you ever get scared or need me to stop at any point in time, just say so, and I will," he continued in a soft but firm voice. "We may have a contractual obligation to fulfill, but coupling between husband and wife should always be first and foremost about pleasure and consent. If I do something you're not comfortable with, you must speak. I cannot read emotions like a Temern. In the throes of passion, the line between pleasure and pain can quickly become blurred. Do you understand?"

I nodded. "Yes, Kronos. I understand. If I get uncomfortable, I will speak up."

"Good girl," he whispered as he leaned forward.

My stomach quivered again, but this time with a spark of excitement, as he pressed his lips against mine. His palm on my cheek glided to the back of my head to hold my nape. He released my other hand to draw me against his firm body. The heat of his bare skin against mine had a sigh of delight rising in my throat. But his tongue invading my mouth silenced it.

It felt a little pointier and narrower than a human's, its slightly rougher texture enhancing every sensation as our tongues made each other's acquaintance. He tasted fresh, cool, and yet a little spicy, almost like peppermint. The sharp tips of his fangs grazing against my tongue sent a thrill running down my spine. But it was the feel of the piercing in the middle of his tongue that took me aback. It shouldn't have surprised me, and yet I gasped and pulled back.

My gaze locked on his mouth, which stretched into a slow, taunting smile, revealing his fangs. Kronos parted his lips and poked out his tongue. On top of being a dark shade of gray, it didn't have a rounded tip like ours, but was indeed quite pointy. To my shock, instead of stopping after a couple of inches, Kronos's tongue kept stretching past his chin and neck, all the way down to his jugular notch.

My jaw dropped in awe, and a dull throbbing awakened between my thighs as a flurry of naughty thoughts invaded my mind. He yanked his tongue back inside his mouth, and his face took on that dirty expression that I always found quite the turn on.

"Yes, Malaya. Keep imagining all the ways I'm going to use it on you," he whispered in a tone halfway promising, halfway threatening, that resonated straight in my core.

Without giving me a chance to respond, he reclaimed my mouth, this time in a far more dominant and commanding fashion while his hands slipped under the front panels of my babydoll. The slightly rough feel of his calloused palms as they caressed my skin in a bold and possessive fashion had my skin erupting in goosebumps.

I ran my hands over his body, loving the way his firm and well-defined muscles rolled beneath the silkiness of his skin. He broke the kiss, his lips roaming over my face, then neck. His fangs grazing my skin had another delicious shiver running down my spine.

While still kissing and nipping my neck and clavicle, Kronos unclasped my babydoll. My skin suddenly felt cold and exposed in sharp contrast to the blazing trail of heat his palms left in their wake as he pushed the garment off my shoulders in a gentle caress.

He crouched before me, his mouth closing around one of my nipples. That, too, resonated directly in my core. The rough texture of his tongue as he licked and sucked on my little nub had moisture pooling between my thighs as a soft moan tumbled out of me. I slipped my fingers through the silky strands of his long, silver-white hair, and pushed my chest forward for greater contact.

I gasped when his nails sharpened into claws, which he carefully raked down my back and over my behind, left fully exposed by the nearly non-existent fabric of my G-string. My inner walls contracted with need and anticipation when his claws hooked into the string holding my undies around my waist and slowly pulled it down. Simultaneously, he knelt before me, his wings spreading partially open as he kissed his way down to my navel.

The growling sound of approval he made as he started licking at my navel, flicking my piercing with this tongue, had me growing even more wet, while my nipples felt heavy and achy, deprived of his attention. As soon as my G-string fell to the floor with a soft rustling sound, Kronos wrapped his arms around my legs and picked me up as he rose to his feet.

I yelped, my hands instinctively closing around his horns for support. The effortless way in which he'd done this—from a kneeling position no less—spoke volumes about his strength. Without stopping to kiss and suck on my navel and stomach, Kronos carried me to his bed and carefully laid me on top of the fluffy mattress.

He immediately buried his face between my thighs. No teasing, no making me beg, Kronos went straight for gold. I cried out as the rough texture of his tongue flicked over my engorged little nub. My back arched over the bed while he expertly licked and sucked on it. I latched onto his top left horn with one hand and rolled and pinched one of my nipples with the other. His claws still carefully raked over the tender skin of my stomach and inner thighs. His palms would then soothe the exquisite burn in an endless loop that had my nerve endings perking up.

Riding the waves of pleasure quickly building inside me, it took a moment for my brain to comprehend the probing sensation around my slit. With both his hands still stirring the most wondrous sensation over my skin and his mouth wrapped around my clit, it only left his tail.

A strangled moan escaped me as its rounded tip slipped inside me. The nagging little voice at the back of my mind shouted that this was wrong, unnatural. But my body didn't give a shit. With a will of their own, my hips gyrated in counterpoint to the movements of his tail moving in and out of me, pushing me ever closer to the edge. Sensing my impending orgasm, Kronos accelerated the pace of his tail making love to me, and the intensity with which his mouth and tongue sucked and massaged my clit.

I cried out as my climax swept me away. Waves upon waves of pleasure crashed through me as Kronos continued to masterfully play with my body. As I slowly came back from my high, I lifted my head to stare at Kronos, still crouched between my legs. As if sensing my gaze on him, he peered up at me. His eyes started to glow. He slightly straightened, while his overly long tongue gave my clit a slow, teasing lick.

Hypnotized, I watched him pull his tail out of me. Like a snake swaying to the enchanted music of a snake charmer, its glistening tip came to a stop right in front of Kronos's face. Glowing eyes still locked with mine, my husband opened his mouth. A bolt of lust exploded in the pit of my stomach when he took the tip in his mouth, licking my essence right off it.

An almost malicious smile stretched his lips, the intensity of the glow in his eyes cranking up another notch. My skin tingled, and the oddest dropping sensation swept through me. It felt almost like a rollercoaster ride, that moment right after you've reached the peak, and you suddenly find yourself in that very brief gravity defying moment before you rush downward.

"Ready for round two?" he whispered, his voice so low I barely made out his words.

I never got a chance to respond. At the same time he stabbed his tongue inside me—taking over where his tail had left off—a powerful wave of lust slammed into me. I threw my head back against the mattress and shouted as liquid bliss flowed through my veins. My head rolled from side to side as intense pleasure crashed over me in one endless wave after the other. At a subconscious level, I understood that Kronos was using his *bakaan* on me. But I couldn't think straight.

My skin was on fire, and my nerve endings had gone into overdrive. Each sensation, each touch, even just the feel of the blanket rubbing against my skin was driving me insane with sensory overload. His tongue, plunging impossibly deep inside of me, further fanned the inferno consuming me from within. With supernatural accuracy, his tongue piercing rubbed against my G-spot, both on its way in and on its way out, sending electric sparks coursing through me. My moans and shouts of ecstasy poured out of me in a continuous flow as I writhed on the bed.

Just when I thought my mind would fracture from this excess of pleasure, Kronos finally relented. The room spun. Even as my body continued to shake with involuntary spasms, I felt boneless, as if I'd just reintegrated into my corporeal vessel after an out-of-body experience. My eyelids weighed a ton, and my eyes seemed to want to roll to the back of my head. You'd think I'd just gone on a drinking binge and was completely hammered, minus the headache.

When I finally managed to refocus, Kronos was towering over me, staring at my face. Kneeling between my parted legs, his dark wings deployed, his fangs bared, and his icy-blue eyes glowing, he looked like a fallen god about to feast on his pagan sacrifice. And feast, I believe he had, gorging on the whirlwind of emotions he had stirred in me while I drowned in a maelstrom of bliss.

The savage, almost feral expression on his face should terrify me. And although it did liquify my insides, it wasn't fear but lustful anticipation that fueled it. A tremor shook my legs when his clawed hands—which had been resting possessively on my thighs—gently scraped my skin before moving to the short sarong still wrapped around his waist.

Hypnotized by his glowing stare, it took every ounce of my willpower to tear my gaze away, drawn by the careful movement of his hands detaching his sarong. I held my breath as he parted the panels of the garment at an excruciatingly slow pace. A sadistic smile stretched his lips as he enjoyed torturing me with this crawling reveal.

And then, there it was, in all its glory.

Thick and long, his cock—a slightly darker shade than his gray skin—stood proudly erect. A few patches of chevron-shaped scales—similar to the ones that graced the outer edges of his shoulders and forearms—adorned the upper end of his shaft.

As I had suspected, he had at least one piercing on the underside of his cock, right below the head. Though I couldn't see it from this angle, I believed he had at least another piercing on the topside. However, my stomach dropped at the sight of a series of spikes on each side of his shaft, almost shaped like sawtooth. That would tear me up inside!

As if he'd guessed what thought had just crossed my mind, Kronos wrapped one hand at the base of his shaft, giving it a tight squeeze before stroking himself twice. My fears instantly vanished as the spikes bent with little resistance. Instead, my inner walls contracted with anticipation at what kind of additional sensation they would provide inside me.

My breath hitched when Kronos suddenly moved forward to lie on top of me. A needy whimper escaped me at the feel of the searing heat of his bare skin against mine. I spread my legs wider to make more room for him, my toes curling when his thick shaft rested against my sex. Eyes locked with mine, Kronos rubbed his length a couple of times against me, coating himself with my essence.

To my surprise, he stopped.

"Do you accept me, my mate?" he asked in a hushed tone, his voice even more gravelly from desire.

That simple request messed me up. Contractually, I had a duty to say yes, and he had no obligation to pleasure me the way he already had. But the respectful way he sought my consent touched something deep within me. In that instant, I realized that maybe he was indeed my soulmate and that, in time, I would fall in love with him.

"Yes, Kronos. I do," I replied, my voice filled with emotion.

Once more, his face took on that tender expression that totally fucked with my head. He'd been so cold, so disdainful when I first arrived. And now, here I was, feeling safe, almost cherished, even though the latter wasn't the case.

But all such meanderings vanished from my mind as Kronos

reclaimed my lips in a deep and possessive kiss as he started pushing himself inside me. Despite how wet he'd gotten me and how much he'd prepared me, my body resisted his invasion. Not surprising, considering his non-negligible girth.

Between kisses and gentle caresses, Kronos whispered words of encouragement as he patiently worked his way in with shallow thrusts. At one point, I realized he had started using his *bakaan* again, but not the insane version on steroids that gave me an instant, mind-blowing orgasm, but the light version that made me feel relaxed, dampening my body's natural resistance.

And it worked wonders.

In just a few additional careful thrusts, Kronos was fully sheathed. I gasped at the slight burn and incredible fullness. But hearing him hiss as he closed his eyes, an almost pained expression on his beautiful face fanned the flame of my desire. Judging by the way he clenched his teeth, his upper lip curled up in a snarl, Kronos was fighting to remain still while I adjusted to his girth.

As the burn faded, a plethora of new sensation penetrated my mind from the soft spikes on the sides of his shaft, the scales, and the piercings. My inner walls started contracting with a will of their own. Apparently taking it as the signal I was ready, Kronos started moving in slow, controlled thrusts. Instead of lessening, the tension on his face increased, and he took a hissing breath through his teeth that resonated straight in my core.

This wasn't the face of someone in pain, but of a man straining under intense pleasure. The pleasure he was deriving from *my* body…

It did funny things to me to know I could reciprocate at least in part the mind-blowing pleasure he had given me twice already. Even as his movements accelerated, the insane sensations of his cock rekindling the flame inside me, I stared at his stunning face. His soft moans in my ears acted like a potent aphrodisiac in and of themselves.

My fingers dug into his back as I began to writhe beneath him, moving in counterpoint to his movements. I couldn't tell which, between his piercings or his scales, was doing a number on the sensitive bundle of nerves inside of me, but they were making contact both on the way in and out.

Kronos suddenly opened his eyes. His irises appeared to have shrunk to a tiny dot, his dark sclera having swallowed them as he stared at me with an almost feral expression. He emitted a deep, menacing growl that sent a delicious shiver down my spine before he crushed my lips in a savage kiss.

In that instant, something appeared to have broken in him. Kronos unleashed his passion on me, taking me faster, harder, and deeper. In seconds, he had me cresting again while I tumbled down yet another bottomless pit of sensory overload. His cock was wrecking me. The searing heat of his skin wrapped around me kept me pinned to the mattress while he pounded into me. His hands and mouth seemed to be everywhere at once.

I was combusting from within, as waves upon waves of bliss washed over me. Nothing mattered anymore but our bodies rocking in a timeless dance, the sexy sound of his grunts and labored breath mixing with my moans, and pleasure... endless pleasure sweeping me away.

After he wrested a third orgasm from me, Kronos pulled away, leaving me feeling bereft. But before I could fully comprehend what was happening, the room spun around me. By the time I regained my bearings, Kronos was lying on his back, his wings spread wide. I was sprawled on top of him, while he was taking me from below.

I didn't think I had any strength left in me for another round. And yet, I found myself placing my palms on his chest and pushing myself up. As I began gyrating on top of him, he grabbed my behind with both hands, his claws pricking my cheeks as he pumped up into me. My palms rubbed over his pierced nipples, drawing a grunt of approval from him.

His eyes appeared completely black as he stared at me, his lips parted, and his labored breath coming in short bursts interspersed with growls of pleasure. I realized then that he was finally approaching his own climax but wouldn't topple over without me.

To my shock, his right hand let go of my behind to wrap around my nape. He yanked me down against his chest and pressed his lips to my ear.

"One last time… together," he said, his voice so thick and deep, his chest vibrated against mine.

He'd no sooner spoken those words than his *bakaan* blasted through me. I couldn't say if I screamed, if my body seized, or whatever else happened. It felt like my soul had been knocked right out of my body from the violence of the orgasm that ripped through me. And yet, I distantly heard the savage roar Kronos emitted as his searing seed shot deep inside me.

I felt like a leaf caught in the path of a tornado, swirling in an endless whirlwind of sensations, taking me higher and higher. I was flying too high. Soon, I would reach the sun and burn to cinders. But tender hands roaming over my body kept me anchored, slowly bringing me back down onto firmer ground.

I blinked as I slowly regained my bearings. Feeling wrecked and boneless, my head resting against Kronos's chest, his cock still buried deep inside me, I listened to the thundering sound of his heartbeat gradually slowing down. He was holding me tightly as if he feared I would vanish. Then his wings wrapped around us, sheltering me in their warm cocoon.

I snuggled deeper against him. Kronos tightened his embrace and placed a tender kiss on my forehead. We didn't speak. Words weren't needed. Feeling safe… feeling home, I closed my eyes and smiled as a veil of darkness fell before me.

CHAPTER 7
KRONOS

An insane amount of power coursed through me as I flew to the power core of my Sector. It provided electricity, heat, and cooling to my four Quadrants. It sat on a tiny island in the center of the Quadrants. A small lake, infested with flesh eating creatures, surrounded the island to keep any inmate who survived the forest leading to it from tampering with the system.

By default, every Sector had a similar geothermal power plant. It provided enough energy to supply the basic needs of the inmates within their Quadrants, as required by galactic laws. But the prisoners needed to carefully manage its use not to run out, which could be difficult if the inmates failed to establish and enforce strict usage guidelines among themselves.

Those who worked well together and gathered their local resources could trade them with me for power crystals—among other additional comforts. The crystals provided extra energy, which could eliminate the need to use it sparingly, depending on the size of the crystal they could afford and their ability to pay to recharge it once its reserves were depleted.

As in most Sectors, the inmates from Quadrant One had the biggest crystals, while Quadrant Four was always a gamble.

Either they pushed hard to get extra comforts, despite the frequent chaos that reigned in that area, or they had the worst living conditions because they spent too much time fighting or protecting their rear to be able to perform any work to improve their lot.

My wards weren't supposed to get a refill for ten more days. Quadrants Three and Four had already depleted their crystals, while One and Two still had close to a quarter remaining. If they didn't abuse their reserves, they should make it until then.

Except, thanks to my mate, I was bursting at the seams with *lumiak*—a form of lightning Obosian Warriors like me could generate from the energy we absorbed while feeding on emotions.

And last night, did I ever feast!

Tharmok's blood… Just thinking of Malaya instantly made me hard again. By the gods, it had been so insanely good! Everything about her was perfection. I never pictured myself drawn to a human. And yet, there it was. My mate had me hooked. Her emotions tasted so divine, I'd gorged beyond reason. You'd think I was a juvenile entering his first heat.

I'd heard of hangovers and indigestions from feeding frenzies. To me, only a silly person would show so little restraint as to make themselves sick from indulging too much. But my skin hurt from the excess of energy coursing through me. My hands burned with the need to unleash my *lumiak* and reduce the pressure within.

I raised my palms in front of Quadrant One's power crystals. Electric tendrils emerged from my skin, writhing over it before shooting out in a thundering sound. A grateful moan escaped me as some of the pressure lessened while the crystal greedily absorbed the energy I fed it. This release was comparable to relieving an overflowing bladder after having been forced to hold it in for much too long.

Except, by the time I'd completely filled Quadrant One's

three power crystals, my *lumiak* 'bladder' easily remained ninety-five percent full. While my skin no longer felt overly stretched, I needed to shed some more power. My face heated at the thought that flashed at the back of my mind. I wouldn't even try to pretend I was giving the other three Quadrants power they hadn't earned to avoid waste.

I just wanted to make room to be able to gorge some more tonight.

Blast it! I couldn't stop thinking about her. The way she'd looked, sounded, and responded to me while I was taking her. And her orgasms... Every time Malaya climaxed, her soul glowed like a star going supernova. It felt like the gods themselves were shining their divine light upon me.

I doubted Malaya even realized that her soul systematically reached for mine whenever ecstasy swept her away. More than once, I'd wanted to latch onto it, and intertwine my soul with hers, truly making us one. But humans couldn't achieve that ultimate union unless they bonded with one of us. It was permanent, hence why Kayog had not required us to perform an Obosian wedding, in case I wanted to repudiate her by the end of our six months.

That wouldn't happen.

In the short time we had spent together yesterday, I had further studied Malaya. While the first ten minutes of us meeting had sufficed to convince me of her innocence, that evening together had cemented my suspicions that we were indeed soulmates. It both thrilled and terrified me. Obviously, I wasn't in love with her yet. We barely knew each other. But I'd never been so mesmerized by a soul as I was with hers. I could just sit there for hours basking in its light.

I liked her inquisitive mind and the fire that lurked beneath her controlled façade. Our first night together had been a major source of concern for me. You didn't force yourself on a non-consenting partner. As much as honoring a contract or a word given defined me, I wouldn't have forced Malaya to hold her end of the deal had she backed out at the last minute. The trusting way she had followed me had touched me deeply. And then the passion she had unleashed...

A frustrated growl escaped me as I blasted all the *lumiak* I could into the remaining crystals. Tharmok's blood, where was my legendary control? Even in my first heat, I'd never been controlled by my cock. This little human had ungodly powers over me. It had taken all my willpower to pull myself away from her this morning. I had to use my *bakaan* to keep from waking her, or I would have ravaged her again.

I shifted on my feet to release some of the pressure in my crotch. The memory of how her wet warmth had squeezed my cock as I plowed into her over and over again had a delicious shiver running down my spine. Nightfall couldn't come quickly enough so that I could lose myself in her again.

Will she allow me?

My stomach knotted at the prospect Malaya might not want to share my bed again. Not for the first time since flying out this morning, I kicked myself for having given my mate her own room. Granted, it was standard for Obosians, especially among nobles, for each spouse to have their private quarters. In my case, I'd welcomed that even more as I had expected Malaya to actually be guilty. I couldn't have shared every night with a criminal without being tempted to strangle her. Therefore, leaving her to rot in her room would have spared me of her presence.

Now, I needed to make her *want* to spend her nights with me. Even if we didn't couple—though I hoped that would happen as often as possible—I just wanted to feel her soft body against mine when I fell asleep.

Having shed all the *lumiak* the crystals could take, I flapped my wings and began the long journey to Amreth's Sector. I needed answers. Ever since Kayog had needled me about giving my soulmate to Amreth, many questions had plagued me.

I usually enjoyed the feeling of freedom and power that flying procured me. As an Obosian, I was a sensual creature and reveled in most forms of physical sensations. Flying offered plenty of that, from the strain of the muscles in my back to the caress of the wind on my skin and as it flowed through my hair, and the way the air currents pushed up or down on my wings. Although I'd flown my entire life, it never got old, each flight remaining a unique experience in its own right.

But today, too many conflicting thoughts warred within me, keeping me even from enjoying the otherwise breathtaking view of Molvi's landscape.

In the distance, the silhouette of Amreth's fortress grew bigger. Like mine—and most other Obosian mansions—his residence boasted multiple terraces spread over three stories. Aside from the fact that we enjoyed basking in the sun, we liked open spaces that we could easily take flight from or land onto. Where dark-grays, beige, gold, and various shades of browns dominated the color palette of my domain, Amreth had gone with a much paler scheme, mostly whites and light-beige with the occasional sharp obsidian accents.

Even as I began my descent, I noticed my old friend standing on his main terrace. I couldn't tell if his perimeter surveillance system had warned him of an intruder's approach, or if luck prompted his presence there.

He watched me land with his usual serene expression, then pressed his palm to his chest in greeting as I closed the short distance between us.

"Greetings, Kronos. I wondered who between you and Kayog would visit me," Amreth said in a slightly taunting tone.

"You know about me?" I exclaimed, making no effort to hide my surprise, even as I returned the greeting gesture.

"Yes. Kayog told me they had found Malaya's soulmate," Amreth said while giving me an assessing look. "Frankly, after finding out it was you, it rather shocked me that you actually kept her."

I stiffened, feeling preemptively offended. "Why did that shock you? She is my soulmate. Why would I not accept her?"

"Because you're unbelievably stuck up, and one of the biggest sticklers for the rules, even by Obosian standards," Amreth said matter-of-factly. "You're the last person I expected to marry a convicted murderer."

"She's innocent!" I snapped, feeling overly protective—even borderline aggressive—to have her thus labeled, even though there had been no contempt in his voice.

A strange glimmer sparked in his silver-white eyes, as he studied my features. "She's still been convicted by one of our highest-ranking judges. I'm surprised you even allowed the Temern to bring her to your estate."

I ran nervous fingers through my hair and walked to the stone railing of his balcony. My eyes went out of focus as I looked down. Unlike me, Amreth didn't have a monster infested moat-like lake at the base of his cliff. His Nundars had created a stunning garden of colorful plants that adorned the large clearing past the forest. Every single one of them could kill a target in seconds. Some did so with the spores they released the minute you came close enough. Others ensnared you with their vine-like tentacles in order to slowly digest you. And a last group would infect you with flesh eating bacteria merely by brushing against their leaves or their thorns.

Since I'd gone into overkill mode setting up the defenses in my Sector, I'd also added a smaller version of a similar garden by the shore of my moat.

"Yes, you are correct." I said at last. "I almost didn't let him bring her to my domain. What Warden would marry a murderer?"

"Apparently, you—of all people—would," Amreth said mockingly.

I turned my head to give him a dark look. "From what I hear, *you* were more than open to the idea as well. Except you didn't even have the excuse of her being your soulmate. Why is that?"

He snorted. "I merely considered it. You went through with it. *I* should be the one asking *you* that question."

I huffed, annoyed, then turned sideways to face him, my elbow resting on top of the railing. "I perceived no deception in the Temern's soul. He genuinely both believed her innocent and that she was my soulmate. If he was right, and I denied her, I'd be committing an even greater crime by allowing Malaya to get sent to Dakon's playground."

Amreth nodded slowly. "My reasoning was the same. But I admit I never thought you'd listen long enough to be swayed."

I scrunched my face as I bit back the urge to give him a tongue lashing. As much as I believed myself to be reasonable, it shamed me to admit I'd only allowed Kayog to bring her so that I could kick her out with a clear conscience once I'd confirmed she was indeed a criminal.

"I almost didn't. In truth, Kayog saying you would take her played a large part in me reconsidering," I said, although admitting it scorched my lips.

"Me?!" Amreth exclaimed, surprise settling on his attractive face.

At forty-four—two years my elder—Amreth always drew many covetous glances from our females. We shared a similar height and size, as well as our silver-white hair. But his skin was a darker shade of gray than mine, and instead of the purplish highlights on my scales, his were silver, which matched the color of his eyes. He had a squarer jaw than mine with a superb piercing right below his generous lips.

Yes, much too attractive.

Had Kayog taken her to him instead, would Malaya have responded to his touch the way she had to mine? Would she have been as aroused with him as she'd been with me?

I immediately chastised myself for allowing such toxic thoughts to penetrate my mind. Malaya and I were soulmates. Our chemistry was preordained.

"Yes, you," I said. "Of all people, you are the last person I would have pictured wanting to get involved in any kind of drama. We both know what a shitshow this will turn into if Wuras is proven to be corrupt. So that you would even consider marrying someone who isn't even your soulmate—when you've shunned all our finest females who pursued you—told me there's more going on. So, why would you have accepted her?"

Amreth shrugged. "Kayog is never wrong. Based on his empathic abilities, he confirmed she was innocent. He also stated that despite the fact that Malaya and I aren't soulmates, our personalities were compatible enough that we would have a very happy marriage. It gets lonely up here. And all those females pursuing me are too high maintenance. They would drive my Nundars away with their antics."

I laughed. "Meena would definitely have them fleeing your domain."

He rolled his eyes with a shuddering expression. That female was as beautiful as she was insufferable. She couldn't take no for an answer. In fact, denying her anything was the surest way to get her to hound you endlessly.

"But *your* Nundars must be very happy right now," Amreth continued while shifting his massive black wings. "Even standing two meters away from you, and while you are at ease, I can feel your aura. You're overflowing with *lumiak*. I can only presume things went well with your mate."

I gave him a warning glance, which he completely ignored. That overly protective reaction on my part also didn't make sense. Amreth wasn't fishing for juicy details about my relationship with Malaya.

"She's innocent," I said, shaking my head. "Her soul is so damn pure, how did Wuras not see it? It took me less than five minutes challenging her to know she was wrongly accused. I spent all evening last night and all morning trying to come up with a rational reason for such a gross mistake on his part. But he's not old enough to suffer from the early stages of *gannath*. And no one in his bloodline has ever been diagnosed with that degenerative cognitive disease."

"Wuras doesn't suffer from *gannath*," Amreth said in a stern voice. The obvious contempt laced within it took me aback. "Malaya is not the first person he wrongfully sentenced."

He turned to look towards the forest beyond which lay his Quadrants. He placed his hands on the railing, his claws jutting out from his fingertips as they dug into the pale stone. The searing wave of anger emanating from him stunned me further. What in Tharmok's name was happening?

"Wuras sent me at least one wrongfully condemned inmate," Amreth continued, grinding the words through his teeth.

"He did? When? Where's the prisoner?" I asked.

"Two months ago. The sentence stated he should be remanded to the Dark Quadrant. As I had no reason to question the ruling based on the file, and since I had room, I had the guards deliver him straight there in the early hours of the afternoon. "That same evening during my fly over, I noticed a flickering soul. When I landed, he was dying."

I recoiled. "Already? On his first night?"

Amreth nodded grimly, his claws digging further in the stone. "He didn't have a shred of evil in him. The predators in my Dark Quadrant realized he was prey and descended on him. He died holding my hand and swearing his innocence. The truth of his words shone like the sun at its zenith."

His eyes lost their distant look from reminiscing as he turned his head sideways to look at me. The anger on his face screamed about how deeply this incident still affected him.

"His file claimed he was the foulest of criminals. All lies!" Amreth hissed. "Innocent people *do not* get sent *accidentally* to a

Dark Quadrant. There are too many verification steps designed specifically to avoid tragic judicial errors. Obosians are the protectors of law and order. *This* is deliberate."

I shifted my wings and stretched my neck to release some of the tension knotting the muscles between my shoulder blades. This was turning into an even bigger nightmare than I feared.

"Do you know anything about that male that could have justified Wuras wanting to silence him?" I asked.

He shook his head with an air of frustration. "I don't. He died too soon. And his file is completely unreliable. All of it is fabricated. Even his name is false. The problem is that we can't even try to discover his true identity."

"Why not?" I asked.

"Because it would require us to do a deep reverse search through the central database. That will set off flags," Amreth explained. "If our assumptions are correct, Wuras will be tracking such inquiries."

I narrowed my eyes at him. "Who is 'we'?"

Amreth's face closed off, setting all my senses on high alert. Something bigger was truly going down.

"It's a little late for you to lose your tongue, friend," I said in a harsh tone. "I'm up to my horns in this mess. So if you have information, you need to spill it."

Amreth made a face as if he'd bitten something bitter then gave me a sharp nod. "I started hearing similar rumors circulating. As you accurately pointed out, making open accusations against Wuras would start a major shitshow no one wants to get drawn into. But we have a duty to uphold the law. We needed to gather proof. I started talking with some carefully chosen Wardens, who wouldn't wag their tongue before the time was right. We all agreed to personally check all prisoners that Wuras assigned to our Fourth Quadrants before they are taken there."

"You found more wrongful condemnations?" I asked, already guessing the answer.

"We found two," Amreth said grimly. "Unlike that first male and your Malaya, those two are no saints. They are petty criminals and smugglers. But not Q4 assassins. We've placed them in Q1 where they have a chance to survive."

"What does Wuras have against them?" I asked, hoping for a first clue to follow.

My heart sank at Amreth's dejected expression. "That's the problem. They have no clue why he came after them like this. They were arrested for minor offenses. Once they stood before Wuras, a bunch of trumped-up charges were suddenly added, earning them a life sentence in a Dark Quadrant. Their best guess is that Wuras is taking out people competing with some of his associates, or that he's taking bribes to narrow the playing field."

I heaved a sigh. "This is such a monumental mess. Malaya is hoping to be able to rebuild her file against Wuras, but it won't be easy with her being stranded here."

"Indeed," Amreth said before giving me an assessing look. "Does Wuras know you married Malaya?"

"No. Not yet," I said, tugging at one of the piercings in my right earlobe, a nervous tick that manifested itself whenever I felt anxious. "But it will happen soon, once the public records get updated."

"I can delay it," Amreth offered.

I frowned. "That's illegal."

He waved a dismissive hand. "Delaying publication of sensitive information to protect an investigation is legal," he said matter-of-factly.

I smiled. "You have a point."

"I can buy you six weeks, maybe two months, but no more than that," Amreth said. "Once he finds out, he will come after you *and* her."

I nodded, my frown deepening. "I appreciate it. There's no question he'll want to silence her or try to discredit us."

"He will. I will inform you of whatever new information I get that may help with the case," Amreth offered.

"Thank you, my friend. This was enlightening. I must go. We'll be in touch."

I pressed my palm to my heart in farewell. He echoed my gesture, and I took flight.

CHAPTER 8
KRONOS

I finally got back home, a little annoyed with myself for staying out much longer than expected. I had hoped to return before Malaya had awakened. Considering it was quickly approaching lunchtime, I had epically failed on that front.

As I began my descent, I spotted my mate sitting on one of the chaise lounges on the private terrace outside her room. She was reading something on her tablet, then typing a few lines before appearing to be reflecting some more. My pulse immediately picked up with an irrational joy at seeing her. Simultaneously, an even more irrational nervousness descended over me. For an overly confident—not to say cocky—male like me, this behavior on my part was truly confusing. In that instant, I would have given anything to possess the Temern's ability to know exactly how people felt.

Malaya's head suddenly jerked up. The flapping sound of my wings had undoubtedly alerted her to my presence. The most pleasant heat spread through my chest when her face lit up upon recognizing me. She put the datapad down next to her and rose to her feet. The way she nervously ran her fingers through her hair as if to fix it was beyond adorable.

I landed, unsure how to greet her. My fingers itched to sink into her lustrous hair, and my arms ached to draw her supple body into my embrace.

But would she welcome it?

She clasped her hands before her as I approached. Eyes flicking between mine, Malaya licked her lips nervously. I didn't have to be a mind reader to understand she, too, wondered how to greet me. The safest route would be to keep my distance. But how boring was safe? I wanted my mate to share my bed tonight and every other night. Setting the tone now seemed like the wisest approach. Her reaction would also give me a clear hint as to where she stood on that front.

Eyes locked with hers, I advanced slowly, stopping a couple of steps in front of her, invading her space. Malaya's lips slightly parted while she stared at me with an expectant look laced with tension. I slipped a hand around her nape. When she didn't balk or stiffen, I drew her closer as I leaned forward. To my delight, Malaya unclasped her hands, her palms gliding over my chest in a gentle caress before resting on my shoulders while I claimed her lips.

I had only meant to give her a tender kiss in greeting. But the moment we touched, a burning desire ignited my blood. With a will of its own, my free arm wrapped around her slender waist, and drew her soft body against mine as I deepened the kiss. While our tongues mingled, Malaya gently scratched my scalp, just above my nape, and pressed her chest against mine.

I almost picked my mate up and carried her to her bed to give in to the unrelenting desire that had plagued me all morning. However, Malaya wasn't just a fling, a temporary hunger I wanted to sate. She was my soulmate, and an innocent victim whose life hung in the balance. While I would make sure to keep her well-aware of my desire for her—as I had just now—I also needed to show her that I wanted to lay strong foundations for our future that rested on far more than lust.

With much reluctance, I broke the kiss. It had barely lasted ten to fifteen seconds—much too long for a greeting kiss, but far too short to sate me.

"Good morning, my mate," I said, my hands caressing her nape and back as I dropped them before taking a step back.

She licked her lips as if to catch one last taste of me then smiled in a way that I couldn't define, but that pleased me, nonetheless.

"Good morning, Kronos. Well, late morning," she added with a nervous laugh.

"Apologies. I had meant to return sooner. But I had some matters to discuss with a neighbor," I replied.

"Ah! That's why you came from over there. I was sitting facing north-east so that I could see you flying back when you returned from your Quadrants," Malaya said sheepishly.

"Were you missing me already, dear wife?" I asked teasingly.

She opened and closed her mouth a couple of times, taken aback by the question. I felt stupid that her not immediately saying yes stung me.

"Well, yes," she said at last.

I frowned and narrowed my eyes at her. She lifted her chin defiantly in response.

"You can remove that frown and spare me the suspicious eyes. I'm not lying. I *did* miss you. First, because once you stopped being a douche yesterday, you actually turned out to be pleasant to hang out with. And I would like to get to know you better. Second, I'm many things, but an introvert definitely isn't part of it. In case you haven't noticed, you're the only person I know here. And third, your Nundars would put Houdini to shame," she said firmly before waving her index finger at her face. "Go ahead, do your soul peeping thing to see if I'm lying."

The way Malaya put her fisted hands on her hips and stared at me with a dare in her eyes was incredibly sexy. I loved that fire in my woman. I didn't need to examine her soul to know she'd been honest in her tirade.

I crossed my arms over my chest and lifted my chin with a deliberate haughty attitude.

"First, I do not 'peep' at souls. Second, I wasn't a 'douche'—whatever that means—but merely circumspect under highly unusual circumstances. And third, who in Tharmok's name is Houdini?"

She chuckled and waved a dismissive hand. "He was a human magician, famous for his disappearing acts."

I nodded, understanding dawning on me. "Unless you openly call them, or if they need to communicate something to you in person, you will never see them."

"But are they just like lurking around spying on us?" Malaya asked, looking a little uncomfortable. "I mean I found breakfast all laid out for me in the dining room this morning. It was still warm, as if it had been freshly made. How did they know I was on my way to get food unless they were observing me?"

"They do not spy on us. Thoughts and intentions have frequencies. They perceived you waking up. For them it would be like a distant nudge," I explained. "Your hunger would be more potent. And the moment you started thinking you were going to get food, it would have sent a very specific signal that would reach the Nundars. They would have started cooking the moment they felt it and brought the food on heated plates so that it would be ready for you the moment you entered the room."

"So what are they doing right now?" Malaya asked, hardly looking convinced.

I shrugged. "Doing whatever Nundars do in their spare time."

"But they're perceiving the conversation we're having right now, right?" she insisted.

I shook my head. "No. It doesn't work that way. If living with them was this invasive, this arrangement would not work.

They are oblivious as to what is currently taking place here. Specific emotions will trigger a response from them. Everything else they dismiss as white noise. They would only be distraught by what was happening in the house if there were extreme negative emotions being generated. For example, if you and I were having a very serious argument, if either of us was mourning someone, or any other situation that could cause severe fear or trauma, they would feel it and act accordingly."

Malaya chewed her bottom lip. Her eyes flicked from side to side while a million thoughts appeared to be racing through her mind. When the most adorable redness started creeping on her cheeks, I immediately guessed where her thoughts had wandered.

"Happiness… or pleasure… will not prompt any intervention on their part. It will merely make them happy, and they will go on with their business. To them, whether our pleasure comes from listening to a masterful musician, watching an amazing movie, or indulging in more intimate forms of entertainment all feel the same to them. Happiness is happiness."

"Oh, good," she said, her cheeks reddening a bit more.

I fought the urge to kiss her, she was so unbelievably adorable. Turning to the chaise lounge she had been lying on, I pointed to the datapad with my chin.

"Reading?" I asked.

She shook her head. "No. Actually that was the fourth reason I was looking forward to your return," she replied, looking both sheepish and a little nervous.

My mate fetched the tablet and brought it back to show me the contents displayed on screen. I took it from her hand.

"I've been making a list of the various cases I investigated in connection with Judge Wuras. I tried to jot down everything I remembered, including the various contacts and ways I used to obtain all the information needed. But this will only take me so far. I would need network access and the ability to communicate with some of my contacts off-world."

She said the last few words in a small voice, while she stared warily at me. Normally, an inmate wouldn't even dare make such a request, it was so outlandish. Since coming to the conclusion that she was innocent yesterday, I'd been debating how I would answer such a request. As she was living with me in my dwelling, network access was not a problem whereas it would have been impossible inside one of the Quadrants. However, her efforts could trigger some red flags from the judge and whoever else was in on whatever shady business they had entered into.

"It would only be for things that are legal," Malaya added quickly when I didn't respond right away. "Kayog gave me a username and access code to the UPO's galactic network. I cannot access anything inappropriate with that. And anyway, I suspect all the activity through such a username and network will be closely monitored. I'm an investigative journalist. The only way for my articles to hold up is for me to have proven and legally acquired facts. Although the people I work with can occasionally be iffy, what they do for me is entirely legit. I swear I will not do anything that could get either of us in trouble."

"Where is that code?" I asked.

"Inside, with the computer!" Malaya said, her eyes widening with hope that I hadn't flat out refused. She pointed at the tall glass wall of her room before heading there.

I followed her, trying to hide my amusement at her hopeful excitement. She made a beeline for her desk, which she had already properly set up. The efficient and uncluttered workspace brought a smile to my face. My father had always been the messy type, with all kinds of trinkets and paraphernalia making it impossible to find anything on his desk. But woe unto anyone who dared tried to put it in order. Then he couldn't find anything.

Malaya picked up the holocard in front of her monitor and handed it to me. I glanced at it before looking back at my mate.

"Breathe," I said tauntingly. "Passing out from lack of oxygen isn't going to help you in any way."

Although her face heated, Malaya glared at me, even as she complied. Without another word, I tapped a few instructions on her tablet, which I still held, to grant it access to my network. In turn, this would allow her to log into the UPO's network with the credentials provided by Kayog.

She gasped, her eyes widening when she realized what I was doing.

"Log into your computer," I ordered.

My mate didn't have to be told twice. She all but launched herself at her desk chair, her fingers frantically typing to unlock it.

"Done," she said, eyes wide and hopeful.

"There you go," I said, handing her the fully connected tablet.

Malaya stared at it as if she couldn't believe it was real, her lips quivering. I hated that it revealed she'd held little hope I would grant her this request. I gently pushed her rolling desk chair, startling her out of her dazed trance, so that I could connect her computer as well. She got up and held the tablet to her chest like a shield while I completed my task. When I turned back to look at my mate, my throat tightened at the sight of tears welling in her eyes.

"Thank you," she whispered in a trembling voice.

I frowned, distraught to see her this upset. "You do not have to thank me. As your husband, it is my duty to protect you and provide all that you need. This is an essential tool to help you prove your innocence and bring down Wuras. I wouldn't deny it to you. You just need to be careful not to do anything that could alert Wuras and whoever works with him that you have resumed your investigation."

To my surprise, Malaya threw herself in my arms and buried

her face in my neck. Tharmok take me! She was shaking. I embraced her and closed my wings around her.

"It's okay, Malaya. Everything will be okay," I said, caressing her back in a soothing fashion.

Malaya lifted her head and wiped her wet cheeks, looking embarrassed. "I'm sorry. I didn't mean to make a spectacle of myself. It's just… The past few weeks have been horrible. I've felt so helpless… So alone."

Although I opened my wings, I kept my arms around her.

"You do not have to apologize to me, my mate. I vowed to stand by you, for better or for worse. If you need comfort, it is my duty to provide it. You do not have to ask for it. It is yours to take whenever you require it. You are not alone anymore, Malaya. We will get through this together," I said in a firm but gentle tone, while wiping the lingering wetness on her cheeks with my thumbs. "This, I pledge to you."

"So you… you believe me?" she asked, an almost pleading glimmer in her eyes.

I heaved a sigh and nodded. "Yes, Malaya. Yesterday, you convinced me that you were innocent. I wouldn't have married you otherwise. But this morning, I got confirmation that you're not the first to have been framed by Wuras."

She recoiled, a million emotions flashing over her features. "WHAT?! Confirmation? Who? How?"

I sighed again and released her from my embrace. I led Malaya by the hand to her bed and sat down at the edge before pulling her into my lap. It had not been a calculated gesture, but it pleased me tremendously that she didn't balk at it. In fact, she wrapped an arm around my shoulder and stared at me expectantly.

I gave her a quick summary of the conversation I had with Amreth. She hung on to my every word, only interrupting to ask smart, pointed questions. In that instant, I got a glimpse of the talented journalist she had been before Wuras turned her life upside down.

"Is there a chance I could speak directly with Amreth?" Malaya asked.

The instant jealousy that flared up at that request shamed me. It made complete sense for her to want to talk with anyone who could have more insight into related cases.

"I want to find out who that innocent man who died was," Malaya continued, oblivious to my inner turmoil. "I have people who can look into it without tipping off Wuras or any of his goons."

"Very well. I will ask him. But now, I need you to tell me your story. How did you end up investigating Wuras?"

"It was a complete freaking fluke!" Malaya said, shaking her head as if she couldn't believe the words coming out of her mouth. "I'd just finished writing an article about some big fraudster and impersonator. The editor contacted me to say I didn't need to rush getting the final editing and proofreading in because a different article would be published first. It was some 'What are the odds?' redemption story about some smuggler escaping her twenty-year sentence on Molvi by marrying the Great Chieftain of some primitive species on the verge of self-destruction."

"Ah yes, Rihanna and Zatruk," I said. "Their story stirred many heated debates here and on Vargos and a lot of resentment towards the United Planets Organization and the Prime Mating Agency."

She recoiled. "Resentment? Why?"

"Because they cheated the system to get a convict off the hook without her serving a single day of her sentence," I said in a self-evident manner. "It created a dangerous precedent that other convicts were all too eager to try and exploit. As soon as the word spread, inmates were demanding to be signed up with the PMA, or their families submitted their application directly to Kayog in the hope he would get them out of there."

"Oh, wow! I never even thought of that," Malaya exclaimed.

"We didn't make it public to avoid even more people trying to use that loophole," I explained. "But Wuras was swift to remedy it by adding a clause ensuring that all sentences had to fully be served on Molvi, no exception."

She frowned and pursed her lips while reflecting on my words. "So he actually had a valid reason to change that law. It wasn't just spite."

I hesitated. "People had mixed feelings about it. Yes, Rihanna got off easy. She wouldn't have survived twenty years on this planet, especially since she'd also been sent to a Dark Quadrant. But shifting her sentence helped to save many lives and enabled the species who inhabit the planet to achieve peace and greater prosperity. What does it matter if a convict's time is served on Molvi or elsewhere? So long as their sentence serves the greater good, it should be all that matters."

Malaya gaped at me. "I had not expected to hear that coming from you."

I snorted. "I may be rigid in my beliefs, that doesn't make me stubborn or narrow-minded. The problem was she only had to complete the trial period of that arranged marriage to have her sentence and entire case expunged, whether she remained with Zatruk or not. *That* was too powerful a loophole. And that's how Wuras was able to make the new law be adopted where the sentence had to be served in full *and* on Molvi. Many of us felt that so long as the sentence had to be served in full, where it happened didn't matter."

My head jerked right as movement at the edge of my vision drew my attention. Malaya immediately tensed in my lap.

"What? What is it?" she asked, fear seeping into her voice.

"Peace, my mate. There's nothing for you to worry about. You are safe in this house. I merely saw movement and realized it is the Nundars setting the table for lunch," I explained.

She recoiled and glanced in the direction of the wall before looking back at me. "You see them all the way in the kitchen?"

I nodded. "I see souls up to five hundred meters away. But I can sense their presence within a hundred-meter radius."

"Wow! Doesn't that make things noisy when you're in a crowd?" she asked, looking a little distraught.

I chuckled. "It would be if we couldn't turn it off at will. Come, let's go feed you."

"But how do they know to set up the table now? Did you tell them? Is there some kind of schedule that they follow?" Malaya asked.

Just as she spoke those words, her stomach growled. I burst out laughing at the stunned look on her face.

"That's how they know," I said mockingly.

I caught myself leading her by the hand again. This was a strange behavior on my part. I'd never been one for displays of affection. But I liked touching her. As she didn't seem to mind it, I would continue to indulge. Plus, it would count towards my genuine efforts to make this relationship work.

"So how did this story about Rihanna land you in this mess?" I asked as we made our way to the dining room.

"I was just really fascinated by it," Malaya said with a shrug. "The last few cases I'd investigated all involved scumbags or gruesome murders. A happily ever after fairy tale between a human and an alien minotaur would be a great palate cleanser. The first article focused mainly on the business side of this entire story. How Rihanna leveraged her contacts to help generate the funds the Yurus needed to finance their project, the benefits of collaboration between primitive species for the greater good of their planet, and how to turn gratuitous violence into something positive. I wanted to write Rihanna's story. How she went from smuggler, to convict, to Clan Mistress of the Yurus."

I smiled at Malaya's reaction as we entered the dining room

to find only one meal set on the table, with an extra glass of wine.

"Wait, did they not realize you've returned?" she asked, confused.

"They're aware," I said, amused, as I led her to the table.

"But…"

"This meal is for you, my dear. Sit," I said, pulling her chair for her.

She complied, more as a reflex than anything else. My woman continued to frown as she watched me circle around to the other side of the table to sit across from her.

"Aren't you eating?"

I shook my head. "I'm still full from last night," I replied with an intense stare that made clear what I was referring to.

"Still…? Oh… Oh!"

I laughed at the adorable way in which her face heated.

"Well, it's kind of awkward for me to just eat in your face," she mumbled.

"Eat, woman. You're starving. I'll accompany you with a drink," I said, pouring wine in each of our glasses. "Better?"

"Yeah," she said, scrunching her face.

"So, about Rihanna?"

"Right," she said while uncovering her plate.

The hungry look on her face put a smile on mine. Although I hadn't prepared that meal myself, it was my resources feeding her. I had not expected to derive such satisfaction from providing for my mate.

"I started looking into her case, and it didn't take long for me to realize something didn't add up," Malaya said while cutting her meat. "Rihanna had not committed any crime. Gabe, her sleazeball business partner, had hidden contraband weapons aboard their ship without her knowledge. They were only supposed to be carrying replacement parts and electronics. When he realized they were about to get caught, he vanished and let her take the fall. Her lawyer provided all the proof that Gabe was in fact the one behind all of this. But even if Wuras had deemed that, as the captain of the ship, it was her responsibility to know what cargo she transported, twenty years was way too much for this."

"They were smuggling weapons on Grubrya, the planet with the strictest anti-armament laws in this sector," I argued. "Twenty years may seem excessively harsh, but not for that specific crime on that particular planet. It is their greatest deterrent against arms proliferation."

"But twenty years in a Dark Quadrant?" Malaya challenged after swallowing a mouthful.

I pursed my lips as I weighed her argument. "Dark is excessive. This would warrant imprisonment in a Q1 or Q2. For that crime, they would only send someone in a darker Quadrant Three or Four if they'd been trafficking in weapons of mass destruction, planet killers, or dirty weapons that would leave lasting environmental damage beyond the mass killings."

"There was none of that, not even remotely," Malaya replied. "It was all just your standard blasters, assault weapons, grenades, tactical bracers, you get the idea. Small potatoes in the greater scheme of things."

"Fair," I replied cautiously. "Then why would Wuras go after her?"

"*That* was precisely the question. I asked Rihanna—lovely lady by the way. She's a tiny little thing but quite the firecracker. She's got the smartest and sharpest tongue in the galaxy. I think you'd like her."

"Mmhmm," I said in a non-committal fashion, which made her smile further.

I took a sip of wine, while giving her a chance to take a few more bites of her meal.

"According to Rihanna, Wuras was punishing her because of some guy named Jasper Lumley, who had allegedly wronged him. Apparently, she was dating Jasper when he got arrested and tried by Wuras. When Jasper got off on a technicality, Wuras was livid."

"But why retaliate on Rihanna? She had nothing to do with whatever happened between him and Jasper. Were they still together at the time Gabe let her take the fall?"

Malaya shook her head and gestured for me to hang on while she finished chewing and swallowing.

"No. Rihanna dumped Jasper as soon as the trial ended because it had revealed a lot of shitty things about him. And that got me super curious." Her voice filled with excitement, giving me a glimpse of the passion she bore for her profession. "That guy was involved in every possible kind of illegal dealings you could imagine. But he was really good at hiding it. Trying to pin him down was like opening one of those nestled Russian dolls or peeling an onion. Every time you thought you'd reached the bottom, there would be another layer."

"I'm not sure I follow you."

"Jasper ran a lot of different deals and cons, but for many of them, he used various aliases or holographic disguises so people wouldn't know who he truly was. I started cross-referencing all those names with anyone that might have dealt with House Wuras and couldn't find any matches. Since that was a dead-end, I wondered if maybe Wuras was just jailing people to get a cut out of it. Maybe he needed to meet a certain quota to keep himself living comfortably. I understand Molvi is semi-private. You 'own' your Sector and the credits generated by the prisoners' labor, right?"

I hesitated. "We do own our Sectors—or rather our noble house does. And yes, as I previously explained to you, our inmates earn their living and comfort by exploiting the natural resources in their respective Quadrant. Their wages are on par with galactic standards based on the volume they produce. We then either sell those raw materials or transform them first into more complex merchandise. But the judges don't get a direct benefit from that. While we do give the courts a percentage of our profits, it goes to the justice system as a whole to finance its operations, including the salaries and bonuses for judges, clerks, and guards, maintaining the facilities, and all other expenses. There is no direct payment to Wuras that would justify him trying to pack the prisons."

Malaya nodded slowly, seeming not overly surprised. "Okay, that confirms why I failed to find any proof to support that particular theory. But it's still what helped me nail him."

"How so?" I asked with undisguised curiosity.

"The best way to figure out if he was indeed milking the system was to check his tax filings and bank records. While some of it is part of the public records as it is mandatory for someone in his position, the bank statements were trickier to access. But once I did—and again, it was all done legally—I found an unusual transfer of five million credits to someone named Pasquali. That total amount had been sent in smaller payments from multiple accounts, the same day, within minutes from each other, so it wouldn't raise any flag from each financial institution."

I whistled through my teeth. "That's a huge amount of credits, even for a noble house as wealthy as Wuras."

"Huge. And the best part? That Pasquali turned out to be another one of Jasper's aliases that I hadn't found yet! At first, I thought Jasper was blackmailing him, and using the proceeds to further his contraband. After all, he spent those millions buying unmarked weapons to resell on the black market. I couldn't see the connection."

"I can't either. But the blackmail theory has potential," I replied.

"Nope," she said between two sips of wine. "With blackmail, once they get their victim to pay the first time, they will continue milking them until one of them dies, or the secret is exposed.

This was a one-time deal. I was getting nowhere, but my gut said there was something there. So I decided to review all of Wuras's cases over the past decade. And that was the first thing that gave him away."

I frowned, taken aback by that. "Why? What was so special about them?"

"As you know, cases are usually randomly assigned to the judges by the automated case-management system," Malaya explained. "However, judges can request to hear a specific case, usually because they have an expertise in the type of conflict being litigated. Wuras had an unusually high number of such requests, but for very generic cases that anyone else could have handled."

"Hmmm, that is unusual. I'm surprised nobody raised concerns about potential bias if he had no specialized knowledge to justify him adjudicating that particular case," I mused aloud.

"Which is what got me digging further into each of those cases. And guess what?"

"The defendants all ended up condemned to a Dark Quadrant."

"Exactly! Half of those cases should have warranted no more than a slap on the wrist. But somehow, new far-more serious charges would suddenly appear minutes before the trial started, with no additional time for the defendants or their lawyers to prepare against those new charges."

"That's illegal!" I exclaimed.

"Tell me about it," Malaya replied, bitterness audible in her voice.

"But why those people? Surely it wasn't random."

"It wasn't. It seemed to be at first, but the more I dug and the more I saw a pattern. All those people worked directly or indirectly for criminal cartels involved in illegal substances and weapons trafficking."

"So Wuras was being overzealous in jailing people he knew were criminals?" I asked.

"No. He was eliminating competition."

Malaya's words struck me like a boulder to the head. Since this whole mess started, I tried to find any number of justifications to explain the judge's questionable actions. I could see him becoming so obsessed with eradicating crime that he would give excessive sentences to people he thought would cause greater harm if set free. If a law should be broken, better it be against criminals in order to protect the innocent. Obosians who served too long and dealt with too many egregiously macabre cases could start displaying such behaviors. Once that happened, they were *strongly* encouraged to retire or go on an extended leave of absence while they recentered themselves.

People with the degenerative cognitive disease called gannath also act that way.

But Amreth was adamant that Wuras didn't suffer from it.

"Look, I can see that you struggle accepting Wuras could be this corrupt, but I promise you that he is," Malaya said in a sympathetic tone. "Those five million credits he gave Jasper were meant to buy unmarked weapons to flood Grubrya's market as well as to purchase a full cargo of Edocit downs. Jasper bought the goods, but instead of handing them to Wuras so that he could complete his deal, Jasper sold them to a third party and pocketed all the proceeds. What was Wuras going to do? Call him out publicly?"

My stomach roiled upon hearing those words. Beyond the fact that I struggled to accept this tale as fact—even though I had no reason to doubt my mate—the mention of Edocit down reminded me of my own recent captivity as a slave.

Once they entered puberty, juvenile Edocits—a dryad species —produced down leaves in the vines adorning their hair. Those leaves acted as a potent recreational drug that was extremely popular for the pleasurable high it provided and the fact that it wasn't addictive. Therefore, drug dealers would often attempt to kidnap those younglings, keep them prisoner throughout their puberty to harvest their down leaves to resell on the black market. In an effort to modify those leaves to make them addictive, such a drug dealer had kidnapped me and a few other species hoping to give some of our genetic traits to the young Edocits.

"That opened the Pandora's box which allowed me to unravel the entire scheme," Malaya continued, seeming unaware of my inner turmoil. "Wuras is associated with the Komoro Cartel for weapons, and with the Fingram Cartel for drugs. He's a shareholder in all of their 'legitimate' companies that launder their illicit money. And they pay him through dividends. Note that, in all the cases Wuras requested to preside, the ones involving members of Komoro or Fingram were the only ones that ended up with a lenient verdict from him."

I sighed heavily, my head hurting at the thought of the shit storm exposing all this would trigger.

"And you had irrefutable proof for all these extremely serious allegations?" I asked.

"I did," Malaya said with an air of frustration laced with anger. "Once I had put together the most solid case possible, I set up an appointment with the Enforcers to present it to them. As I'd obtained copies of Wuras's bank records online, I needed authenticated documents for them to be irrefutable. The morning of that meeting, my contact Pavel Roman was supposed to give me those physical documents signed and sealed. We had set up a rendezvous one hour before my meeting with the Enforcers."

"And that's when you got arrested," I guessed.

She nodded, a haunted look descending over her beautiful face. "When I got there, Pavel was already dead. There was blood everywhere. When I rushed to give him first aid, someone attacked me from behind. I fought back, but my attacker was much too strong and knocked me unconscious. By the time I woke up, I was covered in blood, and the cops were cuffing me."

"Pavel's blood?" I asked, already guessing the answer.

"Yes. His blood was on me, and mine on him. Bruises covered my body, as if I'd fought him before killing him," Malaya said bitterly. "Obviously, all his documents and mine had pulled a disappearing act. They'd wiped our disks, datacards, and even the online backups we had. Just like that, an entire year of hard work had vanished, and I'd become the villain."

"You think you can find this information again?" I asked, anger simmering within me.

She flicked her hair over her shoulder and frowned while slowly nodding. "Having done this once before, I already know where to look for some of this information. I'm just worried he has moved the bank accounts. That will make it really hard. For the rest, I won't know until I start digging. But I know of a few innocent inmates incarcerated on Molvi. I want to talk to them, and hopefully to anyone else Amreth may find."

I stiffened and shifted my wings uneasily. The thought of bringing my mate anywhere near those prisoners didn't please me one bit.

"First, see what you can find of your old files. For the inmates, we'll see," I said in a non-committal fashion.

Malaya opened her mouth as if to argue, then closed it and gave me a stiff nod instead. I didn't think for a second that she had simply caved in. Although I didn't know my mate well yet, she wasn't a pushover or submissive. She knew when to choose her battles. Right now, Malaya was merely biding her time before requesting this again.

"However, I must caution you again about your online searching," I said in a stern voice. "You say you trust all your sources. Yet, Wuras found out what you were up to and knew of your meeting both with Pavel and the Enforcers. Either someone ratted you out, or your searches raised a flag that set him on your trail. Either way, be extremely careful. Few people know of our current arrangement, but the word will spread sooner than later. Once that happens, a lot of people will come after both of us."

Malaya shuddered and peered at me with an air of guilt and fear. I hated doing this to her, but she needed to understand the seriousness of our situation.

"I'm so sorry—"

"Do not be," I interrupted in a gentle but firm tone. "Defending justice is rarely all fun and games. This is a worthy cause. As much as it distresses me such a thing should be happening, it is my duty as a Warden and an Obosian to help set it right, whatever the cost."

Her face softened, and the grateful—almost tender—expression she took wrapped around me like a warm blanket.

"You're a good man, Kronos," she said in a hushed voice.

"Of course, I am. But I'm glad you noticed," I said smugly.

She half huffed, half laughed. "Aaaand you're also quite full of yourself."

"Acknowledging one's awesomeness isn't vanity, if it is factual," I said in a taunting voice. "Am I not awesome, my mate?"

Laughing, she shook her head. "I'm pleading the fifth on this one."

"I will take that as an admission," I deadpanned before gesturing at her plate with my chin. "All done?"

She nodded. "Yes, I'm beyond full. That was very good."

I smiled. "I'm glad you enjoyed it."

"Most definitely. But… hmm…"

I narrowed my eyes at her. "But?" I insisted when her voice trailed off.

"I was wondering if it would be okay for me to cook my own meals from time to time," she asked sheepishly.

My back stiffened, and I frowned. "Why? Is the food lacking?"

She vehemently shook her head. "Oh, no! Not at all. It's really good. But, besides the fact that I actually enjoy cooking, from time to time, I'd like to eat some traditional dishes from my culture. So…"

I scrunched my face at her. "You like cooking?"

She burst out laughing. "Don't look at me as if I'd grown a second head. Yes, some people like cooking. If I'd not become a journalist, I would have gone into culinary school."

"You are a strange creature," I said, shaking my head in amusement. "But if toiling over a hot stove entertains you, have at it, my mate. This home is your domain to use and enjoy as you see fit."

"Thank you!" she said, beaming at me.

I loved how happiness lit up her face. She glowed from within. Unable to resist, I tasted her emotions. Tharmok's blood, she tasted divine. The urge to gorge on them rode me hard.

"My pleasure, my mate. But I must go back out," I said, standing up to fight temptation.

"Okay," Malaya said, imitating me. "I want to get started on this research as well. The sooner I can nail that jerk, the better."

If she found the proof she needed in the next few weeks, or maybe days, would she immediately ask to nullify our union and regain her freedom? The instant possessive anger that surged deep within left me reeling.

"Indeed," I replied, proud that my voice didn't betray the shameful emotion her words had stirred.

To my delight, Malaya accompanied me to the terrace to see me off. It touched me all the more that it didn't come across as something forced or performed out of a sense of duty.

"Will you be gone long?" she asked as we exited the house.

"I should be back around dinner time."

"Oh good! Will you be eating?" she asked.

I turned around to face her, my gaze boring into hers. Her

breath hitched when I cupped her face with both hands and leaned forward.

"Whether I eat regular food and how much of it I require entirely depends on *you*, my mate. *You* tell *me*, Malaya," I said in a hushed tone.

Before she could answer, I gave her a passionate kiss, erasing any lingering doubt she might have as to my meaning. The heady scent of her blossoming arousal had me instantly hard. I broke the kiss, battling the burning desire to push my woman onto her back and have my way with her right here and now.

"Until later," I whispered, my lips a hair's breadth from hers.

Eyes still locked with hers, I released Malaya and flapped my wings, flying away backwards with a smug smile.

CHAPTER 9
MALAYA

I watched him fly away while mentally calling him every name in the book. How dare he turn me on like that just to leave me hanging? That wretched man owned me. My girly bits were still singing from last night. I'd never thought any man could so utterly wreck me and still have me begging for more. Sure, he was an incubus type of deal, but we still barely knew each other. I'd never been the bang-on-the-first-date sort of girl, so this overwhelming addiction to my brand-new husband baffled the hell out of me. But I wanted more. A lot more.

And why the hell not?

We were married, and he clearly appeared to be down to get busy again. I wasn't too proud to enjoy a good thing when it finally entered my life. God knew things had been beyond shitty for me of late. Plus, according to Kayog, we were soulmates. And even if we weren't, who fucking cared? We were both consenting adults and—I couldn't repeat it enough—we were married.

Yep. I'm totally banging my man again tonight.

That decision made, I headed back to my room, trying to

ignore the dull throbbing between my thighs that Kronos had awakened merely with a kiss and a few words spoken in a suggestive tone. I'd heard people refer to hot women as sex on legs, but this title definitely suited my husband. Even my tongue tingled at the memory of those sexy pierced nipples of his. I didn't even get to properly admire the ones he had on his peen. That would need to be rectified tonight.

I groaned in annoyance as I settled in front of my computer. Such wandering thoughts were not helping douse the flame burning low in my belly. There would be plenty of time tonight to explore the sexiness I'd initially been so reluctant to get hitched to.

As I connected to the UPO network, my computer beeped, and an icon blinked at the bottom of my screen. I clicked it, stunned to see it was a secure message from an Enforcer named Maeve Riley.

I straightened in my chair, my eyes all but popping out of my head. I remembered that name. A few months ago, she and her new husband—an Edocit named Helio—had interrupted their honeymoon to go rescue a young Edocit who had been kidnapped from his homeworld. Their intervention had led to the dismantling of a major drug and people trafficking organization.

Heart pounding, I quickly read through the brief message informing me that she had been assigned to assist me with any information gathering I might require for my investigation. The thrilled shriek that came out of my throat hurt my own ears. This was beyond phenomenal. Kronos pointing out I would need to be careful about my browsing to avoid raising any red flags had not fallen on deaf ears. I'd been worried sick that, despite my best efforts, I would trip some kind of tracker and set off an alarm that would set Wuras on my scent.

If memory served me right, Maeve was some kind of computer whiz who could hack her way into pretty much anything. With her Enforcer credentials, she would have legal access to the kind of files and data a simple journalist like me could only dream of. This would significantly increase our chances of keeping this secret until it all blew up in that bastard's face.

I immediately responded, telling her how excited and grateful I felt for her assistance. As time was of the essence, the message included the things I wanted her to prioritize such as acquiring data or documents to help me rebuild the previous file I had on Wuras. While I obviously didn't recall his account numbers, I provided her the names of the establishments and locations. I also sent her a list of people whose court cases Wuras had presided over, and that I would love to get the records of.

Within seconds of me sending the message, Maeve replied with a simple "On it".

Filled with a renewed sense of hope and purpose, I got to work rebuilding my files. As I already knew what to look for and where, I started compiling dates and names at record speed. In less than an hour, I had accomplished what had previously taken me months. At this rate, and assuming Maeve came through for me, I could have the entire file rebuilt in a couple of weeks.

That said, it would still take a while longer for me to be exonerated of the crime I'd been wrongfully accused of. First, we would need to get Wuras indicted and tried. Then, I would need to file an appeal to get my case retried. It could take weeks, maybe even a few months, but for the first time since this entire nightmare began, I had a clear path forward and concrete steps beyond just making sure I'd survive a while longer.

As I filled in the details of one of the reference cases I'd initially used, it struck me once more how important it would be for me to speak with current inmates who had wrongfully been condemned like I had been. Their testimony, and what evidence we could gather to support their claim could make our case foolproof.

Although he hadn't said it in so many words, Kronos was

obviously reluctant to let me do this. My gut said he was being overly protective. I mean, in his shoes, I probably wouldn't want me anywhere near the people he'd been interested in keeping away from the general population because of the horrendous crimes they'd committed. Considering the type of protective measures he'd erected between the Quadrants and this dwelling, my husband clearly did not underestimate the inmates' capabilities.

And here I was, smiling wistfully at the thought he wanted to keep me safe. Only twenty-four hours ago, I'd been thinking what an epic douchebag he was. It was crazy how much he'd grown on me in the short time since he finally started showing his nicer side.

As much as I wanted my name cleared and to regain my freedom, I didn't actually mind that it would take a few weeks or months for it to happen. This would give Kronos and me time to get to know each other better. Being rather extroverted and a bit of a social butterfly, I hated how isolated and alone I felt here. If I planned on staying with him for the long run, this would need to be sorted out. But I could see myself falling in love with Kronos.

With him or with that massive shlong of his that had you singing arias all night?

There was no question Kronos had ruined me for any other man. I immediately berated myself for allowing my thoughts to wander down that naughty road again. I wanted to get a bit more work done before he got back. In truth, I'd considered cooking for us tonight, but I didn't want to ruin his 'other' appetite.

Just as I was refocusing on my work, the distant sound of flapping wings outside drew my attention.

Already?

A quick glance at the time on my computer indicated Kronos shouldn't be back for at least another couple of hours. Happy nonetheless, I caught myself shooting out of my chair and rushing out the already opened large glass doors that led onto my private terrace. To my surprise, I didn't see him anywhere. Taking a few additional steps forward, I stretched my neck to the right to see if he'd once again gone to visit his friend Amreth, which would explain why he wasn't flying in from the forest.

Then the strangest shadow stretched on the ground over me, moving forward past me. I jerked my head up to see what could be casting such an odd shape. My eyes no sooner made contact with its owner than my blood turned to ice.

At least four or five meters long, a winged hydra-like creature was gliding overhead. Its long, narrow body could have belonged to a giant insect, along with three sets of short, spindly legs. Three pairs of translucent wings lined the upper side of its body. The jagged edges of the larger set of front wings looked like they could inflict serious damage on anyone foolish enough to rub against them. At the end of its pointy tail, a sharp, vicious stinger glistened with what could only be some lethal toxin or venom. It didn't have a neck, only a flat head directly attached at the other end. It had two globular eyes and tiny holes as nostrils. Instead of a standard single mouth, five of them protruded in the form of snake-like tentacles at the top of its head.

In the split second it took me to take in this information, the flying hydra tilted its long body, circling back to face me as it continued to quietly glide. Breaking out of my horrified paralysis, I spun on my heel and ran back inside, my scream of terror drowned by the multiple heads screeching menacingly at having found their prey.

My blood turned to acid in my veins at the quickly approaching sound of its wings flapping again. I burst into my room, latching onto the door handle, and yanking it shut. Another scream of terror tore out of me when the hydra smashed headfirst into the glass of the closed door. I stumbled back, lost my footing, and fell hard on my ass. I hadn't managed to lock the door.

For a split second, as I scrambled back onto my feet, I considered trying to lock it—not that I expected that creature to be smart enough to be able to slide it open. However, the creature flapping its wings backwards before smashing itself into the glass wall once again erased any such thought. Lightning-shaped cracks appearing in various places on the glass, with radial cracks at the point of impact had me screaming again and running to the other side of the room. As I reached the door leading to the hallway, another thumping sound resonated behind me. Panicked, I struggled to activate the opening mechanism of the luminous stone by the door.

When I finally succeeded, the sound of shattering glass behind me drowned the discreet swish of the bedroom door's fancy unraveling motion. The 'whoop-whoop' of the creature's wings closed in as I tried to squeeze out of the slowly opening pattern of the door. I barely got one foot out before a sharp, stabbing pain shot through my ankle and up my leg. I screamed, both in pain and fear as the floor rushed towards me. I faceplanted, more pain radiating from my palms and up my arms from throwing my hands in front of me to stop my fall.

Another shriek of terror tore out of me as I felt myself get yanked backwards by the right leg. I started sliding back into my bedroom. On instinct, I threw my hands out, my fingers hanging on to the base of the door frame. Screaming for help, I blindly kicked back with my left foot at what I knew to be one of the hydra heads having latched onto my ankle.

The creature shouted as it lost its grip. Pulling myself forward with all the strength in my arms and my good leg, I tried to get back up only for even more intense stabbing pains to explode in both my legs. The creature yanked me again, making me fall back on my stomach. I tried to kick myself free once more, but a stinging sensation behind my thigh had my right leg almost instantly going numb.

The hydra pulled again, hard. My left hand slipped, losing its grip on the doorframe. Hanging on with one hand, I screamed and scrambled to find anything else to cling to but only ended up on my side with a much too good view of the creature. It twisted my arm, triggering a new pain in my wrist and fingers desperately hanging on to the doorframe. They started slipping in turn as a burning sensation gradually climbed up my legs from where the creature's sharp teeth had sunk into my flesh. In that instant, I realized I was staring my death in the face. My life flashed before my eyes.

This could not be it. This could not be how it ended. Not now, not when just moments earlier I'd finally found hope that everything would be all right. I was supposed to be free, exonerated, and maybe even build a new life with Kronos. Instead, he would find my room destroyed, covered in blood and gore, and maybe some of my desecrated remains after the beast was sated.

Tears of pain, terror, and sorrow gushed out of my eyes as I gradually lost purchase.

"Nooooooo!" I shouted when my fingers finally lost their grip on the door frame.

I began to slide back inside the room, pulled by the hydra, only to be stopped seconds later. A sharp pain radiated from my wrist down my arm, and from my right ankle up my leg. It took me a moment to realize something had grabbed my right wrist, stopping me from getting dragged away by the creature. I tilted my head back to see what was happening. Through blurred vision, I first saw the oddest pair of hooved feet walk past me, followed by a second pair.

My skin tingled, and my hair stood on end, as if caught in a static storm. Strange bipedal creatures dressed in almost medieval-looking robes raised their right hands at the hydra. They only had two extremely long fingers with dark, forked claws. Whooshing sounds resonated above me, and the hydra screeched. It didn't register at first that the hooved beings' fingers had caused that sound. But when the hydra screeched and let go of my ankles, I finally noticed the air blurring in front of their fingers, almost like a ripple in the water.

Although this had all occurred in seconds, it felt like time had stretched to a trickle. I yelped when the hand holding my wrist dragged me backward out of the room. I screamed and tried to free myself. Then a voice resonated inside my head.

"Peace, Mistress. Nundars help. Nundars take to safety."

I stiffened, my mind freezing as the words slowly made their way through my brain. No, not words. It hadn't been an actual voice. And yet, I'd clearly understood the message. I tried to get up, but the pain in my left leg had me screaming again, while the right leg wouldn't respond.

Four pairs of hands reached for me and picked me up, two Nundars on each side. Although humanoid, they had a very long, striped neck that stretched into a cone which also served as their heads. Two big eyes stared at me with infinite wisdom. Their mostly flat faces gave the hint of a snout above their thin-lipped mouth, which was framed by a fur-like long mustache, a paler beige color than their skin.

Carrying me, the Nundars started running down the corridor to the main hall. Behind us, I could still hear the hydra screeching and thrashing. Despite the sort of kinetic power they'd displayed, fear coursed through me for the two Nundars who had remained behind to hold off the beast. Even though their faces hinted at them being mature adults, maybe even elders, their slender bodies and shorter stature gave them a frail appearance.

"Peace, Mistress. Nundars protect. Master comes."

This time, I knew for a fact I hadn't actually heard their words, even though I 'heard' them clearly. I finally understood what Kronos had meant when he said hearing them communicating was more like an instant knowledge, a transfer of thought.

"Kronos is coming?" I exclaimed, shocked to find my words slurring.

"Master comes soon."

Even as I rejoiced, a different fear sparked in my heart. What if the creature harmed or killed him? Granted, being noble born didn't guarantee you the right to become a Warden on Molvi. Only the finest Obosian Warriors could earn that privileged position. But I still couldn't help worrying about him.

My head swam as the Nundars carried me to the other end of the mansion, and into the interior garden. My legs were on fire, as if acid was eating them from within, while my stomach roiled with a nauseous feeling. Struggling to focus, I vaguely wondered why they were carrying me to the draped sculpture at the back of the garden. It was too big to be a door, and we were exposed, out here in the open.

As if in response to that thought, a screech overhead had me jerking my head up. I should have screamed and panicked at the sight of the hydra circling above us like a vulture before it dove down. But I felt too sluggish to bother. My skin tingled and burned as if I'd swallowed the sun, and its heat radiated through me.

Two Nundars appeared out of thin air. No, not appeared. They walked right out of the swirling stone carving, as if it had been a curtain of water. They immediately did that whoosh-whoosh thing, their left hand resting on their right wrist, while they pointed at the flying hydra with their two fingered right hand.

Seeming oblivious to the danger ahead, the Nundars carrying me ran straight into the stone wall. The pain I expected as they rammed my aching feet straight into it never came. The wall just vanished, revealing a long corridor in an incline leading to a massive underground lair I never suspected existed.

Had my mind not been so foggy, I'd likely have marveled at how big, spacious and luminous it was. Carved directly out of the stone shaping the mountain, the ribbed texture of the ceiling gave the illusion we were walking under a sandy desert. The off-white polished walls gave it that sense of width and purity. The furniture made of pale wood and light beige pillows all had soft and rounded angles. Large windows in strategic locations allowed daylight to flood in. And glowstones imbedded in the walls bathed the areas deeper inside the mountain with a dreamy light.

Countless Nundar silhouettes hastened in front and around me as my rescuers continued to carry me through one arched doorway after another. The screeching of the hydra faded in the distance, replaced by the soothing sound of trickling water. Its origin finally revealed itself in the form of a small cascade running down pale rocks into an interior pool.

The Nundars laid me down onto a divine cushion by the water. More shadows moved in front of my face before something cool pressed to my lips. Only then did I realize I'd been talking. I had no idea what words I'd spoken. Why had no one answered me?

"Drink, Mistress. Tea breaks fever, cleans poison."

I opened my mouth to protest that I didn't have a fever, and that I was too hot to drink tea. But the moment my lips parted, cool liquid poured into my mouth. The rabid thirst that took over me silenced anything else I might have wanted to say. I greedily gulped down the contents of the bowl, vaguely aware I begged for more once it was gone. Another bowl pressed against my lips, and I welcomed the bounty.

Halfway through, an unpleasant feeling settled on my ankles, then on my legs. It reminded me of wet clothes sticking to my skin after getting drenched in the rain. I wanted to protest again, but moving my tongue felt like a herculean effort. Water trickled down the sides of my mouth and down my neck. The odd pressure against my lips vanished. My eyelids grew heavy as I tried to recall what I'd been doing before the unpleasantness on my legs distracted me.

"Rest, Mistress. Nundars watch over you. Master fights."

Who was Mistress? Who was Master? Why was he fighting? I couldn't tell if they answered me. A veil of darkness descended before my eyes. I stopped fighting and welcomed its embrace.

CHAPTER 10
KRONOS

Biting the inside of my cheeks to repress an amused smile, I watched Seelo prancing about right outside the security zone by the landing pad. As the 'leader' of the Q1 inmates, the Nazhral female was putting on this display to make sure the others would give her credit for their impressive productivity.

Quadrants One and Two contained large reserves of soridium, a highly sought after metal to build integrated circuits and other electronic components. Being far more conductive than copper, it allowed for finer wires without losses, was less vulnerable to electromigration, and was far less likely to fracture even under intense stress. While my family also dabbled in other fields, the sale of refined soridium and its derivative products constituted our main source of income. It had made us extremely wealthy. There was a reason our less problematic inmates were assigned to work in those mines.

Usually, it took the combined weekly haul from Q1 and Q2 to fill the hold of the transport shuttle. But this week, the Q1 inmates had managed to fill it entirely. Even now, Zolran was finishing loading the last crates, getting creative in their placement to fit it all in. While such an unexpectedly high productivity pleased me, I burned with curiosity as to how Seelo had convinced the others to more than double their productivity without getting her authority challenged.

What did you promise them, little Nazhral?

Zolran closed the hold's doors then cast an inquisitive look my way. I nodded in response to his unspoken question. Having worked as my pilot for years, he didn't need extensive explanation to know what to do. We still had to visit the other three Quadrants to collect the resources they had also gathered. Zolran flapped his wings once to propel himself up the ramp of the shuttle instead of walking. This time, I didn't repress a smile. That move betrayed his cheerful mood.

As I'd always been a proponent of profit-sharing and wealth trickling down, on top of their set wages, my guards and pilots always received a share of my profits. Such a haul from Q1 alone promised a nice little bonus for him. Being low-born, Zolran didn't have generational wealth. But working for me had allowed him to steadily build a nest egg. He intended to use it to help his offspring launch the business they had been dreaming of once they completed their education in two years.

As the shuttle took off, Seelo strutted back my way with that naturally seductive gait of hers, her fluffy white tail slowly swaying from side to side in an almost hypnotic fashion. Everything about this bipedal feline species screamed sensuality. Although generally pleasant to the eye, they didn't hold too great a reputation across the galaxy. Many of them were involved in some form of smuggling or contraband. More still actively worked as space pirates or slavers. The sad part was that Nazhral weren't fundamentally evil. In truth, a majority of those I'd encountered—Seelo included—had a generally nice soul. Unfortunately, their culture condoned and encouraged behaviors deemed criminal by the galactic community.

But some of their people—like Saydi—were the foulest beings I'd ever encountered. I immediately clamped down on that thought. I wouldn't allow memories of the wretched Nazhral who had enslaved me to mar the pleasant mood sharing lunch with my mate had put me in.

I couldn't wait to be done with my tasks and return home. My little human was really growing on me. And that kiss goodbye…

Maybe I should deplete even more of my energy reserves to make extra room for tonight.

The Nazhral stopping in front of me at a non-threatening distance forced me to clamp down on my wandering thoughts. While the souls of none of the other inmates surrounding us showed any signs of potential aggression or foul play, I should know better than to allow myself to become distracted while in a potentially dangerous environment. Even if this was Q1 with the least problematic convicts, they remained criminals.

"You've been very productive," I said in a slightly taunting tone.

She ran a clawed hand over the dark patch of black fur that spread from her forehead, between her feline ears, and down the back of her head, before crossing her arms over her chest with a smug expression. That patch and her pawed feet were the only spots of color on the otherwise pristine white fur that covered her body.

The vertical slit of her golden eyes widened as she smirked at me. "We like our comforts," she purred. "Rain season approaches. We want to make a few upgrades and additions to our facilities before it does."

"Do you, now?" I asked, raising a curious eyebrow.

"Mmhmm," she replied in a non-committal fashion. "But before we get to that, we noticed an unusual bump in our energy resources this morning. Is there something you'd like to tell us, Warden?"

I shrugged. "Consider it a gift."

She narrowed her eyes at me, her long eyelashes casting a

shadow over her high cheekbones. Someone less familiar with her might have misinterpreted that look as being flirtatious, a grievous mistake that could have—and had—resulted in some people getting their faces viciously clawed.

"Obosians—and especially Wardens—*never* give freebies. What's the catch?"

I chuckled. "There genuinely is no catch. Enjoy it while it lasts as it's not likely to happen again any time soon. Now state what you want. I have other Quadrants to visit," I added quickly to change the subject. She didn't need to know I'd given myself indigestion feasting on my mate's pleasure.

Or that I am hoping to do so again tonight...

Seelo pinched her lips, displeased with my lack of cooperation. I couldn't even blame her for it. In the world she evolved in, everything came at a cost, hidden or otherwise. One thing I'd learned about her in the seven years she'd served here, the Nazhral female hated being indebted to anyone. It gave them power over her, which she didn't like one bit.

Knowing she wouldn't get anything else out of me, Seelo huffed and handed me a holocard.

"This is our shopping list," she said in a slightly clipped tone. "It also contains the breakdown of everyone's contribution."

I nodded while quickly browsing the list of goods, furniture, and tools they wanted their credits spent on. The rest of the payment I would owe them for the soridium they mined would be divided according to each prisoner's contribution and sent to their personal accounts. For some, these funds would be their savings after they completed their sentence. For others, it provided income for the families they had left behind.

"On the last tab, you will see additional resources we require to expand both our dwelling and the factory," Seelo added, a hint of defiance in her voice.

My brow shot up as I perused it. "This is going to cost you!"

She shrugged. "Thanks to all that extra energy *given* to us, we have a lot more credits on hand."

I snorted and bowed my head in concession.

"We also have the skills to perform most of the construction ourselves," she continued, this time with the serious glimmer of a professional businesswoman in her golden eyes. "We only need the material and a few hours from an expert to optimize our design for the refinery."

I tilted my head to the side, intrigued by this unexpected request. "Why? What prompted this sudden desire?"

"Credits, of course," she said as if it was self-evident. "We'll get a lot more for refined soridium than the rough stones we give you. She waved at a wizened human standing in the middle of the sprawling square in front of the main building that served as their dwelling. "Mika only has one year left to serve in his sentence. He wants to pad his savings for when that day comes so that he may live his remaining years comfortably and out of trouble."

I nodded. "Understandable. But what's in it for the rest of you? Altruism isn't a thing among you lot."

It was her turn to snort. "That much you got right, Warden. We don't like his shriveled ass enough for that. But we will get fifty percent of the proceeds you pay for the refined soridium he produces until his share of the construction cost of the refinery has been repaid."

"And after that?" I insisted.

"We get twenty-five percent of the proceeds while he trains us to refine our own soridium," she replied.

"And then?"

"And then everyone keeps a hundred percent of their own production," she said as if it was self-evident. "Once he's gone, we will not let this go to waste. I regain my freedom in three years. I intend to have a very comfortable little nest egg of my own by then."

"Very well," I said in an approving tone. "You will provide a detailed written agreement that *all* must sign. I will get you a quote for the total cost by morning. As this constitutes a permanent improvement to your Quadrant, and since it will benefit future inmates past your own sentences, I'll refund fifty percent of the construction cost incurred. *But* only after your first successful delivery of refined soridium,"

Seelo beamed at me, her small fangs peeking between her pink lips, while the other inmates cheered.

"Thank you, Warden," she purred.

"But that will also require an adjustment to the percentage you will deduct from Mika's contribution, as his share will have been repaid faster," I warned. "As for the expert—"

A beeping sound on my bracer interrupted me. I jerked my head down as I raised my wrist before my face, convinced I'd misheard the sound. That specific tone indicated perimeter breach at my fortress. That *never* happened. No inmate could ever get past my security measures. And inmates with flying abilities—not that I currently had any in my Sector—either had their wings regularly clipped while serving their sentences or wore implants that would inflict debilitating pain if they flew past a restricted height or zone.

My blood turned to ice at the sight of the surveillance system's report. I soared, flapping my wings furiously. Seelo's alarmed voice calling out my name quickly faded as I raced home. Two Faernychs had been detected entering my Sector, each one coming from opposite sides of the area. This was impossible. Those fearsome creatures were bred and trained on Vargos, my homeworld. I had acquired eight of them to protect the forest surrounding my playground, two per Quadrant. A rapid verification confirmed mine were still where they belonged.

Faernychs would never wander or hunt beyond their assigned territory. Therefore, these two would only be closing in on my residence because someone had ordered them to do so. Only one person would be insane—or desperate—enough to commit such a crime.

Somehow, Wuras had already found out about my marriage to Malaya.

Fear and seething rage flooded through me. Fifteen years I had managed this Sector, and such a breach had NEVER happened. As far as I knew, no Warden's dwelling had ever been attacked by a creature. That it occurred today, to *my* dwelling, the day after Malaya arrived wasn't a coincidence. Wuras had crossed an unforgivable line for which he would answer.

The twenty-minute flight back never felt so long. If only I hadn't already sent Zolran away. But calling him now would be pointless. Not only would it take him too long to get back to my house, but he also wasn't a Warrior like me and wouldn't survive the encounter.

When I'd first designed the security system around my fortress, Father had chastised me for going overboard with the aerial perimeter breach detection alert and camera systems. As no threat would ever come from the air, he'd deemed it a waste of credits to have anything past the moat and the cliff. While I had held my ground on implementing those two features, I had not bothered fully integrating the system with remote devices like my bracer. This meant I couldn't play the actual camera feeds here. The scanner only indicated the creatures' location.

And one of them was headed straight for Malaya's terrace. If she'd once more elected to work outside on the chaise lounge to enjoy the warm afternoon sun, by the time she realized what danger lurked, it might be too late. I remembered all too well how long it had taken her this morning to even notice me arriving behind her.

My stomach twisted with dread as I flapped my wings even harder. If anything happened to her…

I tried to cast the horrible thought out of my mind. If the beasts found my mate, my Nundars would feel her distress and come to her rescue. I refused to even contemplate the possibility that they might be too late.

In direct response to that thought, my bracer beeped again, this time confirming a physical breach. I roared in helpless rage and terror when it indicated critical damage to the external wall of Malaya's bedroom.

As the outline of my domain finally appeared in the distance, I was drowning in an ocean of self-loathing and self-recrimination. Tharmok curse me! I'd grown so complacent, so confident in my invulnerability within my own domain that I'd grown lax. I no longer even bothered carrying a staff or any type of weapon when I visited my playground, despite it being filled with hardened criminals. Between my energy shield and my *lumiak*, I'd always been able to easily handle every situation. But now, lethal beasts stalked my mate.

My heart soared when the distant echoes of the pained cries of a Faernych reached me seconds after I finally cleared the forest. I needed to believe this confirmed the Nundars had intervened in time and were keeping the beasts at bay. The muscles in my back burned as I crossed the moat in a sharp ascending angle to clear the cliff. The moment I shot past the railing, the Faernych screeched and stumbled back out of Malaya's room, as if recoiling from a violent blow.

As I dashed forward to cross the two hundred meters or so between us, a metallic glow in the wide, open space of the main terrace caught my eye. A victorious roar escaped me, and I implored a blessing from the gods upon the Nundars for this gift.

Alerted by my war cry, the Faernych turned to look in my direction just as I was swooping down to scoop up the battle staff my familiars had left for me. I grabbed it in a fly by while continuing to dash towards the beast. When collapsed, the staff resembled a short thirty-centimeter-long baton. With a flick of my wrist, I activated it, stretching the baton to its full length of a hundred and eighty centimeters. I pressed the central button of the staff, and sharp blades jutted out of both extremities.

In the seconds it took me to perform these actions, the creature jerked its head left to look inside the room then right back at me, seeming unable to decide which prey—or rather threat—it should battle. It hissed at me, having rightly realized it was staring its death in the face. To my horror, as the beast bared the needle teeth of its five mouths, I noticed the bright red spots marring at least three of them. Blood. Human blood.

It got to Malaya. It hurt my mate!

The enraged cry that tore out of my throat failed to fully cover the pair of whooshing sounds that resonated from within Malaya's room. The air blurred, and the Faernych hollered as the invisible kinetic force of the Nundars struck it again.

The air crackled with static energy as the back of the beast smashed against the stone railing. It landed sideways, its three right wings stuck under its long body. Using its spindly legs and its main left wing, the Faernych twisted and contorted until it righted itself. But before it could take flight again, I threw my left hand forward and welcomed the prickling heat of my *lumiak* blasting out of my palm.

The beast screeched again and lost its precarious footing. Angered, even as it scrambled to regain its balance, the Faernych whipped its five mouths forward in an all too familiar movement. I dodged out of their path a split second before they all spit a stream of acid my way.

Impossible!

I activated the energy shield on my bracer before charging the beast. It *never* should have been required. From the moment they hatched, Faernychs were trained not to attack Obosians, unless for combat training purposes. And even then, they were never to use their acid against us, and only as a last resort against prisoners. Something truly nefarious was happening. But there would be time to sort it out after I'd dispatched the creature.

Not to mention the second one.

I slammed my energy shield on the side of its face and immediately flew upward out of the path of its tail. As expected, even as it recoiled from the impact, it attempted to stab me with its stinger. I couldn't allow it to get me, or the numbing effect of the toxin covering it would spread, gradually paralyzing me. I swiped my staff behind me, the lower half connecting solidly with its flank as I zipped past the creature in the opposite direction it was facing.

The time it took its much longer body to turn around allowed me to put a bit of distance between us. The beast gave chase, its heads spraying their acid in different angles to increase the chances of catching me, whichever direction I flew in. If not for my shield, it would have done a number on me.

We began an aerial dance of lunge and dodge, while I blasted my *lumiak* at the Faernych. While most lifeforms would have been reduced to cinders by my power, the Faernychs' scales protected them from it. Granted, it still hurt them, and if applied repeatedly at the same spot on the body, it would eventually crack the scales. However, the Warrior would have likely depleted all his reserves long before that happened. This was the reason Obosians had eventually tamed these formidable beasts.

The only way for me to kill it was to pierce the softer scales of its under belly with the bladed tip of my staff, and channel my *lumiak* through it. We'd specifically designed this weapon to multiply the power of the energy coursing through it. Naturally, my foe wouldn't make that an easy task.

I flew higher, over the house. Another wave of anger surged through me when I spotted the second Faernych getting repelled in the interior court garden. While my Nundars had feasted well this morning from all the excess energy Malaya had given me last night, they wouldn't be able to sustain this for long.

Without hesitation, I dashed toward the garden with the first Faernych hot on my tail. A hundred meters away, I pointed the tip of my staff at the second creature and poured my *lumiak* through it. It shot out like a laser beam, striking true right below the beast's main wing. In a one-two punch, my Nundars' kinetic blast slammed into it as well, sending it spinning in a disarticulated mess. It crashed against the rockface of the mountain, right next to the waterfall.

Although half-stunned, the Faernych valiantly flapped its wings to avoid plummeting to the ground. I zapped it again, drawing its attention to me. With a furious screech, it finally focused on me and charged, flying half-drunkenly while it recovered. I spun around in an ascending fashion to avoid getting sprayed by the first creature chasing me.

I zigged and zagged, herding them towards the only trap that would see me getting out of this unscathed—or at least mostly. Once both beasts were but a couple of meters behind me, I flew over the edge of the main terrace and dove down towards the moat. With my wings flattened to reduce friction, I shot down like a boulder, increasing the distance with my pursuers.

As the surface of the water came rushing towards me, I braced for what would be an excruciatingly painful recovery. I blasted my *lumiak* over the surface of the otherwise still water, counting the seconds. Waiting until the very last minute, I changed my angle and spread my wings to turn into a glide over the surface of the stirring lake. I cried out in pain as my wings felt on the verge of tearing right off my back in protest as gravity tried to keep them plastered against my body.

As I had hoped, instead of following me into a glide, the Faernychs crashed into the water, thanks to an insufficient turn radius. The loud splashes they made as they attempted to recover and take flight again, finished the job my *lumiak* had initiated. I spun around just in time to see a Faernych take off, only to have its underbelly sliced open by the claws of a nevianaar, its massive three-clawed limb shooting out of the surface of the water.

The beast screeched as yellow blood gushed out of the gaping wounds, some of its guts peeking out. In a desperate move, it flew towards the shore in an erratic flight pattern. Under normal circumstances, the nevianaar would have finished it off, but another prey called to the aquatic hunter. Although I believed this first Faernych wouldn't make it too far, I couldn't risk it surviving and wreaking havoc in my forest.

As soon as it reached the 'garden' adorning the shore, I fired a light *lumiak* blast at the plants, enough to trigger the release of their noxious spores, but not enough to harm them. In seconds, an orange foam formed around the wound of the creature's underbelly. It ate through the flesh and organs, the edges darkening in almost instant necrosis. Its body shaken with violent spasms, the Faernych flew another short distance past the garden before plummeting to the ground, its dying scream buried by the one of pain from its companion.

As it had sunk much deeper into the water, the second Faernych took much too long to recover. Although it managed to take flight, its ascension was quickly halted by the massive maw of the nevianaar closing around the lower half of its tail. Its beady eyes—tiny in its otherwise gigantic triangular head—stared greedily at its prey and tried to drag it under water. Screaming in pain and fear, the Faernych desperately flapped its wings in a useless effort to fly away vertically.

Realizing its sharp teeth were sawing too quickly through the narrow tail, and that once it tore, its dinner would fly away, the nevianaar stabbed its central hooked claws into the sides of the Faernych's tail before yanking down again. In one last ditch effort, the Faernych aimed its five mouths downwards and showered its predator with acid.

The nevianaar roared, involuntarily releasing its prey in the process. The Faernych flew up. But the hooked claws, still stuck on each side of its tail, ripped long gashes the entire length. I could have helped the nevianaar secure this unexpected feast, but as I was approaching the creature to stab its exposed underbelly, I noticed something… or rather the *absence* of something.

The creature should have been branded by its trainer. Now that I thought of it, I couldn't recall seeing a brand on the first one that had died in the garden. Even though my body cam would have recorded it, once I demanded reparation for this egregious attack, a video recording without a corpse would be too easily challenged as having been tampered with. As I didn't know how much the garden's toxins would damage the corpse of the first Faernych, I needed a clean kill on this one and to preserve its remains.

Wounded and pissing blood, the creature had entered survival mode and wanted nothing more than to flee as far as possible from the source of pain… which was up. Escorting it from a short distance below, and slightly behind, I spurred it forward with weak blasts of *lumiak* on its wounded tail. It almost felt unfair as its pace gradually slowed and its wing movements became sluggish.

With only fifty meters or so left to ascend, I didn't want to risk the Faernych going into shock from blood loss before it reached my terrace. Accordingly, I dashed forward, moving slightly in front of the creature. Leveraging my momentum, I thrust my staff upward. The bladed tip easily pierced through the softer scales of its underbelly. Its scream of agony died in a startled hiccup when my *lumiak*—enhanced by the staff—blasted directly inside it. The Faernych went limp as electric tendrils slithered over its body with a crackling sound before fading away.

Gritting my teeth, I strained under the heavy weight of the beast still impaled on my staff as I ascended the last few meters to safety. I hurled the carcass over the railing, a hiss of relief escaping me as the burning ache in my arms and shoulders seemed to first peak before finally relenting.

But now wasn't the time to wallow in my aches and pains.

Abandoning my staff embedded in the Faernych's remains, I flew over the house to the interior garden, gliding through the narrow opening of the stone entrance to the Nundars' lair, before landing into a run down the descending corridor.

Three of their Elders already awaited me at the bottom, having no doubt felt my victory.

"Malaya?" I asked.

"Mistress wounded. Much poison. Nundars heal Mistress."

Another wave of fury surged through me upon hearing the confirmation to what the traces of blood on the Faernych had hinted. I had failed to protect my mate. Because of me, Malaya suffered.

"But she will live?" I insisted, following the Nundars as they hastily led me to their inner sanctum built around a hot spring.

"Yes. Mistress fully recovers. Five or seven suns."

Five days to a week?! Tharmok's blood! Just how extensive were her injuries? The answer quickly became apparent as the haunting sound of the Nundar healers' humming grew louder as we approached the sanctum. Leaving my guides behind, I ran forward into the room. Lying on plush cushions, Malaya was shaking, a constellation of plump beads of sweat covering her forehead.

Thick strips of nillag—a natural sponge that fed on poison and toxins—were wrapped around both of Malaya's ankles and calves. Another layer, this one much thinner, bandaged part of her right thigh. They had strategically placed a series of stones on her chest, stomach, arms, thighs, and forehead. Most of the ones on the lower half of her body had an angry red color, while those closer to her head and chest had an increasingly paler shade of pink, edging towards white.

"Malaya! I'm here, my mate!" I exclaimed while rushing to her side.

I knelt next to her makeshift bed and took her hand. It felt cool and clammy. I released my *bakaan* at a low intensity, wrapping her in its aura. Malaya's features instantly relaxed, even her strained breathing eased.

"Thank you, Master. Now Nundars heal faster."

Their humming immediately intensified. In seconds, the pinkish hue of the stone on her forehead completely bled out, leaving the stone pristine white, while the stone on her neck grew redder. The pitch of the humming shifted. And while the stone near her neck and chest continued to grow redder, the ones on her arms grew paler. This indicated the poison was being channeled along a specific path by the vocal modulations of my familiars. Slowly, methodically, they would guide it down my mate's legs to the nillag, that would drain the toxin out of her.

"Thank you, my friends. Thank you for protecting my mate," I said, my voice thick with emotion.

Although they didn't stop their humming, they looked at me with gentle eyes filled with endless wisdom.

"Mistress bright star. Soothing light. Master chose well."

Despite the situation, my heart filled to bursting with gratitude. They, too, could see the beauty of her soul. Her aura soothed them, a rare occurrence with non-Obosians. Yes, I had chosen well by keeping her. And Tharmok smite me, I would protect her better going forward.

CHAPTER 11
KRONOS

Fuming, I restlessly paced my room, unable to rein in the anger that simply wouldn't abate. The perimeter alarm finally going off did little to comfort me. I almost ran outside to wait for Amreth to land on my personal terrace, but I couldn't move too far away from Malaya. She needed my *bakaan* to numb her discomfort.

I glanced at her beautiful face. She looked so small and fragile as she lay peacefully in my humongous bed. This should have been a lovely tableau I would have awakened to after a night of passion with my new bride. Instead, it was the deceitful illusion of a worried night spent watching over her to make sure she didn't have any additional adverse effects to the toxins the Faernych had infected her with. Despite their amazing healing powers, Nundars knew little of human anatomy.

The flapping sound of wings drew my attention back to my terrace where the large glass doors stood wide open. Amreth landed gracefully moments later. By the way he jerked his head left and right, eyes wide and mouth gaping, my friend was taking stock of the unusual scene of my Nundars hard at work in the open to repair the damage caused by the beasts. He turned his head to look inside my room and found me staring at him with a grim expression.

"What in Tharmok's name has happened here?" he exclaimed while marching towards me.

"Two Faernychs attacked Malaya in her room yesterday."

"WHAT?!" Amreth exclaimed, his entire body tensing with shock and outrage. "Whose? Who dared?!"

"No branding, no owner's seal on either of them," I said with seething disgust.

Malaya sighed and shifted her head on the pillow. The medicine the Nundars had given her acted as a sedative.

"Is that your mate?" Amreth asked, his voice softening as he stretched his neck to look behind me, before taking a few steps towards the bed.

My spine instantly stiffened, and a growl rose from my throat as I bared my fangs at him.

He froze and gave me a stunned look. "Peace, friend. Surely you know I'm no threat to her?"

I stopped, both shocked and shamed by my primal reaction. Of course, he would never harm her. However, beyond the fact that yesterday's events had rattled me, having another male near my woman while she lay in bed and in a vulnerable state had my protective—and possessive—instincts going into overdrive.

"Yes, it is Malaya," I grumbled.

The look of wonder on his face made me uneasy and once more fanned my irrational jealousy.

"Tharmok's teeth! You were not exaggerating when you said she had a beautiful soul. It is stunning," Amreth said. "Anyone with eyes could see it."

"Anyone but that vermin Wuras," I hissed.

Amreth frowned. "What's wrong with her?"

"Poison," I snarled. "Two wretched Faernychs attacked while I was touring my Quadrants for our weekly trades. Before my

Nundars could rescue Malaya, one of the creatures bit her multiple times."

A series of foul curses in Obosian tumbled out of Amreth's mouth while the same anger that had been simmering inside me since last night settled on his face.

"Poison means that they were adults," Amreth mused out loud. "Are you saying that two unbranded mature Faernychs came to your home to attack your mate?"

"Yes. I know all the Faernych breeders on Vargos. There are only a handful of them. None of them would have raised any of their beasts to maturity without them being branded," I said.

Amreth nodded slowly. "This means there's an underground market somewhere."

"My thought exactly. But it surely cannot be on Molvi," I countered.

My friend frowned as he reflected on my words. "Hmmm, I would tend to agree with that assessment. It would have been impossible for someone to run such a ranch here without being noticed. That means they were brought here. But how did they get here so fast?"

"Those questions have plagued me all night," I said in a frustrated tone while running a nervous hand over my top right horn. "If they were flown in from Vargos, the journey would take at least twelve hours. That means they were either dispatched late in the evening two days ago, or early yesterday morning."

Amreth shifted his wings, his frown deepening. "Which would then mean that Wuras was informed right away when your mate arrived two days ago."

"That's also what I believe. It must have been one of the guards during triage," I said pensively.

"During triage?" Amreth echoed, seeming confused. "What makes you think that?"

"I told them not to brand Malaya before they brought her here. As I expected her to be guilty, I didn't want my brand on her when I sent her off to you or Dakon. And I also didn't want her marked as a criminal in the highly improbable chance that she turned out to be innocent. Obviously, I didn't give my reasons to the guards. I merely said not to mark her."

"Right. That would have definitely raised flags."

"The fact that I had her flown to my house in a private shuttle instead of to Dakon's Sector certainly didn't help," I said.

Amreth stiffened and eyed me warily. "Could Dakon have made a stink over you taking one of his inmates?"

I shook my head. "No. I swapped another one of my new Q4 inmates for Malaya. I wouldn't steal from him. So long as he gets the right headcount, Dakon doesn't care whether he gets this inmate or that one. And if he'd had a problem with the swap, he would have confronted me directly about it. He has no qualms speaking his mind."

"I concur with that assessment. But the 'who told' and 'how' Wuras found out is the least of your problems right now," Amreth said grimly. "You must report this in all haste."

I sighed and rubbed my face with both hands in frustration before resuming my pacing. "Honestly, I don't know what to do. I'm fucked if I do, and I'm just as fucked if I don't. We both know what's going to happen once the word spreads I married a convict."

"Yes," Amreth said in a sympathetic tone. "They will question your suitability as a Warden. And your family's detractors will seize the opportunity to try and bring your entire House down. Your Sector is highly coveted for its natural resources and productivity. If there's even a hint that House Aramon could be deemed unfit, any support you might otherwise have enjoyed will quickly erode."

"Exactly. I haven't slept all night just trying to sort out this entire mess in my head. But any way I look at it, we lose. We don't have a case to present yet against Wuras. Malaya had only just started when the attack occurred."

Amreth absent-mindedly rubbed the dark scales adorning his forehead has he weighed my words. "Which is undoubtedly why Wuras attacked so swiftly. Given time, you could expose him. But by forcing your hand, he puts *you* in a vulnerable position. And if you accuse him now without a solid case, people will think you're just lashing out in a desperate attempt to save face."

"Now you understand my dilemma," I said in angry frustration. "But keeping it quiet not only welcomes another attack, but also implies I—"

My bracer and vidscreen simultaneously going off interrupted me. Accrued tension stiffened my spine as I recognized the ringtone of an urgent incoming call. I stepped over to the seating area of my room and gave a vocal command to turn on the vidscreen.

My blood turned to ice at the sight of my sire's stern face filling the screen. As cocky and self-assured—not to say arrogant—as I often came across, a single scowl from my father sufficed to make me feel like a petulant youngling. And right now, his icy-blue eyes—which I'd inherited—were leveled on me with a hard glint that made me want to squirm.

"Son, what is this blasphemy I hear?" Father asked in a tone cold enough to instantly freeze molten lava.

However, it was my brain that froze as I wondered how in the world he had already heard of last night's attack. Aside from the Nundars, and now Amreth, no one else knew of this outrageous assault.

Except the attacker...

"You heard?" I asked, baffled.

"Obviously, I heard! And so has everyone else," my father hissed. "What in Tharmok's name would possess you to commit such an unforgivable sacrilege? It wasn't enough that you stole one of your fellow Warden's prisoners, but you compound this insult by marrying her? You gave our name to a foul murderer?"

I felt my blood drain from my face as I stared at my father in shock. Ever since I consented to this marriage, I'd debated on how to inform my parents of the situation. Knowing they would go berserk under the current circumstances, I'd planned on delaying it until we had a solid enough case so that there would be no question I had taken the right course of action. I'd been a fool not to realize sooner what a formidable foe we were pitted against. Wuras once more demonstrated that he remained three steps ahead of me at every turn. By controlling the narrative, he kept us on the defensive.

I heaved a sigh and repressed the urge to allow my shoulders to slouch. Any display of weakness now would undermine my chances of rallying my father to our cause. Although this had not been how I had wanted to break the news to him, now that everything would be out in the open, we could greatly benefit from his wisdom in handling this crisis.

"I did not steal anything," I said in a calm and controlled voice. "I merely swapped Malaya with one of my prisoners. Yes, I married her according to human customs. We are not bonded yet, although I intend for that to also happen at a later date. But she is *not* a criminal."

"She is *convicted*!" my father exclaimed. "She has been tried and condemned. It is clearly written in the official records. That female is a criminal... a murderer!"

"No, Father. Malaya is innocent. She has been framed and falsely convicted. Wuras set her up in order to silence her," I countered.

Instead of launching into the furious rant I had expected, my father stared at me with a crestfallen expression, his anger bleeding out of him to be replaced by an air of sorrow. It struck me all the harder that, in my forty-two years of existence, I had never seen him display this type of vulnerable emotion.

"Do you hear yourself, Son?" Father asked, his voice filled with pain. "I should have listened to your mother. You were not ready to resume your duties so soon after—"

"I am *not* having a crisis," I interrupted sternly. "I am not suffering from PTSD following my previous abduction. This isn't a burnout, and I'm certainly not affected by *gannath*. I promise you that Malaya was set up, just like I am now by Wuras."

"How can you speak such outrageous words and not realize that you are clearly having a mental breakdown? Who in their right mind could possibly attack House Wuras—"

"Last night, my house was attacked by two unbranded adult Faernychs," I interrupted again in a harsh tone. I pointed an angry finger at the bed behind me where my mate still lay unconscious. "They were sent to murder my mate while I was supervising the trades in my Quadrants. If not for the timely intervention of my Nundars, she'd be dead right now!"

A look of horror descended over my father's features as he glanced over my shoulder before looking back at me. Conflicting emotions battled over his face so similar to mine.

"That's not possible," he said, his voice hesitant.

"I have the full footage of me fighting them on both my surveillance system and body cam," I retorted, lifting my chin defiantly.

This time, my sire visibly paled, shock and outrage settling in. "You do?"

"I most certainly do. I told you it had been a worthwhile investment. My mate is currently fighting for her life from the beast's poison. The only reason she's not currently writhing in pain is the sedative my Nundars gave her and my *bakaan* soothing her."

He shook his head as if struggling to come to terms with these revelations. "She nonetheless remains a murderer. A murderer you married…"

"If I may, Lord Aramon," Amreth interjected in a soft and respectful voice. "Your son is correct. Malaya Velasco is undeniably innocent. Her soul is pure. I have rarely seen one so beautiful as hers. Had Kronos not married her, I would have done so to save her. But they are soulmates. Therefore, it is as it should be."

"You, too," my father whispered, studying my friend's face as if he'd turned into some sort of twisted creature.

"Yes, my Lord. Me, too. A Temern confirmed both Malaya's innocence and the sacred bond she shares with your son," Amreth insisted. "He speaks the truth about Wuras."

In that instant, I could have hugged my friend. Instead, I gave my father a detailed rundown of the events that had taken place over the past few days from the moment Kayog first approached me about her situation. Through it all, Amreth provided confirmation and his support to my statements.

"Innocent or not, this is a monumental mess," my father said at last. "This scandal is all everyone talks about on Vargos. The Conclave has already received multiple calls to have you removed. Many of our clients have either paused or canceled their orders with us. Our rivals are seizing this opportunity to try and bring our entire House down."

I flinched. Of course, Wuras would wage his public opinion campaign on our homeworld. Gossipmongers would throw themselves at this latest scandal like carrion feeders on a rotting corpse. On Molvi, Wardens tended to be too tight-knit a community, most of us having no time or interest in petty rivalries. But on our homeworld, fortunes could be made and destroyed with a single word.

"I am sworn to protect the innocent and uphold justice, whatever the personal cost. Malaya is innocent, and Wuras is corrupt," I replied.

"Can you prove it?" my father replied, a dare in his voice.

"As I explained to you, Wuras disposed of her original files on him. We are regathering the evidence. It will require about two or three weeks," I said.

My father's face twisted into an angry snarl. "Are you daft?!

You barely have three days, so forget three weeks. The Conclave is summoning you. They demand you appear before them at once. Send me your recordings and security logs. I will try to buy you some time, but it will not be more than three days."

This time, I didn't prevent my shoulders from slouching in defeat. "Very well, Father. I will send you the recordings and prepare my journey to Vargos."

"Bring the human," he added in a clipped tone.

"What? No! She's ill!" I exclaimed, outraged.

"THEN FIX HER! If her soul is so *pure* as you claim, it will be clear for all to see," my father hissed. I ground my teeth at the contemptuous way he said 'pure' but kept silent. "In that case, it will prove bias or misjudgment on the part of Wuras. A proper judge would have seen it and not sent the female to a Dark Quadrant, least of all Dakon's. She *will* stand before the Conclave."

As much as I wanted to challenge his command, I couldn't argue with his logic. We'd never manage to find sufficient incriminating evidence against Wuras in such a short time. The purity of Malaya's soul constituted our only solid proof of his corruption, or at least of his inadequacy as a judge.

Once more defeated, I gave him a stiff nod.

"You have three days. Do not fail your House or your people… for a convicted human."

With these final harsh words, my father ended the communication.

CHAPTER 12
MALAYA

I slowly emerged from the oddest dream. My entire body tingled, my limbs feeling heavy, just like my head. You think I was recovering from a serious hangover, thankfully minus the splitting headache. I forced my heavy eyelids open, confused by my strange surroundings and the steady beeping sound in the background.

Then my memories returned with the violence of a tsunami. I jerked up into a sitting position in what appeared to be a medical bed. The room spun around me from the suddenness of my movement. I tried to plant my palms on the mattress beneath me to help me keep my balance only to have the movement blocked by the straps shackling me to the bed. I fell on my back and took a few deep breaths while the dizzy spell slowly faded.

By the looks of my surroundings, someone had taken me to the small medical bay of some spaceship. Two other medical beds lay empty to my left and right. I couldn't see or hear anyone else in the room.

Spaceship or prison ship?

The last things I recalled were the violent attack by a dreadful beast and the Nundars coming to my rescue. Then things blurred, likely as a result of my injuries. But more importantly, where was Kronos? Why was I on a spaceship and above all shackled? My heart seized as a horrible thought crossed my mind. The Nundars had mentioned something about Kronos coming or fighting... maybe both. Had he gotten injured? Was this why they had taken me?

As panic began to set in at the thought Kronos could have been hurt because of me, the door opened on a stern-looking Obosian female. Her dark blue uniform instantly identified her as medical personnel, likely a nurse.

"Good, you're finally awake," the female said in that less-than-friendly tone people used when addressing someone they deemed contemptible or inferior.

"Where am I? Where's Kronos?"

Completely ignoring my questions, she flipped the blanket still covering my lower body, casting it aside.

"Do you feel any pain?" she asked, poking a finger in different spots around my ankles and calves.

By the mostly faded state of the scars, their healing was fairly advanced. Even with using the finest healing nanobots, it would have taken a few days to achieve such fantastic results.

How long have I been out?

"Where's Kronos? Why am I here?" I reiterated.

"*I* ask the questions, Convict!" she snapped, glaring at me. "Now, do you feel any pain?"

I swallowed hard and shook my head, while panic steadily grew within me. Why wouldn't she answer such simple questions? Did it mean that Kronos indeed got injured or, worse still, that one of the beasts killed him? Was that the reason for her contempt and obvious anger at me for bringing death and chaos into his life.

The nurse proceeded to run a series of cognitive tests. I absent-mindedly responded, tears pricking my eyes as my overactive imagination ran wild with one horrible speculation after the other. Once done, she went to fetch one of those wretched prisoner uniforms and matching pair of shoes. She placed them on the stand next to my bed before proceeding to free me from the straps restraining me.

"Do not get any weird ideas. Misbehave, and I will make you regret it sorely," the nurse warned.

"I won't," I said in a shaky voice before looking at her pleadingly. "But please, please tell me Kronos is okay. I don't care what happens to me, just please tell me he's not hurt."

The nurse glared at me. She paused detaching my restraints, the pale gold of her eyes going out of focus as she examined my face. Moments later, she blinked rapidly, a frown marring her scaly forehead while a troubled expression settled over her features. She turned her gaze back to the strap around my left wrist and finished untying it.

"Lord Kronos is unharmed," the nurse begrudgingly said at last.

"Oh, thank you, God!" I exclaimed with a shuddering breath.

The nurse glanced back at me and seemed even more troubled. She finished freeing me then helped me get up, making sure I was steady enough on my feet.

"Any dizziness?" she asked, her tone significantly nicer than the contemptuous way she had previously addressed me.

"Not anymore," I said. "I did when I first woke up. Now, it's just my legs that feel a little wobbly. Otherwise, I'm fine."

"Good. Put these clothes on. There isn't much time," she said, pointing at the inmate uniform she had brought me.

Without a word, I removed my tunic and donned the uniform while the nurse went to operate some machine on the counter a short distance away. When the aroma of food wafted to me moments later, I realized she was likely using some kind of replicator. The nurse returned, carrying a tray, just as I was finishing putting the flat shoes on.

"Sit and eat," she said, in a semi-grumpy tone, like she didn't know how to address me anymore.

I sat down and studied her face as she placed the tray on an overbed table, which she positioned in front of me. She was pretty. Tall and slender, she appeared to be in her late thirties like me—although it was difficult to accurately guess the age of an Obosian.

"Can you tell me anything at all as to why I'm here and what's going on?" I asked in a timid voice.

She stared at me with an unreadable expression, her gaze going out of focus once again for a few seconds. In that instant, it finally dawned on me that she was looking at my soul. Had I not been so frazzled, I would have figured it out sooner.

"It is not my place to discuss such matters. Eat and drink. You will need your strength," she replied.

Although her voice lacked the earlier aggression she initially addressed me with, the finality in her tone made it clear she wouldn't be swayed. Despite the worry gnawing at me, I forced myself to eat. By the third bite, I found myself gulping down my food, suddenly struck by just how famished I felt.

As I was washing down my meal with a refreshing glass of water, the door swished open, startling me. My eyes widened at the sight of the familiar silhouette.

Kronos!!

I put my glass down on the table with a bit too much force. But as I pushed it away, the joy soaring in my heart instantly faded. I swallowed painfully the water left in my mouth as my eyes locked with the icy stare so similar to Kronos' yet clearly not his. I instinctively knew this male to be his father. The resemblance was uncanny. He was bigger and taller than his son —a standard feature among Obosians, who continued to grow throughout their lives. Even more piercings adorned his face and ears, including a few golden studs in his horns. The harsh and contemptuous way he stared at me felt like a déjà vu of my first meeting with Kronos.

"Leave us," he said to the nurse, his eyes remaining locked with mine.

His voice cracked like a whip and with the authority of one used to people obeying his every command.

"Yes, Lord Aramon," the nurse replied in a submissive tone.

She bowed her head, cast a nervous—almost sympathetic—glance my way before scurrying out of the room. I swallowed hard again and slid off the edge of the bed onto my feet, not wanting to remain in such a vulnerable position.

"You are his father," I said, stating the obvious. It was the first thing that came to mind, and I felt the irrational need to be the one initiating the conversation, if only to give myself the illusion I still had some kind of control over something. "Is Kronos okay?"

"Do you care?" he challenged.

I recoiled. "Of course, I care!"

"Why?" he challenged, taking a menacing step forward. "Do you love him?"

I blinked, taken aback by that question. "Kronos and I just met. It's too soon for that. But I don't have to be in love with him to genuinely care about him. Plus Kayog... a Temern says Kronos is my soulmate."

He scoffed. "And you believe it?"

"Yes, actually, I do," I said with conviction, holding his gaze unwaveringly.

Although his eyes never went out of focus, I strongly suspected he was examining my soul while assessing the honesty of my responses.

"Did you kill Pavel?"

That question struck me hard. It shouldn't. God knew I'd had time to mourn his untimely loss, but something in the brutal way he asked the question hit differently.

"I did not. I swear it. He was my friend," I said, a tremor entering my voice.

"And Judge Wuras is corrupt?" he insisted.

"Yes! He framed me before I could reveal all the crimes he has committed."

Lord Aramon scrunching his face with repressed anger was the last reaction I expected from him. He sighed with disgust before averting his eyes.

"You're disappointed," I whispered, flabbergasted. "You wanted Wuras to be right!"

Although he glared at me, his anger didn't quite feel personal. He couldn't seem to decide how he actually felt about me… or this situation.

"What I wanted is irrelevant. Either way, you've brought complete chaos to this House," he said through his teeth.

"*I* brought *nothing*!" I hissed, taking a determined step towards him with my hands fisted, fed up with the bullshit. "*Wuras* did this! I am just one of his countless victims, who refuses to go down quietly. I am sorry that Kronos and your House got dragged into this mess. But the blame belongs at Wuras's feet, not mine."

Once again, his reaction didn't match the outraged anger and self-righteous indignation I expected. Instead, he pursed his lips and gave me a slow, assessing look.

"See that you show this much spine before the Conclave," he said sternly.

I blinked, completely taken aback. "What?"

The Conclave? I was to stand before the Conclave? But why? As far as I knew, it acted both as a strange mix of the Supreme Court and the Senate for the Obosians. The thirteen males and females who sat on that body had almost complete power over their people. Their word had the power of law. But they only addressed matters of major importance to Obosians. While Wuras's corruption could possibly fall under that category, was this an important enough case to warrant the attention of the Conclave? Either way, I wasn't ready to defend this case. I didn't have any evidence, and my brain was still foggy from my recent ordeal.

"You have one chance, little human. Don't fail," he warned in an imperative tone. "Come."

Little human… Like father, like son.

As soon as I exited the room, four immense guards I hadn't noticed before closed in around me. To my relief, they didn't shackle me, but their forbidding expressions broadcast loudly I'd better not get any funny ideas or give them cause to discipline me. That was one spanking I definitely wouldn't enjoy.

Shrinking in on myself, I quietly followed Lord Aramon who was marching down the short hallway with determined steps, as if he owned the place. As we approached the reinforced door at the other end, it finally dawned on me that we were indeed onboard a vessel. It wasn't a traditional door but a hatch. It parted before us, revealing another corridor, this one much longer, riddled with a series of security features, as well as more guards armed to the teeth standing watch. You'd think we were entering a secret vault containing some national treasury or the type of technology that could destroy the galaxy as we know it.

My anxiety level skyrocketed as we approached another set of reinforced doors. The guard standing watch next to it released the security lock. Heart pounding, I stretched my neck to see beyond Lord Aramon's humongous wings what awaited me on the other side. To my shock, I stepped into a shell-shaped room.

Despite its huge size, domed ceiling, and abundance of glow-stones lighting the space, the chamber felt ominous. The somber floors and dark gray walls undoubtedly played a part in this. Straight ahead in the rounded end of the room, thirteen Elder Obosians sat behind an elevated, semi-circular table. On the left and right sides of the room, two rows of seats lined the walls. A dozen Obosians sat on the left side, but I only had eyes for the right side where Kronos sat, surrounded by his own set of guards.

Our gazes connected. The obvious relief in his eyes took me aback. Did he think I wouldn't come? No... He feared I wouldn't be *able* to come. After all, I'd just awakened from who knew how long I'd been unconscious since the attack. Despite the lingering panic stiffening my spine, Kronos's reassuring smile did wonders for me. Hell, his mere presence in the room, seeing him unscathed soothed a great deal of the tension knotting the muscles of my nape and shoulders.

The sound of my footsteps resounded loudly in the otherwise silent room, their sound echoing slightly. I realized the architects had done a fantastic job with the acoustics so sound would carry perfectly and spare the need for microphones—or so I suspected. For some stupid reason, I tried to lighten my steps, feeling self-conscious that I should be so loud while the much bigger Obosians escorting me were all but gliding over the floor. Even my grumpy father-in-law, marching with a determined gait, hardly made any noise.

Sometimes, I have the dumbest sense of priorities.

At a subconscious level, I understood that my survival instincts had prompted this reaction in an involuntary effort to draw less attention to myself in a hostile environment. Considering all eyes were already on me and that there was nowhere to hide, it was a pointless endeavor.

My father-in-law stopped about four meters away from the Elders. I absentmindedly noticed he was standing on a slightly paler patch of stones in the middle of the floor. Four more similar paler patches—though discreet—adorned the floor at equal distance from each other. I realized then they likely served as marks for prisoners or supplicants to stand on.

Imitating the guards escorting me, I stopped a couple of meters behind Kronos's father.

"Honorable Elders of the Conclave, I bring you the human

female Malaya Velasco, wedded to my firstborn son, Kronos Aramon, according to human customs, and convicted of murder by Judge Wuras. She stands here as a witness in the case against Kronos."

Case against KRONOS?!

What the fuck was going on? It should be a case against *me* or Wuras. Not against Kronos!

With those final words, Lord Aramon glanced at me over his shoulder, a warning in his eyes, before he walked over to the benches where Kronos sat with the guards watching him. He didn't sit with his son, but separately at the other end of the front row.

"Convict Malaya Velasco, step forward," said the Elder male sitting to the right of the female in the center.

Heart pounding, I obeyed, advancing a few steps to the same paler spot where Lord Aramon had stood. To my surprise, the guards didn't follow, content to stay a short distance behind me. Thankfully, I appeared to have guessed right about taking position on that spot as they seemed content with my behavior.

He turned his head right to look at the dozen or so Obosians sitting on the opposite side of the room from Kronos.

"Nurse Drula Volgir, step forward," he said in that same commanding tone.

Only then did I notice her presence amidst the small crowd. She cast a strange—almost commiserating—look my way as she complied, stopping on one of the paler spots to my left.

"Nurse Volgir, do you recognize this human female standing before us?" the Elder male asked.

"Yes, Elder. Her medical record identified her as Malaya Velasco. I was entrusted with her care on her journey from Molvi to Vargos," Drula replied.

"What were you treating the convict for?" the Elder asked.

"Neurotoxicity and cytotoxicity resulting from multiple venomous bites by an adult Faernych," the nurse said factually.

"Based on the amount of venom she received, its toxicity level, and her weaker human immune system, left untreated, death would have normally been expected within two to three hours after the first bite. Thanks to the timely intervention of Warden Aramon's Nundars, neurotoxic damage to Convict Velasco's nervous system was minimal. Cytotoxic cell necrosis was also mitigated by their efforts over the first twenty-four hours. Our medical pods and advanced nanobots were able to repair most of the lingering damage she sustained over the past forty-six hours."

My jaw dropped upon hearing all of this. I knew my injuries had been bad. Frankly, I thought the hydra had bitten right through my bones, but cell necrosis because of its venom? A quick calculation also made me realize that I'd been unconscious for at least three days.

"Most, but not all damage?" the Elder insisted.

"Neural damage has been fully mended. There is some mild tissue damage left that the nanobots should fully heal in the next forty-eight to seventy-two hours without requiring further intervention on my part," she replied.

"Is the convict able to stand before this Conclave?" he asked.

"The convict was chemically awakened from sedation. I have performed the standard series of tests on her. Malaya Velasco's vital signs and cognitive functions are normal. She's fully operational."

"Thank you, Nurse Volgir. You are excused," the Elder said.

While grateful to finally get this assessment of my status, I also felt offended and somewhat violated that it should have been revealed publicly before anyone would even share it with me. What if the news had been terrible instead? What if I'd just found out that I was getting eaten alive from within by some necrotic toxin destroying every cell in my body?

However, the Elder turning his glowing eyes my way put an

end to my self-righteous indignation. I braced for what would follow.

"Convict Malaya Velasco, you stand here as a witness for Warden Kronos Aramon. What do you have to say in defense of his crimes?"

I recoiled, utterly baffled. "His crimes? What crimes?"

"You were condemned to a life sentence in Warden Dakon Kothor's playground. On the day of your transfer, Warden Aramon stole you from your assigned Warden. He forbade the guards from branding you, as required by law. Then instead of sending you to his Dark Quadrant to serve your sentence, he took you to his home to live as his wife, in contravention of your sentence. Only two things could justify such aberrant actions: mental issues or moral ineptitude. So what do you have to say in his defense, Convict?"

Each of his words struck me like a freight train. While technically true, worded like that turned them into something foul and completely detached from reality. Anger and a rabid need to defend Kronos swelled within me.

"With all due respect, Sir, your assessment of Kronos's actions couldn't be more wrong. You state there are only two options to justify them. I beg to differ. There is a third option and the true reason for this behavior which, I concede, appears totally contrary to his personality and values. Kronos Aramon is the most righteous, honorable male I've ever met. He has devoted his entire life to upholding the law and defending justice. And it is in the pursuit of that very objective that he has taken the actions you have enumerated, though not in the dark spirit you presented them to be."

"Are you branded?" he challenged.

"No, I am not."

"Were you brought to a Dark Quadrant to serve your sentence?"

"No," I repeated, annoyed by his obvious tactic.

"Did Warden Aramon take you to his private residence to live by his side as his mate according to human customs?"

Grinding my teeth, I once more forced myself to answer, waiting for the opportunity to counter the point he was trying to make.

"Yes, he did."

"And yet, you've been duly judged, convicted, and sentenced by an honorable Obosian judge—"

"No, I have not," I interrupted in a clipped tone.

Shocked gasps resonated in the room from the attendees on the right, while the thirteen Elders of the Conclave stared at me with outrage.

"You lie?!" the Elder hissed.

"I do not lie," I replied firmly.

"Are you not a convict?"

"Yes, I am," I said.

"You just denied it!" he snarled.

I lifted my chin defiantly. "No. I do not deny being a convict, as per the judgment I received. I deny being tried by an *honorable* judge. Ask better questions, and you'll get clearer answers."

More gasps greeted my last sentence. Although I flinched inwardly at my wretched mouth running away again, I only felt bad to the extent too much attitude could backfire and hurt Kronos's case. But I couldn't stand a bully or a kangaroo court.

"Tread carefully, Convict. You may have avoided serving your sentence for now, but *we* are not so blinded," he hissed.

"Or what? I'll be wrongfully accused of more crimes I never committed? You'll add an extra life sentence in Q4 to be served consecutively to the one I've already been given by the judge who framed me for murder? I thought Obosians were the guardians of justice."

"You dare question it?" he exclaimed.

"I have no choice but to," I retorted, incensed, before pointing an angry finger at Kronos. "If Kronos is sitting over there, and I'm standing before you, then you already know of my claims. Yet, the moment I woke up in the infirmary, every Obosian I've encountered has made it obvious they already deemed me guilty. And I see the same condemnation on your face, both when you look at me, and when you speak of Kronos. Whatever happened to innocent until proven guilty?"

"You were condemned," he countered in a haughty tone.

I threw my hands up in aggravation. "By a corrupt judge! And I'm not his first victim! Where is your appeal system? Where is your check on ethics and corruption? If such an accusation is being raised, you should *want* to investigate it and find out the truth, whether to prove his innocence or end his corruption."

I took a deep breath and ran shaky fingers through my hair to try and rein in my seething anger. I was tired of repeating this same bullshit over and over again only to be met by more people doubting me. Proving one's innocence shouldn't be this painful.

"Do you think Kronos Aramon wanted to marry a human and a convict at that? He and I had that very conversation shortly after our wedding. Had we randomly met on the street, he wouldn't have spared me a second glance. He only agreed to see me—with much reluctance—because a Temern vouched for my innocence. He believed speaking to me would confirm my guilt, at which point he would have sent me to Warden Dakon's sector with a clear conscience. You didn't even grant me that courtesy. Are you so afraid to acknowledge that Obosians are not perfect? That one in your midst could be rotten?"

"You are standing before us, are you not?" the Elder snapped back, earning himself a few approving nods from both his fellow Elders and some of the attendees on the side benches.

I waved a dismissive hand. "Pfft. You're still not giving *me* a chance. This is only a show to take *him* down," I added pointing once more at Kronos. "You can read souls. You can see I speak the truth!"

"The only thing your soul shows is anger," he replied with that same obnoxious tone.

"YES, BECAUSE I'M MAD!" I shouted, startling everyone including myself.

I closed my eyes and took a few deep breaths to regain my composure. Squaring my shoulders, I looked back at the Elder and resumed talking in a controlled voice.

"I am angry because, like the rest of the galaxy, I used to put Obosians on a pedestal. You were the embodiment of righteousness and honesty. The hand, eyes, and heart of justice. And now I see it was all a lie. You're like everyone else. You're quick to condemn others for their sins but turn a blind eye to your own. I expected… more. So much more from you…"

"Why should we side with a convict over a respected judge?" he challenged.

"No one asked that of you. I'm asking you to side with the *truth*, with the *facts*," I countered. "I've always respected the law. Until this mess, I had a flawless record. I've never even had a speeding ticket. But on the very day I'm supposed to hand over an incriminating file about Wuras to the Enforcers, I suddenly decided to commit a gruesome murder? With the help of Temerns, I get a second chance at trying to prove my innocence. But the day I start putting my file back together, I get attacked by venomous beasts? Is it common for a Warden's home to get attacked by wild beasts? Are Temerns known to lie about someone's innocence? Do you honestly believe that Kronos is the type of male who could be easily swayed by a murderer?"

"Kronos Aramon is recovering from a traumatic abduction. It could explain his otherwise aberrant behavior," the Elder said dismissively.

"Seriously? After all the valid questions I've raised, *this* is the explanation you want to go with? But I'm the one being dishonest?" I said with disgust.

The Elder slammed his fist on the table. "You go too far, Convict!"

"Enough!" snapped the female Elder to his left.

As she sat in the central position, I could only assume she was the leader of the Conclave.

"However unpleasant this entire situation may be, anyone with eyes can clearly see she's no murderer," the female said with a disgruntled expression. "This means either Wuras's judgment is slipping, which may indicate the need for him to retire, or he is indeed guilty of the serious crime you accuse him of. Can you back up your claim? Without proof, it is slander and defamation."

"They took my file the day he framed me for murder. I was starting to rebuild it when I was attacked," I said with helpless frustration. "But the nurse confirmed I've indeed been attacked by those hydra beasts and nearly died from it."

She shrugged with an unimpressed expression. "There is no question you were bitten by a Faernych. That doesn't mean Wuras, or a random other assassin, set them after you. Every Warden has a few trained Faernychs in their forests. While I am *not* making an accusation, I can think of at least two other explanations that would have nothing to do with Wuras. One of Warden Kronos's beasts could have become rabid—which is known to happen with older Faernychs—and gone on a rampage, making you one of its countless victims. Or a more nefarious one would be that Warden Kronos deliberately set his beast on you to frame Wuras. They are trained to obey him, after all."

I paled upon hearing those arguments. While I didn't believe for one minute that Kronos would have staged this, could the faer… whatever-she-called-it truly have simply gone rabid? But it felt like too convenient a coincidence.

Kronos stood, instantly setting his guards on high alert. While they also stood, his calm and composed demeanor seemed to appease them.

"If I may interject, Elder Ozra, I have proof that I didn't stage this attack and that it was not a case of Faernych dementia," Kronos said with poise. "My domain's surveillance camera and the body cam I always wear when touring my playground recorded the entirety of the events. I've made a montage video to show you the shortened version. But I also have the full recording, if you require it."

"Videos can be tampered with," the Elder male countered, making me want to punch him in the throat.

Kronos gave him a smug smile that didn't reach his eyes. "They can be, which is why I also brought the remains of the two *unbranded* and *unsealed* mature Faernychs that attacked my domain and my mate."

"Unbranded?!" Elder Ozra exclaimed.

"Unbranded and unsealed... In my home..." Kronos repeated with barely repressed anger.

This time, a truly troubled expression flitted over the faces of all thirteen Elders.

"Present your evidence, Warden," Elder Ozra said.

Kronos handed a small data stick to one of his guards. The guard tapped a few instructions on his armband then connected the stick to it. A giant holographic screen appeared a meter above me, and about two meters in front, making it hover at an equal distance between the Conclave's table and the spot where I stood. Seconds later, the footage started playing. It took me a second to realize at first that it was from Kronos's body cam point of view.

It showed him looking at the warning message on his armband—or so I guessed since I couldn't read the Obosian text it displayed. As Kronos took flight, I got a brief glimpse of the Quadrant he had been visiting. The image then cut to the various camera feeds outside the house. They showed the two beasts coming from opposite ends of our Sector, and clearly not from the forest. However, the height from which they descended implied they had been dropped from a cloaked vessel.

My heart started pounding, and I felt myself shaking when I saw myself running out of my bedroom with a smile on my face, thinking Kronos had returned early, only to see death had come knocking. I hugged myself while watching the beast ramming its body against the glass door, hearing it shatter, followed by my agonized screams moments later. I could almost feel the teeth sinking in my flesh all over again. At least, there were no cameras inside my room. We could only see the terrace with the shattered door and hear my screams interspersed with the thumping sound of the beast flapping its wings while trying to drag me out.

At last, I stopped screaming, the beast toppling over while the Nundars pushed it out of my room with their power. The camera feed switched to an aerial view of the interior garden. I rubbed my eyes only to realize tears had made them blurry. Although I vaguely remember being taken through there, a single look at my face sufficed to understand why my memory was so fuzzy. I looked drugged and in pain. No wonder, considering what a mangled mess the beast had made of my legs.

The moment the Nundars carrying me vanished inside their cave, the feed switched back to Kronos's body cam. The next few seconds displayed an accelerated footage of his remaining flight home, then battle against the creature. However traumatized I'd felt reliving these dreadful moments, watching Kronos fight mesmerized me. I knew Wardens had to be exceptional fighters, but I'd never imagined he would be this badass. It was almost like watching an action movie.

When he went to lure the second beast, I feared my heart would beat its way out of my chest. Despite knowing he would make it out alive—as proven by the fact he was standing a few meters from me, I still felt faint with fear for him when he nearly crashed in the water and some even more fearsome aquatic creature wrecked the flying hydras. Once he tossed the dead creature over the railing onto the main terrace of the house, I thought the footage would end there. But it continued a while longer.

Seeing Kronos rushing through the maze of the Nundars' lair searching for me turned me upside down. But the way he held my hand, visibly used his *bakaan* to ease my pain, and thanked the Nundars for saving my life wrecked me. More tears ran down my cheeks as I turned to look at him. Gratitude, wonder, and a deep emotion that was far too early to name burned fiercely inside me. Our gaze connected. The tenderness in his eyes melted me from the inside out while a communication I couldn't put into words passed between us.

I wanted to run and throw myself into his arms.

The holographic screen vanishing broke the magic. I blinked and wiped my cheeks, feeling embarrassed by this display of weakness.

"Her soul is reaching for yours, Warden," Elder Ozra said pensively.

I frowned, confused by her comment.

"Yes, it does," Kronos said with pride. "The Temern, Kayog Voln, says we're soulmates. I concur."

"You didn't bond with her," she challenged.

"We just met. Malaya doesn't know our way or the implications of bonding with one of us," Kronos said in a factual manner. "I intend to bond with her once we've proven her innocence so that she can freely choose to make our union official out of love and not as a means to survive."

That, too, hit me hard, but in the most wondrous way. He was right, we barely knew each other. Yet, hearing he wanted to keep me for the long haul moved me deeply. It felt… right.

Elder Ozra pursed her lips while she weighed his words.

"It is undeniably disturbing footage you presented here," Elder Ozra conceded at last. "While there is no denying your domain and your mate were attacked—by unbranded Faernychs, no less—there is still no proof Wuras is behind any of this."

"You are correct. While it is an overly convenient coincidence, we cannot directly link this attack to Judge Wuras… yet," Kronos said. "We believe he appropriated Malaya's original incriminating file and is going out of his way to prevent her from putting it back together."

"So what do you expect from this Conclave?" she insisted.

"I want the Conclave to publicly acknowledge that I am not mentally impaired. I want you to condemn the attack against my domain and against any interference with our investigation," Kronos said forcefully. "Furthermore, I want you to make the full roster of Wuras's past and present cases publicly available, as well as freeze his off-world assets."

Elder Ozra frowned at that last request while the other members of the Conclave visibly recoiled or bristled.

"The latter request is excessive without proof of wrongdoing," she countered.

"While my mate was fighting for her life, a UPO Enforcer provided us legally obtained certified bank records from Wuras displaying a number of dubious transactions," Kronos argued. "They clearly show he receives regular payments from Komoro and Fingram subsidiaries, the two most powerful drug and contraband cartels in this sector of the galaxy."

Elder Ozra shifted her wings in a movement that hinted at her growing unease with the situation. Kronos was making a solid case for us. We needed her to grant this request.

"While it does sound suspicious, it isn't proof of wrongdoing. House Wuras has investments in many businesses. A subsidiary of a questionable organization may not be involved in illegal business. Without solid evidence against said subsidiary, there is no ground to freeze his assets."

"Fine, but we *need* a few weeks without interference to rebuild the file that was taken," Kronos insisted. "And Wuras needs to be closely watched. He tried to silence my mate twice. First by trying to send her to Dakon's playground, which we all know would be a death sentence for a pure soul like my Malaya. Then by sending wild beasts to my house. He *will* try again. Failing that, he might flee. Freezing his assets would make that harder for him."

"We will *not* freeze his assets until you can provide strong enough evidence to support such an action," Elder Ozra said in an imperative tone. "We accede to your other requests. But be fairly warned, Warden Aramon. You have one month to bring substantial evidence to support your grievous accusations. Fail to do so, and you will be stripped of your title. Your Sector will be confiscated from your House and awarded to House Wuras as reparation for this defamation."

"WHAT?!" I exclaimed, flabbergasted. "That's not fair! *I'm* the one accusing Wuras of corruption. If we fail to gather enough evidence in time, punish *me*, not *him*!"

Elder Ozra tilted her head to the side while staring at me with an undefinable expression tinged with a smidge of mockery. "Then make sure you find proof, Malaya Velasco. Your case will be retried the same day."

She turned her head left then right to look at her colleagues, before looking back at me.

"So say we all," she said with a finality that made it clear the Conclave was at an end.

"So say we all," the others repeated in unison.

Then as one, they all stood up and filed out of the room through a secret passage behind their seats.

CHAPTER 13
MALAYA

Stunned, I watched the four guards who had escorted me here turn on their heels and walk out of the room the same way we had arrived. None of them paid me any mind as if I no longer existed. The four guards who surrounded Kronos also simply walked away, but through a different door near their seats by the right wall.

Seeing Kronos take a couple of steps towards me broke the paralysis that kept me glued in place. Without thinking, I broke into a run and threw myself into his arms. He caught me as I slammed into him. His muscular arms closed around me seconds before his massive wings wrapped around us.

I instantly felt safe, protected... home.

I tightened my embrace. My face buried in his neck, I inhaled deeply his fresh scent with a hint of sandalwood and pine. He gave me a gentle squeeze then caressed my back in a soothing fashion. I lifted my head to look at him. Our gazes connected. His icy-blue eyes shone like the full moon in the dark sea of his black sclera, hypnotizing me. I couldn't tell who leaned towards the other or if we simultaneously did it, but our lips met in a tender kiss filled with devotion and unspoken promises.

Too soon, it ended, but the spark it had lit in my heart lingered.

The moment Kronos opened his wings, I not only felt bereft, but also exposed and vulnerable. One arm still wrapped around me, he brushed a rebellious lock of hair from my face.

"How are you feeling, my mate?" he asked in a gentle voice filled with concern.

"A little tired, probably because of the sedation, but otherwise surprisingly well considering what the nurse described," I said.

He slightly leaned away from me to glance down at my ankles, despite the dreadful convict uniform that covered them.

"And your wounds?" he asked.

"They tingle a little, but they're fine, otherwise. I had a look when the nurse examined me earlier, and the scars are mostly faded," I said sincerely.

He nodded. "The Nundars worked on your wounds."

"It shows. They did a wonderful job and saved my life," I said, my voice shaking a bit with gratitude and emotion.

"They certainly did," Kronos said with warmth before his smile slightly stiffened.

Movement at the edge of my vision made me realize the reason for his sudden mood change. Although he kept one arm around my waist, Kronos turned to face his father who had approached us.

"Malaya, you met my father, Lord Destar Aramon. Father, this is my mate Malaya Velasco."

My face felt like it had been dipped in cement as I smiled politely at his father. Aside from the fact that the man was freaking massive, he also intimidated the fuck out of me. While Kronos held an undeniable badass aura, his father's was on steroids. Even his resting face looked like he was ready to bash my head in and use my bones as toothpicks.

"Hello again, Lord Aramon," I said in a subdued voice.

I'd hoped to take my cues from Kronos as to how to address his father, but I didn't know how to interpret his reactions. There was undeniable deference on his part towards his sire, but it didn't tell me much about how *I* was supposed to act towards him.

Lord Aramon gave me a slow once over that seriously made me want to squirm.

"You've got yourself an interesting mate, Son," he said, although his gaze never strayed from me.

I didn't know how to interpret that, or the fact that he hadn't responded to my greeting. Kronos snorting and amusement sparkling in his eyes in response somewhat reassured me. Had he looked offended, I would have gone into full panic mode.

"That, my Malaya certainly is," Kronos said, his hand tightening possessively around my waist.

That did wonders for my shaky self-confidence.

"Interesting in a good way I hope," I said in a slightly nervous tone.

His father pursed his lips as he continued to stare at me. Was he seriously just going to ignore my words and act like I was just some prop next to his son?

"You cannot be this arrogant when addressing the Conclave," he said sternly to me. "Moxan may be obnoxious, but he's still an Elder. They hold your fate—and ours—in their hands. See that you remember that when next you stand before them."

I flinched. That Elder had seriously gotten under my skin. Even as I'd lost my shit, I'd known it was reckless of me to let my emotions get the best of me, especially with the dreadful threat Elder Ozra dumped on us at the end if we failed to find proof.

"Apologies, Sir," I said sheepishly.

"Hmmm," he said in a way that I didn't know how to interpret.

I cast a sideways glance at Kronos, but he was staring at his father with an unreadable expression.

Lord Aramon waved his hand for us to follow him. "Come. Let's go to your vessel."

Without waiting for our response, he headed out of the room through the same side door the guards who had been watching over Kronos had used. As soon as we exited, I peered at the reinforced doors to our left with more security checkpoints that seemed to lead to a great hall where civilians and others could mingle. Lord Aramon headed in the opposite direction. I realized the section we were in allowed vessels to dock directly to this secured area so the people coming to stand before the Conclave couldn't wander off in the city without a thorough security check.

At the end of each corridor a single hatch connected with a visiting ship. We followed Kronos's father through the third corridor outside the room we just exited and entered a different vessel than the one I'd awakened in.

As soon as we were all inside, Lord Aramon stopped and turned to face us. Once again, I felt like a little girl about to be scolded by her dad when his gaze turned to me.

"I'm sorry for causing trouble for your House," I blurted out.

He waved a dismissive hand. "*You* didn't. A human proving an Obosian corrupt, especially one as high-ranking as Judge Wuras, would hold little value. But another Obosian noble house will force action. You convinced the Conclave."

"Could have fooled me," I mumbled with a huff.

Lord Aramon snorted. "Their reaction is due to the fact that your word and their opinions are not enough. They need irrefutable proof to bring down as powerful a House as Wuras. They cannot allow this to go on. By putting the burden on my

House, they make sure we will leave no stone unturned to provide the evidence they need."

"But it's still unfair that they should dump this responsibility on you," I insisted. "Why can't they interrogate Wuras like they did me? They'll see he's shady."

Both Kronos and his father shook their heads.

"Obosians can naturally block others from seeing their souls, or how much of it can be seen," Kronos explained. "We normally only share our light with our mate once we bond."

"Damn," I said, my shoulders drooping. "It just feels so unfair that they are pinning my accusations on your family."

Kronos smiled. "It's actually a good thing. House Wuras is powerful, but so is ours. By giving us an official mandate, the Conclave has made it okay for people of lesser Houses to speak up about what they may have seen or know."

My eyes widened in understanding. "Like the courthouse guards and clerks that Wuras is blackmailing!"

"What?!" Lord Aramon exclaimed, eyes wide.

"Torgal—my Temern lawyer during the proceedings—said that many of the guards and clerks both hated and feared Wuras. He believes they would love to bring him down but are afraid to act against him, probably because he's blackmailing them."

"We need their names," Lord Aramon said in a commanding tone.

I shifted uneasily on my feet. "I can ask Torgal, but what if Wuras tries to get them killed, too?"

"Do not worry. We'll protect them," he replied with confidence before turning to Kronos. "My fleet will escort you home to avoid you encountering any *unfortunate accident* on your journey. You will reinforce the defenses around your dwelling as well as your playground. A second attack directly against your house will cause a riot, but all your inmates suddenly dying because of your 'negligence' will undermine all of us."

"Yes, Father. We already started with the upgrades around the house," Kronos said, his scaly brow creasing. "But you make a valid point about the Quadrants. I will tackle those as well as soon as I return."

"Good, and keep your female safe," he added before shifting his attention back to me. "As for you, see that you find that evidence. If you need help with anything, speak up. Understood, little human?"

"Understood. And it's Malaya," I replied.

"Excuse me?" he asked, his tone implying he couldn't believe I talked back.

Refusing to be intimidated, I held his gaze, although I forced myself to speak in a respectful tone instead of a belligerent one. "My name is Malaya, not 'little human.'"

He tilted his head to the side. How the fuck could this male make me feel like I was shrinking where I stood with a single stare defied logic.

"Are you not human?" he challenged.

I gave him a 'What the fuck' look before conceding. "Well, yes."

"And aren't you little?"

"I'm not lit—"

The way he raised his pierced eyebrows in disbelief before casting a meaningful glance between me, his son and himself shut me up.

"Well, compared to you guys, I *am* smaller, but—"

"So that makes you a little human, does it not?" Lord Aramon said smugly, interrupting me.

I scrunched my face in annoyance, while his smug smile broadened.

Dismissing me, he glanced back at his son. "Keep me apprised of your progress."

Without waiting for Kronos to respond, Lord Aramon turned on his heel and headed for the hatch to leave. I shook my head in aggravation as we watched him walking away.

"I don't call you big Obosian," I muttered under my breath.

To my horror, despite already being a few meters ahead of us and about to exit the vessel, Lord Aramon stopped dead in his tracks and turned to look at me. My stomach dropped, and I braced for the well-deserved tongue lashing that awaited me.

"You just did," Lord Aramon said, his icy gaze boring into me.

"I… I'm sorry," I said, wishing the ground would open beneath me and swallow me and my dumb mouth whole.

Far from mollifying him, my words only had his scowl deepening. "You're sorry? Why? Are you saying I'm not big?"

My eyes widened, and I opened and closed my mouth a few times, unsure how to answer that unexpected question.

"Yes, you are," I blurted out at last when he raised an impatient eyebrow in reaction to my failure to respond.

"And am I not an Obosian?" he insisted, his voice just as stern.

"Well… yes," I said in a small voice.

"So why are you apologizing for making an accurate statement?"

This time, I squirmed, having no idea how to respond. I scratched my nape, and cast a desperate glance at Kronos, hoping for him to rescue me from this mess of my own making. He was merely staring at his father with an unreadable expression.

Lord Aramon huffed, reclaiming my attention. "Your little human clearly needs more rest, Son. See that she gets it."

With that, Lord Aramon walked out of the ship. I exhaled the breath I hadn't realized I'd been holding.

"That went well," I mumbled.

"It did," Kronos concurred.

I jerked my head towards my husband. "That was sarcasm, in case you hadn't noticed. It couldn't have gone worse! Your dad hates my guts!"

To my shock, Kronos chuckled, and his eyes sparkled with mischief.

"My father likes you… *a lot.*"

His smile broadened when I just stood there, gaping at him in disbelief.

"I'm the one who's supposed to be delirious from the flying hydra's venom! What the fuck could possibly make you think he likes me?"

"He teased you! My father only has two moods: grumpy and ultra grumpy," Kronos said with a laugh in his voice. "It usually takes months, if not years, for him to start showing his more relaxed side to a stranger."

"*That* was his more relaxed side?!" I exclaimed.

He nodded. "Actually, that was his humorous side."

He burst out laughing at my flabbergasted expression. Then to my shock, he picked me up in his arms and carried me deeper inside the ship.

"But he has a point. You need rest. The nurse forcefully pulled you out of sedation with some drugs. You still have some recovery to do," Kronos said in a tone that brooked no argument.

I almost argued, but more out of principle than anything else. The thought of curling up in bed held an undeniable appeal. On our way to his quarters, we passed a crewmate to whom he spoke in Obosian, likely giving him instructions for our departure.

Just like his bedroom on Molvi, this one boasted dark brown and gray colors, with a massive window looking out onto space. Surprisingly, there was no workspace in the room, although I suspected he had a full office on the other side of one of the connecting doors.

I didn't argue when he helped me out of the wretched convict uniform I'd been forced to wear again. If I never had to touch another one of those for the rest of my life, it wouldn't be too soon. Wearing nothing but my undies, I crawled on top of his humongous bed while he removed his leather breastplate. Sadly, he didn't remove his pants, content to kick off his boots.

He didn't get into bed with me. After tucking me in, he sat at the edge and simply held my hand. I wouldn't have minded a bit of snuggling. Kronos was truly a gorgeous male. To think I hated his guts when I first met him.

"It will take about twelve hours for us to get home," Kronos said in a gentle voice. "I suggest you try to sleep through as much of it as you can. The Nundars wanted you to remain unconscious for at least four to five days straight for your body to fully heal. I hated that we had to wake you up early for this."

"You were so badass fighting those beasts! And the Nundars were amazing, too. If they hadn't arrived when they did…" I took a deep breath when my voice threatened to break. Kronos gave my hand a comforting squeeze, to which I responded with a shaky smile. "They look so inconspicuous, almost fragile. And yet they are so powerful! I was fairly out of it during the attack, but that video you showed blew my mind. The power with which they knocked those beasts back is incredible!"

"The Nundars are indeed great," Kronos said with a wistful smile. "The power they displayed was impressive. But that's all thanks to you."

I recoiled. "To me?!"

"I had an excess of energy that morning. So I overfed them before leaving. Which came in handy," he deadpanned.

The lascivious look that descended over his features had my toes instantly curling. Damn the man. He chuckled at my embarrassment. But I refused to let him get the last word.

"Then I better keep you overfed all the time," I said in a singsong voice.

Instead of laughing or taking on a playful expression, Kronos's face took on an intensity that had me instantly hot and bothered.

"I'll make sure to remind you of that statement once you're fully rested, my mate."

Kronos leaned forward and gave me a kiss that had me melting from the inside out.

"Rest," he whispered against my lips. "I'll be next door if you need anything."

After brushing his mouth one last time against mine, Kronos stood up and walked into the adjacent room, which I'd accurately guessed to be an office. He left the door open as he went to work. Feeling safe and content, I closed my eyes and let sleep claim me.

After what felt like mere minutes, I woke up with a start, only to see we'd actually reached home. Kronos had wrapped me in the blanket to cover my nudity and was carrying me out of the shuttle. I snuggled against him, still feeling a little groggy.

As we exited the ship—which had taken up almost the entirety of the landing pad, I finally noticed the slew of vessels darkening the early evening sky. Lord Aramon hadn't been kidding when he said his fleet would escort us back up. And I suspected more vessels had stayed in orbit or hovered a little higher up in the sky.

However, at least a couple of them were flying towards the Quadrants, likely to scout for any trouble lurking around. As Kronos carried me down the inclined ramp to the house's main terrace, I got a glimpse of the fully repaired glass wall of my own private terrace. Additional technology had been cleverly added to the house's main structure so that it wouldn't clash with the harmonious design. I couldn't tell what they were, but I suspected some of them to be long-range automatic weapons.

Around the railing, I recognized discreet shield nodes. Whenever a breach was announced, an energy shield would form, connecting each node. Based on the few nodes I'd been able to spot, the shield would entirely cover every terrace and other open areas of the house. Had this system been in place prior to the flying hydras attack, the shield would have prevented them from ever getting close enough to even be able to break down my glass door.

All these visible upgrades should have reassured me. Instead, as we approached the door to the main hall, my pulse picked up, and my stomach roiled with a growing sense of panic. It made no sense, and yet the moment Kronos stepped into the hallway leading to our bedrooms, the discreet tingling around my ankles steadily increased in intensity until it turned into a full-on throbbing, not to say burning sensation. A heavy weight settled on my chest, making it harder to breathe. I could almost hear the beast screeching in my ears.

A whimper escaped me, and I realized I was shaking and crying when Kronos tightened his arms around me as we approached my bedroom door.

"It's okay, Malaya. You are safe. The Faernychs are dead. They can't hurt you anymore," Kronos said in a soothing voice.

When he stopped in front of my room, the panic that had been growing inside me just blew up. I started kicking and screaming, even as I latched on to Kronos like a drowning woman. Heavy sobs choked me as he moved away from my door and headed towards his room instead.

A wave of peace washed over me. My brain understood it was Kronos trying to soothe me, just like it knew my panic was unfounded. I'd seen him kill the creatures. I'd seen the enhanced defenses around the house. And with the Nundars nearby, I truly had nothing to fear anymore. But I hadn't had a chance to process everything that had happened that night. After the attack, I'd first been delirious then sedated, only to wake up moments before being thrown in front of the hostile panel of the Conclave.

After watching the recording Kronos had played for the Conclave, I thought I'd gotten over the trauma. It had shaken me but not as brutally as it was now. On the video, it had felt almost like watching an action movie I'd just featured in a small part of.

But being back here, right where it had happened, truly made the reality of it sink in.

"I thought I was going to die. I could feel myself die all alone," I said between two sobs.

"But you didn't," Kronos whispered, tightening his embrace. "You are not alone. You are not going to die. The Nundars and I will never allow it."

"I'm sorry," I said, unable to stop myself crying.

"Don't be, my mate. It's okay. You had a traumatic experience. Let it out. You are safe with me."

And let it out I did.

It took me a moment to realize Kronos had taken me to our shared hygiene room instead of his bedroom. It was only once the sound of running water pierced through my foggy mind that it finally sunk in. As the large, recessed tub filled with warm water, Kronos tossed the blanket wrapped around me onto the floor and rid me of my panties before sitting me on the counter. He quickly stripped out of his own clothes before taking me back in his arms.

While water filled the tub, Kronos walked around the room while whispering comforting words and kissing the tears drenching my cheeks. Although it didn't take long, by the time he lowered us into the tub, my sobs had deescalated to sniffles. I felt drained, my entire body aching from having cried so hard.

Kronos settled me in his lap. I buried my face in his neck, surrounded by the warmth of his strong body, and of the bubbling water submerging us up to my shoulders. For the next eternity, he hummed a peaceful melody I didn't know, the vibrations of his chest and his *bakaan* lulling me into a sense of bone-deep well-being.

My head still resting on his shoulder, I looked up at his beautiful profile, moments after he stopped humming. "I'm glad Kayog found you for me," I whispered.

He smiled and lowered his head to look at me with a tender

expression. "I'm glad he shamed me into stopping my idiocy, because I'm glad I married you."

A silly smile stretched my lips. "I intend to make you fall in love with me, you know that?"

"I'm counting on it," he said before gently kissing my lips.

When he broke the kiss, I lifted a hand to caress his cheek, but Kronos caught my wrist and frowned as he stared at my pruned fingers.

"Let's finish washing up and get you out of the water before you're wrinkled to oblivion," Kronos said with false severity.

"Okay," I breathed out.

I made to reach for the soap, but Kronos playfully slapped my wrist. He spent the next few minutes washing me, his touch tender but devoid of lust. He made me feel utterly cared for, almost cherished. He dried me and brushed my hair before thankfully carrying me back to his room. I didn't think I would have had another mental breakdown had he taken me to my own room, but I wasn't ready for that just yet.

He didn't bother putting clothes on either of us and carefully placed me in his bed before joining me. I came willingly when he drew me into his embrace.

"Sleep, my mate. You are safe."

As I closed my eyes, snuggling deeply against his strong body, a single thought replayed in my mind. Yes, I was glad Kayog had found my soulmate for me.

CHAPTER 14
KRONOS

A fluttering sensation drew me out of my slumber. Although instantly alert, I kept my eyes closed as my mate's dainty fingers traced the contours of the piercing in my left nipple. She carefully shifted not to wake me as she lifted her head from my chest. Her hand glided over to my right nipple, and she once more played with its piercing. The pad of her index finger followed the ring of my areola. I repressed a smile when the wet tip of her tongue replaced her finger.

My abdominal muscles involuntarily contracted. Malaya froze. Despite my eyes still being closed, I felt her lifting her head to look at my face. With a great deal of effort, I managed to maintain a relaxed expression on my face, as if I were still asleep. Apparently fooled, my female resumed her naughty endeavor, giving my nipple one last lick before she carefully pulled down the blanket covering us.

She got it as far down as the middle of my thighs before giving up. As my left wing trapped a part of the blanket, she wouldn't be able to get it unstuck without shifting me. For the briefest moment, I considered pretending to conveniently move in my sleep at that time but decided against it not to give myself away too soon.

Malaya was naturally curious about my body. The first time —although I should say times—we'd made love, I hadn't given her much chance to explore. Beyond the fact that I'd been too focused on pleasuring her while evaluating her responses to my touch, I'd also been too busy gorging on my woman's emotions to let her have her way with me.

She traced the grooves of my abdominal muscles, lingering for a second on my navel. I didn't have a piercing there but couldn't deny feeling tempted to add one since seeing hers. Assuming everything went as planned with us taking down Wuras, I might just do it then. After all, piercings were trophies marking our major achievements.

The delicious flame of arousal sparked low in my belly when Malaya's wandering hand traveled further south. She was still only using her fingertips to draw the dark scales and spikes on the top and sides of my cock. Even though there was nothing sexual to the way she was touching me, blood was quickly rushing to my groin.

"Molesting me in my sleep?" I asked, my voice made deeper from freshly waking.

Malaya gasped and yanked her hand away before looking back at me. I plastered a neutral expression on my face, eager to see what she would do. The initial guilt of having been caught in the act vanished almost instantly on my mate's face, replaced by an unrepentant expression.

"While I can see why you would interpret it that way, I actually wasn't molesting you," she said boldly.

I raised an eyebrow. "You touched and licked my nipples, caressed my chest and stomach, and just now were fondling my cock. If that isn't molestation, I don't know what is."

Her eyes widened, and her cheeks reddened as she realized

I'd been awake longer than she thought. To my delight, rather than cowering, she doubled down in her lack of remorse.

"I did all of the above, but it's not molestation. It's exploration. As I have not been given the opportunity to get a proper look at my husband so far, I decided to seize it. You can call it educational research," she said shamelessly.

"Educational, is it?" I asked, amused.

"Mmhmm. But clearly, *you* are in need of some education. As you do not seem to know the difference between research and molestation, it is my duty to rectify that," she said, batting her eyelashes with an exaggerated innocent look.

"Do tell!" I replied with a chuckle.

"See, when I licked and touched your nipples like this, it was research," Malaya said.

She teased my left nipple by slightly brushing her index finger over the nub and touched my right nipple with the tip of her tongue, like one would carefully taste something they were not sure they would like.

"See? Short, sweet, and educational…" Malaya said, looking at me as if I was a particularly difficult student. "Now, for the molestation version…"

My stomach fluttered in anticipation as my mate lowered her head over my chest. Obviously, I knew the difference between the two. And yet, I wasn't quite prepared for the bolt of lust that exploded between my thighs when her mouth closed around my nipple. Malaya didn't play around, and immediately began sucking on it while she rubbed her palm on the other nipple. In between suctions, she would run her tongue over my areola and flick its tip on my piercing. Simultaneously, she would pinch and tweak the other nipple, her ministrations resonating directly in my cock.

I never noticed when my hand found its way through the soft strands of her long hair to keep her in place. Malaya suddenly gave me a sharp nip. I took a hissy breath, and my abdominal muscles contracted in response.

She lifted her head to smile smugly at me.

"Should I continue the demonstration?" she asked in a teasing tone.

"Educate me, my mate," I whispered, my entire body tense and hungry for more of her touch.

Malaya smiled and immediately resumed caressing my body. A part of me almost regretted she didn't resume sucking on my nipples. They were quite erogenous for me. But the bold way she caressed my chest and stomach while her mouth traced a blazing trail downwards had a different, even more sensitive part of my body aching for attention.

As she teased my navel and nipped at it, the heavy weight of anticipation settled on my chest, making my breathing deeper and more labored. The timid flame of arousal in my stomach swelled into a roaring brazier as her lips continued their journey towards my pelvis. Her blunt nails raking the scales on the side of my left thigh sent a shiver coursing through me.

Kneeling next to me, Malaya leaned down to get a closer look at my crotch. With the greater distance, my fingers slipped out of her hair and down the slender curve of her back. I took another hissing breath when she boldly covered my cock with her palm, rubbing it over its length. She finally closed her hand around it, my girth too great for her fingers to touch. But that didn't stop her from giving it a good squeeze.

A strangled moan escaped me when she started stroking me while maintaining a firm grip around my cock. It gave my *xinnix* —the small spikes lining the sides of my length—the perfect stimulation. Each of them, five on each side, didn't just provide additional sensations to our mates, they also procured the male with the same type of pleasure a clitoris did for a woman. Each friction sent electric pulses through my loins, fanning the fire burning in my veins.

Malaya bowed lower and, holding my cock straight, she gave the upper side one long lick, from the base to the tip, tearing another moan out of me. She repeated the motion a few times, then started tracing the scales and piercings on my cock with the tip of her tongue, driving me mad with need. When the inferno of her mouth closed around the tip of my cock at long last, I threw my head back and fisted the blanket with my left hand as intense pleasure surged through me. My stomach contracted some more from the lava swirling within as my woman bobbed greedily over me.

Tharmok's blood, that was good!

My right hand, still caressing Malaya's back journeyed down to the plump cheek of her behind, giving it a good squeeze, before venturing between her thighs. My fingers found her slit already soaking with her essence. A shiver shook her gorgeous body when I grazed her clit.

As was my wont when I became increasingly aroused, the tip of my tongue peeked out with a will of its own and started rubbing the central bump of my upper lip, right below my cupid's bow. Except, it wasn't my lip I wanted to lick, but my mate's delectable ones. The memory of how delicious she tasted as my tongue had dipped in and out of her on our first night made my mouth water.

Unable to resist, I leaned sideways and lifted her rump. Malaya gasped around my cock, the exquisite vibration almost wresting an orgasm out of me. I growled while tightening my pelvic muscles to rein myself in. My mate let go of my cock and slapped her palms on the mattress so she wouldn't faceplant. But even as she was turning to look at me in outrage, she realized what I was doing as I pulled her leg over me and on the other side of my face.

She didn't resist—not that I would have given her the choice —and got into a comfortable position before her mouth dived back on my cock. I wrapped my arms around her lower back, bringing her pelvis down closer to my face, and my tongue darted through her opening. A tremor coursed through Malaya as my tongue sank deep inside her.

The tart taste of her essence exploded on my taste buds while the intoxicating scent of her musk filled my nose, making me ache with need. My tongue couldn't get deep enough inside my woman. Tharmok's teeth, I wanted to devour her whole. At the same time, I was fighting the urge to thrust upward into her mouth as she continued to suck my cock. Each time she grazed my *xinnix* with her teeth, my spine seized, and my loins burned with the need to release my seed.

As her moans began to fill my ears, and her legs started trembling around my face, I realized my woman would soon climax. I accelerated the movement of my tongue dipping in and out of her, and pressed two fingers to her clit, rubbing feverishly. In seconds, Malaya cried out with my cock still inside her mouth. The vibration had me roaring in turn.

Although I refused to climax just yet, something broke inside me. Holding Malaya's thighs up, I partially sat up and flapped my wings backwards twice to pull out from under her. She fell face down against the mattress, but with my hands still holding her rump up. I had meant to go slow and be gentle with her, especially considering the ordeal she'd just gone through over the past few days. But I made the mistake of tasting her emotions while she was still riding her climax.

Something wild and rabid took over me as the divine taste of her emotions struck me like the purest form of liquid lust shot directly through my veins. Kneeling behind her, I slammed myself home in one powerful thrust. Malaya cried out, the sound muffled by the mattress pressed against her face. The taste of her pleasure-pain clawed my skin raw with bliss. For a split second, I feared I would spill within a couple of thrusts from the insane sensation overload I derived from my female.

I should stop gorging on her emotions, but I couldn't. Even if it killed me, I wanted all of her. I *needed* all of her. Although erratic at first, my movements gradually steadied as I started taking Malaya harder, faster, and deeper. Having partially recovered, my woman pushed herself up on her palms and was now rocking back and forth, meeting me thrust for thrust while an endless stream of moans tumbled out of her. They mixed with my grunts and growls both from the physical euphoria of her wet sheath caressing and squeezing my length in its tight grip, and the rapturous energy of her emotions seeping into me, filling me with raw power that had each of my nerve endings on edge.

I'd been so drunk with pleasure, Malaya's next orgasm took me by surprise. The emotional blast that crashed through me nearly had me come undone, wresting a few drops of my seed before I managed to rein myself in. My mate collapsed on the bed while she flew on the wings of bliss. But that wouldn't do. I slipped an arm in front of her and pulled her back up. With her back pressed against my chest, I resumed pounding into her from behind.

Tharmok take me! The searing heat of her skin against mine felt divine. I never wanted to let go. My hands roamed all over her body and fondled her breasts. While my lips kissed and sucked on the tender flesh of her neck, my tail snuck around her front to flick her clit. My fangs ached to sink into her flesh and bind her forever to me. Such a powerful urge made no sense. Despite Kayog claiming Malaya was my soulmate—and even if I also believed it—I still barely knew her. It was too soon. And yet, even now as she flew high, my mate's soul was trying to reach for mine to complete a bond not yet possible.

Once she began coming down from her high, I pulled her off and laid her down on the bed. She looked breathtaking with her hair disheveled, her face flushed, her lips swollen, and her eyes so darkened by passion they almost seemed black. And all this was for me. This woman was mine. All mine.

I spread her legs wide and buried myself deep inside her

welcoming heat. I swallowed her moan in a ravenous kiss, my loins ablaze with the need to fill her with my seed. Malaya clawed at my back, her hands then sliding down to my ass, her nails digging into my skin as she writhed beneath me, wanting all I had to give. She was fucking perfect. Made for me.

And I had not even used my *bakaan* to drive her mad with lust and pleasure.

For a split second, I considered invoking it, but chose not to. Her soul was shining like a thousand suns, her light so bright its heat could burn me to cinders. And it was glowing like this for me, not my powers or any other artifice.

Just me…

Electric sparks coursed through my body as I gave myself over to the divine pleasure of being one with the other half of my soul. Malaya's strangled moans and the urgent way she chanted my name announced her imminent climax. I gorged on the tsunami of emotions pouring out of my woman, pleasure too much to bear tearing me from the inside out.

Malaya suddenly seized in my arms, her mouth forming a silent O as her climax slammed into her. Her inner walls clamping down violently over my cock sent me over the edge. A blinding light exploded before my eyes. I threw my head back as I roared my release. It felt as if lightning had struck my spine, its electric tendrils coursing outward throughout my body and all the way down the tips of my wings and of my tail. I slammed myself deep within my woman as my seed shot out in fiery spurts, while lightning sparks continued to wreck me from the inside out.

I collapsed on top of my mate, and forced myself to roll off to the side, drawing her into my embrace. The room spun, and spasms shook me from head to toe, while Malaya's feverish skin trembled against me. By the gods, this woman would be the death of me. And what a wonderful death that would be.

Malaya snuggled against me, and I tightened my embrace. I would never let her go. She was mine, now and always.

I spent the next few days reinforcing the defenses around my playground, as per my father's request, and the following week trying to gather information from my fellow Wardens. While some of them also had a few stories of shady sentences, things weren't going well. All the inmates given a questionable sentence by Wuras and who had landed in a Dark Quadrant had conveniently died shortly after their arrival. Despite their best efforts, Malaya and Maeve failed to find any connection to shady activity between those inmates and Wuras that could have provided a lead to follow.

The other inmates he had sentenced to any Dark Quadrant were all hardened criminals with a rap sheet the size of a mountain. Their sentence had been well-deserved and wouldn't serve us. We desperately needed to find something that would stick. But time was speeding by with us making little to no progress.

Guilt gnawed at me as I entered Malaya's room and peered at her beautiful profile. Sitting at her computer, shoulders slouching in defeat, my woman was staring at her screen with a crestfallen expression. It had taken her a couple of days to work up the courage to come back to her room to work. I had offered for her to take a different room in the house to set specifically as her office, but she'd declined. First, she didn't need that much room for it, and second, she refused to be cowed out of her own room by that vicious incident. It would be like handing Wuras a second victory over her.

While it had further increased my admiration and affection for my mate, it had also reminded me of my failure to protect her that first time. And here I was failing again by not finding anything to support her case... *our* case.

"Bad news?" I asked, crouching next to her chair.

She turned to look at me and gave me a brave smile that utterly failed to hide her distress. "Things are not good, Kronos. And I don't know what else to do."

The distress in her voice clawed at my heart. I picked her up and carried her to the edge of her bed. I sat down before settling her in my lap.

"Talk to me," I said gently.

Malaya heaved a sigh before resting her head on my shoulder. I wrapped one arm around her, and she took my other hand in both of hers. She stared at it without really seeing it, her fingers absentmindedly caressing mine.

"Wuras outplayed me," she said in a defeated voice. "He's had nearly a month since my arrest to cover his tracks. And I gave him the means to do just that on a silver platter."

"What do you mean?"

"Maeve has pulled up every last one of his old and new records and gone through them with a fine-tooth comb. They account for everything in a legitimate fashion. Wuras used my files to whip up legal explanations for every single one of my accusations."

"But they are forged," I argued.

Malaya shrugged. "We know they are, but we can't prove it. He has a bunch of miraculous new receipts dating back months if not years to justify everything. Maeve looked into those other companies, going as deep as she legally could, even toeing that line, but still came up empty. Some of those companies had a distant link with the Komoro and Fingram cartels, but their business was all clean. We're fucked."

My heart sank. While I didn't doubt Malaya had spoken the truth about her initial investigation, for the first time I wondered if maybe she had misinterpreted what she had found back then. How could Wuras have so thoroughly forged a solid alibi for *everything* without one of the most—if not *the* most—talented hacker the Enforcers possessed managing to find anything that could stick? After all, Maeve and her husband Helio had achieved the impossible task of tracking down Saydi and uncovering her flesh-trading and drug trafficking operation. Without them, I'd still be a slave.

Naturally, I didn't mention those misgivings to her. Not only would it serve no purpose, but my mate also needed my support right now, not to be undermined by my doubts. But something had to give. We only had a little over two weeks left to present our evidence to the Conclave, and what we had so far would be deemed weak at best. I didn't care about what would happen to me, but I couldn't allow my choices to cause the fall of my House… of my father's House. And worse still, I couldn't bear the thought of what would befall my mate. If they tried to take her from me, I would undoubtedly commit murder.

"At least, we still have all those wrongful accusations and condemnations," Malaya said, as if in response to my somber thoughts. "That should help our cause, right?"

The hopeful way in which she asked that last question hurt my heart. As an Obosian male, my duty as husband was to fill my mate's life with comfort, joy, and pleasure. I never lied and wouldn't start today. So it killed me to have to drive home our stark reality.

"They will help remove Wuras from the bench," I said carefully, my thumb gently caressing the side of her arm. "But unless we can prove he personally gained from those incarcerations— be it by eliminating the competition or getting some kind of commission for it—the Conclave will have no choice but to only question his ability to serve his functions. They will blame it all on gannath or a burn out. They will slap him on the wrist, and either put him under supervision for a few years or take away his gavel altogether."

"And what will that mean for your House?" she asked in a worried voice.

"My House will still be held accountable for slander and defamation. We must link him to corruption in one way or another," I said gently, hating how she flinched upon hearing my words.

Malaya's eyes flicked from side to side as she pondered furiously. "What about the guards? All the ones whose names Torgal provided in that list? Any of them agree to speak as to why they hate him?"

"Amreth is handling it. He will hold a party at his estate next week," I explained. "Ideally, we would hold it here, but it would draw too much suspicion, and many people would likely decline. Wardens frequently hold gatherings. No one will question Amreth doing it, since he was due anyway. He has invited them all. Hopefully, we'll be able to talk there."

"Okay, that's great," she said, relief audible in her voice.

I didn't tell her that I held little hope from that either. Those guards undoubtedly *wanted* to talk but likely wouldn't unless we could reassure them that we had enough other evidence to nail Wuras. Most guards were commoners or belonged to humble families. If this whole mess could threaten to bring down a House as illustrious and wealthy as mine, they would be stupid to risk their own families without guarantee of success.

I didn't know where else to look or what stone had been left unturned, but I had a week to find it. Whatever it took, I couldn't fail my mate.

"I'm going to dig more into Komoro and Fingram," Malaya said. "Since we reached a dead-end with Wuras himself, maybe the cartels will reveal something we haven't thought of yet."

"That's a good idea. I will—"

The emergency signal going off on my com interrupted me. My heart skipped a beat as I removed my arm around Malaya to look at the interface of my bracer, fearing the potential attack my father had mentioned on my playground had finally occurred.

To my shock, it wasn't the security system warning of an

intruder or of something nefarious happening, but an urgent call from the leader of my Dark Quadrant. I frowned, wondering what in Tharmok's name Morgir could possibly want from me. Had one of the inmates died, he would have simply said so. Instead, he'd written:

"Must speak in person."

"What is it?" Malaya asked, her voice laced with worry.

I gave her a reassuring smile and gently caressed her hair. "One of the Q4 inmates requests an audience with me," I said nonchalantly. "I'm guessing one of them tried to escape and got himself mangled beyond what their medical pod can handle. I must go see what they want. Hopefully, it won't take too long."

"It had better not!" she said with false severity. "We're having lechon tonight. The meat has been marinating for two days, and the Nundars are threatening to throw me off the railing if I show my face again around the spit. They've kicked me out of cooking my own dish, the little bullies."

I burst out laughing at her overly dramatic but playful pout. Our Nundars adored her and had grown quite fascinated with learning more about Filipino recipes as well as other human dishes. They'd been getting quite creative finding local meats and produce to match those from Earth.

"The Nundars are the sweetest beings in the galaxy. If any bullying is taking place, I bet it's coming from you," I said teasingly. "But I will not meddle in any kitchen fights. So long as we have banana-cue for dessert, we're good."

Malaya snorted. "You know, I never would have pegged you for having a sweet tooth. You were so damn grumpy the first time I met you, I figured you were into burn-your-tongue-and-stomach-spicy and hello-acid-reflux-vinegary foods."

I chuckled and rubbed my nose against hers. "You have

many more things to discover about me my mate. But that will have to wait until I return."

I gave her a passionate kiss to which she responded with equal heat. With much reluctance, I broke the kiss and let her slide off my lap.

"Try not to miss me too much," I taunted, before blasting my *bakaan* at her.

Malaya gasped, her legs tightly closing shut, and her skin erupting in goosebumps. Her face took on such a lascivious expression, I instantly went hard. By the way she squeezed her breasts with both hands, I already knew her nipples had pebbled and were aching. I stopped my *bakaan* seconds later. The tension that had stiffened her body relented, but the damage was done. The delicious scent of her arousal tickled my nose.

"You little shit," she whispered, while giving me a murderous look.

"Oops, I only meant to soothe you before I departed," I said with the least sincere apologetic look. "But that's your fault for feeding me so well. I no longer control the strength of my power." Her outraged look only made me grin further. "See you soon, my darling."

As I turned around to leave, I ran my tail up her leg and used the tip to give a little poke to the apex of her thighs. Peering at her over my shoulder, I burst out laughing when she growled in frustration and attempted to slap my tail. I yanked it away just in time and ran out of her room onto the terrace when she chased after me. I took flight spinning around mid-air to blow her a kiss.

CHAPTER 15
KRONOS

A silly smile played on my lips as I flew over the forest. Since she'd come into my life, Malaya had made me discover a playful side of me I never knew existed. I shouldn't have teased her like that. Unless she gave herself some relief, my mate would be hot and bothered for a while. And I couldn't even feel sorry for it. I loved knowing she was aroused because of something I'd done. I loved even more the thought that right this instant, she was possibly lying on her bed, rubbing her clit and pinching her nipples while thinking of the things I would have done to her had I not been forced to leave.

All the things I WILL do to her tonight when we go to bed...

I adjusted my pants to release the pressure I created for myself with my own silly games. Malaya would make me pay for this later tonight, and I couldn't wait. It scared me how obsessed I'd become with her. I just thanked the gods that, although she'd overcome the trauma of staying in her room, my woman still came to my bed every night. In truth, her room only ever served as her office and closet. Which suited me just fine.

Tharmok's blood, I was falling hard for my mate.

We had played naughty a couple of times in her bed, mostly

from me disturbing her in the middle of her work. So that box was checked. We still had many rooms and surfaces to get wild on. I just needed Malaya to shed some of her inhibitions. While she was open to pretty much any kink, she remained overly worried about the Nundars walking in on us. If she only knew what Nundars bore witness to once Obosians went into their first heat between the ages of seventeen and twenty-one, she would stop fretting.

Before that age, an Obosian's libido was basically non-existent. But once we went into heat, if you didn't want to get dragged into a wild and unbridled orgy, you had better steer clear. Obosian teens in heat were literally put together in a massive room to engage in a crazy sex marathon that lasted at least a couple of weeks, up to a month for the more dedicated people. Everyone banged everyone, pausing only out of exhaustion or if a Nundar dragged you to the side to force you to hydrate, feed, or rest.

It was usually during that time that young Nundars decided which Obosian House they would want to serve. After they'd tasted your energy when you were in your most vulnerable and uncontrolled state, they knew whether they wanted to live by your side for the rest of their lives.

And now, it was Malaya who I wanted to taste my primal energy and to gaze upon my soul in my most vulnerable state. I didn't need to finish our trial period to know I would bond with her. We just needed this mess to be done and over with so that I could take her on our bonding flight.

If she accepts me...

I dismissed that thought even as it popped into my head. However cocky as I could be at times, I felt with a bone-deep certainty that Malaya was also falling for me. It was omnipresent in the way she talked to me, looked at me, touched me, and curled up against me like I was her safe haven.

A part of me wanted to turn around and go right back to my

mate, if only to bask once more in the divine glow of her soul. But that had to wait.

Morgir better have a good reason for bothering me.

Like most Q4 inmates, the Raithean had a very long sentence. The thirty years, in his case, were well-deserved. He'd been neck deep in drug trafficking, although his role had mostly been that of a cleaner. If you needed someone to disappear, be it quietly, painfully, or spectacularly, he had you covered. I'd met few people with such a taste for sadism.

When he first landed in my playground, I'd expected him to either slaughter all the other inmates or for them to take him out quickly out of self-preservation. While there had undeniably been some casualties, I'd been shocked to see him instate some semblance of order in this chaos, which also provided a form of safety for the others.

They were still too unruly to properly exploit the resources in the Quadrant, but their quality of life had noticeably improved since Morgir's arrival. It had nothing to do with any type of altruism on his part. The Raithean simply enjoyed his comforts. And he could only achieve it by raising the level for everyone else.

As I began my descent towards the clearing where their dwelling had been erected, I shifted my vision to assess the threat level. Unlike Quadrants One and Two where trouble was mild to non-existent, the Dark Quadrant always had some level of threat. Unfortunately, our ability to see souls didn't reveal intentions as clearly as a Temern's empathic abilities. At least five of the fifteen inmates gathered around the square in front of the dwelling displayed notable aggression.

The problem was that I couldn't tell if it was aimed at me or one of the other prisoners. Only once in their midst would I know for sure. At least, their aggression levels didn't speak of imminent attack, but I would need to keep a close eye on them in case that evolved into something of greater concern. For their sake, I hoped they would behave.

When I told Malaya earlier that I was having a hard time controlling the strength of my powers since she'd been over-feeding me, I'd only been partially joking. If I didn't rein myself in, I could turn an inmate into ashes with a single blast of my *lumiak*. Furthermore, since that first attack against Malaya, I now systematically carried a staff with me. If trouble came my way, it would find me ready.

A quick glance at the scanner on my bracer confirmed the position of the other twelve inmates not gathered around the square. I landed not too far from their dwelling, its stone wall to my back to avoid anyone sneaking up on me. My gaze roamed over the prisoners while assessing potential threats. It paused for a second on Saydi—the wretched Nazhral female who had temporarily enslaved me. She was curled up at the foot of a large tree. Bald spots now marred her previously lustrous ivory fur streaked with gold. In some of them, a puckered scar could be seen.

The hatred her mere sight previously used to stir in me didn't come. I didn't feel pity for her at finding her broken and scarred, her deceptively youthful appearance and beauty now a thing of the past. I was many things, but not that altruistic. However, as much as I had wanted to see her suffer and pay for what she had done to me and to her other victims, seeing her attempting to assert her authority here only to be savagely put back in her place opened my eyes.

Anger may make you wish for terrible things to happen to those who wronged you, but allowing yourself to start deriving pleasure from other people's suffering will change you into something... someone that you're not. She had hurt me once by taking away my freedom.

I wouldn't let her hurt me further by taking away my morality and sense of self. I didn't need to fuel her suffering or bask in it. She had been sentenced and was serving her time. Abusing my power over her out of revenge would make me a monster like her. Saydi didn't deserve my thoughts or energy. Karma was settling scores with her.

I shifted my gaze to the shallow stream of water where Morgir had been soaking. The amphibian male rose from the water by pushing himself up on the eight long tentacles below his torso. He twisted two sets of three tentacles into a makeshift version of legs, the remaining two tentacles dangling on his sides as he marched in an eerie fashion towards me. It wasn't uncommon for Raitheans to use this unusual method of walking, especially on rough or sandy surfaces that otherwise irritated the undersides of their tentacles. As they also tasted with their suction cups, who really wanted to lick the ground as they walked?

Morgir stopped at a non-threatening distance from me, a smug smile on his face as he leveled his dark eyes at me. He wiped the water trickling down the shorter tentacle-like appendages that served as hair for his species, before crossing his muscular arms over his broad chest.

"I'm here, Raithean. What do you want?" I asked as sole greeting.

"We've seen the news, limited though they are in this fancy place," Morgir replied with a taunting edge in his voice. "It seems like things are getting a little heated for you."

I narrowed my eyes at him. Inmates had extremely limited access to the outside world. Each Quadrant had a vidscreen on which they could watch intergalactic news and a vetted number of popular series and movies. Productive Quadrants like the first and the second had spent part of their income buying a second vidscreen and broadening the selection of shows and channels they had access to. Unfortunately, Vargos's main news channel featured among the default ones every Quadrant received.

Over the past week, reporters had extensively covered our

appearance before the Conclave, and the fact that I'd married a convict 'stolen' from a fellow Warden. Not a single word had been mentioned regarding our accusations about Wuras's corruption, only our questioning his suitability as a judge. I didn't doubt for a moment that Wuras had been fueling this propaganda to discredit our efforts to prove his corruption. With the proper narrative, he could easily recover from temporary misjudgment in the trials he oversaw. By undermining me, he got the popular opinion on his side while making potential witnesses wary of being associated with me.

"It's merely a little squabble," I said nonchalantly.

He frowned, his mocking expression giving way to a sterner one. He performed the double-blink typical of his species, first with his regular eyelids, then with the horizontal ones from his nictitating membrane.

"That little 'squabble' as you so nicely put it could cost you your Sector," he said in a harsher tone.

How in Tharmok's name does he know that?

Granted, the news had questioned my suitability as a Warden for marrying a convict that I had supposedly stolen from a colleague. But they had also mentioned ad nauseam that I likely suffered from PTSD due to my recent abduction. Morgir should have assumed that I'd only be temporarily relieved of my functions while undergoing some therapy to get my head straight. This was too big of a leap to merely be coincidental.

"Why, Morgir, you almost sound like you're afraid to lose me. I am touched," I taunted, waiting for him to show his hand.

He dismissively waved it instead. "Not at all, Warden. I'm merely seizing an opportunity."

My brow shot up, my curiosity genuinely piqued. "Oh? And what opportunity would that be?"

"I have a deal for you that you just can't refuse," Morgir said with a calculating glimmer in his obsidian eyes.

I snorted. "Do you, now? Do tell. I'm all ears."

He gestured at their dwelling with his head. "Nights on Molvi can get quite cold, while days can become scalding hot. But we've been quite comfortable over the past couple of weeks thanks to your sudden generosity when it comes to power. As we've taken quite a liking to that, we feel it should become a permanent thing. We want full charges like this on a regular basis in exchange for some invaluable information."

I burst out laughing. "My dear Morgir, it seems like you've gotten your head smashed once too often by your fellow inmates. Either that, or you're suffering from an acute case of dehydration."

"I can give you irrefutable evidence to take down Wuras and his entire House," he hissed.

His words struck me hard. It took all my willpower not to show how much they had affected me. Until I got a better sense of what he actually had, I couldn't let him guess how desperate we were for any edge against the judge.

"That's quite the boast," I said mockingly. "But whatever makes you think I need your information or that I even want to take his House down to begin with?"

"Let's not play games, Warden. If you had the evidence you needed, you would have nailed him already rather than allowing your father's and your mate's names to get dragged through the mud," Morgir said in a harsh tone, a sliver of cruelty slipping into his voice to add salt to the wound. "You're scrambling for proof, and I bet you're running out of time. We may be locked up here and cut off from most of the world, we still get some juicy information."

"And just how juicy is that information? All I'm hearing is a lot of boasting with very little substance," I retorted with a bored expression.

"Wuras got his hands on the file your human put together on him. By now, I can guarantee you he's covered his ass against all those allegations. Anything she had on him, it's been countered, and it's foolproof. You *will* lose against him. Unless I help you, that is," he added with a shit-eating grin. "But for that, you'll need to pay up. The price is unlimited power supply, all the time, for the remaining twenty years of my sentence. And I want your solemn word on that."

Once again, each of his words struck me like a dagger in the chest. But even as it freaked me out that he should know so much, an impossible hope also blossomed in my heart. I just needed to play my hand very carefully not to get screwed over. You couldn't trust a convict, least of all one in a Dark Quadrant.

"Even assuming I needed—or simply even wanted—what you have to offer, no amount of information you possess would justify such an insane demand. I would *never* grant you that," I said matter-of-factly.

"Fine," Morgir said, flicking one of his hair tentacles over his shoulder with annoyance. "Then make me a counteroffer."

I huffed. "A counteroffer on what? You've said a lot of words, none of it with much substance. Maybe what you have to say is not worth it."

"I assure you it is, Warden. Read my aura," Morgir added in a pressing tone.

When I merely stared at him in a way that made it clear I was about to walk away, the Raithean showed the first crack in his cocky demeanor. I desperately wanted whatever information he possessed—and I genuinely believed he did have something valuable to offer without needing to check his soul. But I needed to negotiate from a position of strength to get all the goods. If I caved in too quickly, he'd skimp on the information and save useful things for later so that he could extort more out of me.

Judging by the number of inmates who were standing here bearing witness, Morgir had likely boasted that he had me by the balls, and he'd whip me into granting them major improvements to their living conditions. If the deal fell through, it would significantly undermine his authority. And that was my leverage. Even though I was calling his bluff, I didn't actually want for him to get toppled. Despite being a foul individual, Morgir had brought a semblance of stability to this Quadrant that I would like maintained for the foreseeable future.

"Look, what I can give you will bring down the judge's entire House. I worked for Wuras for ten years. I know where all the skeletons are buried and every single one of their secrets. Make me a good offer, and you won't regret it."

Once more, I clamped down on my growing excitement. There had been nothing in his file indicating a potential connection to Wuras. Then again, we hadn't delved too deeply into his case as there had been abundant cause for him to get the sentence he received. Over his decades of sitting as a judge, Wuras had passed too many sentences for us to go through every single one that didn't have some kind of obvious red flag.

"Ten years, really? You've been here a while. Why do you want to talk now?" I challenged.

"For revenge, of course," Morgir said as if it was self-evident. "The reason I'm here is because that *mazzath* sacrificed me when a deal went sour, and he almost got caught. I was asked to play along, to take the fall. With Wuras presiding over my trial, he'd take good care of me."

I nodded slowly. "Instead, you got thirty years in Q4 with no opportunities to get even."

"Until now…" Morgir said with malicious glee. "When he turned on me, I swore I would find a way to get him. But speaking up before now would have served no purpose. Who would have believed any accusation I may have laid at his feet?"

I pursed my lips and nodded again. "Fair. No one would have even bothered looking into your allegations. But now you have me curious. Your Quadrant has three small crystals. With your group's weak production, you rarely manage to fill two of them, sometimes even just one. Therefore, if your information is good, I pledge to fully fill one crystal for free, for one year."

Morgir recoiled, a look of outrage descending over his features. "Don't fucking insult me!"

I opened my mouth to reply when I felt a shift in a soul to my left, the sliminess typically emitted by someone on the verge of performing a contemptible act. I jerked my head left, my eyes locking menacingly with those of a human named Bramull.

"Don't even think about it, Bramull," I said in a frosty voice. "I promise you won't like what will happen."

Morgir hissed at the human. He raised the two tentacles dangling from his sides in front of him and pointed the bottom suction cups at the man. Bramull paled and took a step back. Raitheans possessed a number of natural offensive traits that would wreck his fragile human constitution. Their suction cups didn't only serve to taste or allow for adherence on various surfaces to propel them forward, but they could shoot needle thin darts and acid. Uncoated with acid, the darts would cause symptoms similar to malaria for a few hours or a few days, depending on the victim. But when coated with acid, they would also liquify you from within.

"Piss off, you *mazzath*, before *I* deal with you," Morgir hissed at Bramull. "And I promise you that we won't waste energy firing up the medical pod to fix your sorry ass."

Bramull withered and took a few more steps back before sitting on the ground to indicate he would behave. I snorted and shook my head at the human's stupidity. Did he think the others would have joined him in attacking me out of frustration that I wasn't giving in to their outrageous demands?

"I believe you were about to make me a better offer," Morgir said, reclaiming my attention.

I chuckled. "Actually, I wasn't."

"Three full crystals for five years," Morgir countered.

"*One* small crystal for *one* year," I repeated, this time making it clear I wouldn't budge. "If your information is good, I'll bump it up."

Morgir huffed in annoyance. He shifted on his unnatural legs, visibly torn. I had to tread carefully before he called the whole thing off.

"You know, Warden, you're playing hard ball, but without my info, your House is going down."

I lifted my chin and held his gaze unwaveringly. "Assuming you're right and my House goes down, Wuras will get this Sector as compensation. As your Warden, I pay you market wages for what you produce instead of the minimum wages most other Wardens pay. I also give you double the basic energy required by law because I find the default is too low and adds unnecessary hardship—not to say cruelty—to the lives of the inmates. You think Wuras will do the same? And when he learns you're still alive and bitter over how he screwed you over, what do you think will happen?"

This time, I clearly hit a nerve. Morgir hesitated, unsure how to proceed. I couldn't allow him to revert back to his outrageous demands and decided to press my advantage.

"Look, you know I'm honorable. Give me something good and, on my honor, I will bonify it and make it worth your while. You have my word," I said in a firm tone.

Morgir clenched his teeth and finally gave me a stiff nod. "Fine, and may your gods curse you and your House if you break your oath. You're looking at the wrong target. Don't waste your time going after the Judge. Daran Wuras is just a front. Go after his father. Brenor Wuras is the head of Komoro."

"WHAT?!"

This time, I utterly failed to hide my shock and disbelief, not that I even tried to. Of all the bombs the Raithean could have dropped, I never could have foreseen that one. But if it was true…

"You're not finding anything, because Brenor has set up all his illegal accounts under his grandmothers' maiden names. The laboratory where he produces the drugs is located right under everyone's noses. It is in the basement of his wine bottling vineyard on Vargos."

I felt faint, stunned by the magnitude of his revelations. A quick glance at his soul revealed no deception. He believed every last word he'd spoken. No wonder we'd been unable to find anything truly incriminating for Wuras.

Morgir retrieved a holographic card from the waterproof belt around his waist and tossed it my way.

"This card contains the list of all his main customers, the banks and managers that handle his accounts, and the main subsidiaries that launder his money. And since I'm feeling generous, here's a little bonus for you," Morgir continued. "If Cilaug Laktar still lives, you will want to talk to him. He can tell you the location of all the warehouses as well as the name and schedule of all the shipping vessels."

"Cilaug Laktar?" I echoed, memorizing the name.

"He got sacrificed, too," Morgir said bitterly. "Last I heard, he got life in Q4. I don't know in which Sector. But if you find him, please say hello for me. So you see, this is worth a lot more than one measly year. I'll expect a proper bonification of the offer. And once everything I just said checks out, you might want to throw in an extra bonus and bring my buddy over here. I could use smarter company than this riff-raff I'm stuck with," he added, casting a disdainful look at the other inmates observing us.

"If this checks out, then yes, this information will be worth way more than one year. I'll keep you informed. You have my word," I said in a neutral voice, proud that the excitement bubbling inside me didn't show.

"Warden," Morgir said as a farewell.

Without another word, I flapped my wings and flew back to my mate in all haste. The tide had finally turned.

CHAPTER 16
MALAYA

The information Kronos brought back from his visit to Morgir blew up our case. What I had found about Judge Daran Wuras was less than the tip of the iceberg. That son of a bitch had not been the mastermind I'd believe him to be. He'd been nothing more than a fixer… and a disappointment to his father. That five-million-credit deal that went sour with Jasper, Rihanna's ex-boyfriend? That had been a side deal Judge Wuras had attempted to pull off to prove to his dad he had the talent to take over the family business. No wonder he'd been so bitter after getting conned that he had lashed out at anyone even remotely linked to Jasper.

Lord Brenor Wuras, one of the wealthiest and most influential patriarchs on Vargos, was held in high regard by his people and the intergalactic trade community. While he had his hands in multiple businesses, from public transportation to fashion, to gastronomic dining, and a chain of luxury hotels, Brenor Wuras was better known for growing his family vineyard into the biggest name where fine wine was concerned.

If trying to take down Judge Wuras had looked like an

impossible feat, merely thinking of going after his father was suicide.

And yet...

Right now, I could kiss that Raithean, tentacles and all. Had he just pointed us to Wuras, we couldn't have done much, least of all in a timely fashion. Providing us with the name of his banks had been a first step, but it would still have been like searching for a needle in a haystack. His giving us the clue that the accounts were under the names of his grandmothers turned it all around. He had indeed used the last names of both his maternal and paternal grandmothers to form the name Ginak Vokoth. Never in a million years would we have made an association with him as the Obosians were a hardcore patriarchy. A female's birth name pretty much vanished the minute she married.

Kronos was able to find Cilaug Laktar, another Raithean condemned for life in a Q4. He had landed in Dakon's playground. Although he'd gotten pretty banged up during his stay in the toughest Quadrant of Molvi, Cilaug had survived the ordeal. In exchange for the promise of some comfort items, he'd been more than happy to reveal every secret he held about Wuras's father. He knew everything, from the location of every warehouse to the access codes to enter them, the names of the transport ships and their captains, and even the detailed delivery schedules.

With this massive influx of information, we went to work. Even with Maeve's help, it took a week just to identify all the bank accounts, link them irrefutably with Brenor Wuras, and highlight the main fraudulent transactions and money laundering methods for each. The Enforcers tracked every single vessel Cilaug had identified and confirmed they were indeed performing the deliveries according to the scheduled rotations the Raithean inmate had outlined.

Maeve was literally having orgasms rampaging through all

these files. To my dismay, Kronos and I ended up getting partially benched through it all. It turned into such a massive case with the illegal drugs being delivered to multiple planet members of the UPO that the Enforcer essentially took it over. Obviously, we were kept in the loop—to some extent—so that we could put together a strong enough case for the Conclave. But even that got affected.

The Enforcers were putting together a huge sting operation. As it involved multiple planets and space stations, each with their own laws and jurisdictions, obtaining warrants became a massive undertaking. As they would only have a single go at this, they couldn't muck it up. They wanted every single warehouse hit at the same time, as well as the production and refinery facilities.

The biggest challenge turned out to be getting a warrant for the Wuras vineyard. The request should have been posted on the roster of cases in the court where Judge Wuras worked. Saying the Conclave was unhappy to bend the rules for the Enforcers to obtain that warrant was the understatement of the millennium.

For fear their operation might get leaked, we weren't allowed to attend the party Amreth organized or even speak to the guards and clerks who hated Wuras. Whatever information they had to provide paled in comparison with the treasure trove Morgir's revelations had given us. While I understood their logic, I had conflicting feelings about it. A part of me had dreaded the potentially nasty way people would have greeted us, especially me, at that party. To the Obosians, I was still a convicted murderer. But the extrovert in me could have really used some social interactions.

Until my conviction was overturned and my record expunged, I wasn't allowed to leave this Sector. Technically, I wasn't allowed to leave the Quadrant I'd been assigned to. Kronos had mentioned the actual existence of a shopping mall, complete with movie theater, restaurants, dance clubs, spas, and everything else I could dream of. As quite a few Wardens had spouses and offspring living with them here, they even had schools here up to a teenager's senior years. For university and specialty education, students usually returned to Vargos to pursue more advanced studies.

That meant I had a lot of free time on my hands and nowhere to go. As Kronos's Sector didn't exactly scream touristic area, there would be no picnics by the river or stroll in the woods involved. I still remembered all too well the nasty critter in the water that had eviscerated the first Faernych and bitten the tail off the second one. But our home was a tourist haven in itself. And Kronos did make time for us to have romantic picnics in the interior garden, or swim in the insane pool that circled more than half of the house, with water pouring in from our own private waterfall.

Although the Nundars insisted on cooking gastronomic dishes for us every day, they 'allowed' me to cook in my own kitchen from time to time, showing great eagerness in learning the recipes I liked, whether Filipino or otherwise. These little guys had seriously grown on me. Obviously, their saving my life had played a non-negligible part in this, but they had this peaceful and joyous aura about them that instantly put me in a happy place just being in their presence.

However, the fact that they didn't have individual names still messed with my mind. Beyond the fact that both males and females looked alike—I'd literally have to lift their robes for their naughty bits to tell me which gender they were—they acted with a sort of hive mind. Their mind speech always 'sounded' the same, even though it wasn't exactly a voice speaking.

Since Kronos had told me they liked keeping to themselves and felt uncomfortable feeling other people's energy, I made it a point not to pester them. To my surprise, they were the ones seeking my company from time to time. It took me far too long to realize that they would conveniently show up at the times when my isolation started weighing on me, usually when Kronos was off tending to his Quadrants. They would come hum for me with those haunting voices of theirs—the only times I would ever hear an actual vocal sound from them. Other times, they would perform 'magical' tricks which would qualify more as acrobatic tricks balancing objects in the air using their kinetic powers.

The one time they truly got me bawling was the day they showed up with long sticks sculpted to resemble bamboo. Four Nundars took position, each of them placing their bamboo poles on the floor, while another Nundar brought me a set of folding fans, before clasping silver anklets with chiming bells on both my legs. My throat tightened with emotion as I opened the fans and five other Nundars started playing the music to a singkil dance. I had mentioned in passing to Kronos that I used to perform this cultural dance of my people.

As it required people to move the bamboo sticks on the floor in a rhythmic fashion while the dancer navigated skillfully in between them while avoiding getting her ankles bashed by the poles getting knocked together, I obviously couldn't perform it anymore.

Until the Nundars volunteered for it...

It was hilarious having one of those little familiars play the role of the prince in this courtship dance. And yet, the Nundar showed impressive dexterity, effortlessly weaving through the moving poles on his hooved feet. To my shock, halfway through our performance, Kronos flew in and shooed off the Nundar before taking his place. Discovering my husband had secretly learned the dance wrecked me.

Naturally, I properly thanked him later that night.

I was slowly but surely falling in love with my husband. Wuras remained the only dark cloud in our otherwise perfect sky. As he obviously wouldn't be able to leave Molvi, since his job required him to physically remain here, I'd been looking at how I could lead a fulfilling life here. And the three weeks that followed Morgir's revelations allowed me to practice just that.

Despite my frustration at being cast out of my own investigation, I found solace writing an epic article about this entire mess. I couldn't wait to publish it once Wuras—father and son—had been arrested and indicted. Heck, I'd probably end up writing a full book to cover every insane detail, from how such a respectable family turned to crime only to become one of the most powerful drug cartels in this sector of the galaxy. I wanted to know how they managed to build such an empire under everyone's noses for so many years without ever being caught. The stories of the inmates themselves and the blackmailed guards would make for just as compelling tales, both for my book but maybe even for a documentary or vidscreen series.

One week after we'd initially been set to face the Conclave again, the Enforcers raided Komoro's warehouses, boarded their transport ships, and descended on House Wuras's vineyard.

They never saw it coming.

It killed me that I hadn't been allowed to witness any of it firsthand. But Maeve was gracious enough to send us footage from her body cam and from some of her colleagues as well. Seeing Wuras—father and son—rage as they were being arrested was orgasmic in and of itself, especially in the case of Daran Wuras who had been presiding over a hearing when they came to drag him right out of the courthouse.

Only then was I allowed to leave Molvi, but solely to return to Vargos and face the Conclave. Initially, it should have been for us to present our evidence against the Judge, after which they would have reevaluated my case. But thanks to the overwhelming evidence presented by the Enforcers, our presence there was merely a formality.

Or so I thought.

Throughout the journey back to the Obosian homeworld, I mentally prepared for the fact that I would likely have to wear that wretched convict uniform again. At least, I was taking heart in the fact that it would be for the very last time. However, after we docked, a single guard came to fetch us, no shackles, no uniform. I was further shocked to realize we hadn't docked at one of the heavily guarded accesses to the chamber, but the same low security one through which we had left the first time.

I beamed at Kronos as he took my hand to lead me out of the ship. This constituted yet another positive sign this nightmare would soon be behind us. I walked the relatively short distance to the chamber, where another guard allowed us in. We entered by the side door through which we had left last time. Finding the side benches totally empty but for Lord Aramon and a human male I recognized as Tedrick Wilson threw me for a loop. From my understanding, the previous crowd had been official reporters and record keepers.

Why is this happening behind closed doors?

Considering the Enforcers had pretty much taken over my investigation, it didn't shock me to see one of their senior officers present—although I would have loved to meet Maeve in person instead. Judging by the slight frown marring Kronos's brow, he felt just as confused as I was.

He glanced at his father who had, as always, that utterly unreadable expression laced with his usual I-can't-be-bothered-with-anyone's-bullshit edge. We never got a chance to join Lord Aramon and Tedrick on the benches.

"There you are," Elder Ozra said as soon as she saw us enter. "Warden Kronos Aramon, Convict Malaya Velasco, stand before us."

Utterly baffled, we both complied. Kronos escorted me to one of the two central marks on the ground. He gave me a reassuring smile and caressed my cheek before continuing a couple of meters farther to the next mark. Once he'd taken position, we both faced the Conclave.

"Warden Aramon, you are standing before this Conclave to

answer for the grievous accusations you had alleged against House Wuras. You were granted one month to gather irrefutable evidence to substantiate those allegations. We understand that you collaborated with the Enforcers. This resulted in raids performed by the Enforcers. Based on the illegal substances and accounts seized, as well as the incriminating bank records and other administrative documents recovered, this Conclave is satisfied that your allegations have been proven accurate."

I couldn't repress the silly grin that blossomed on my lips. Obviously, I'd already known this would be the case after the historic raid they had performed. But hearing it confirmed removed a massive weight off my shoulders. Beyond the fact that I wanted my name cleared and to regain my freedom, I had especially wanted to lift the threat hanging over Kronos's House.

"Considering the egregious nature of House Wuras's proven crimes, and the reputational harm your own House suffered because of it, the Conclave hereby confirms your soundness of mind, your competence, and your ability to continue to serve as a Warden of your House's Sector," Elder Ozra continued.

My grin further broadened, while Kronos puffed out his chest. It still pissed me off that taking it away from him could have even been a possibility. But it pleased me that they resolved this issue early on instead of allowing this sword of Damocles to hang over our heads for the weeks and maybe even months it would take to try both Daran and Brenor Wuras.

"As compensation for the cowardly and criminal attack perpetrated against your home and your mate, as well as the slanderous campaign run against you, your mate, and your House, the Conclave awards to House Aramon the vineyard and winery formerly held by House Wuras. You shall also receive five hundred grams of algarium to use as you see fit."

My jaw dropped, and my brain froze. Beyond the fact that this was an insanely generous damages award, it shouldn't be happening just yet. Damages were awarded at sentencing *after* the accused had been found guilty. While the evidence gathered during the raid was indeed irrefutable, both Daran and Brenor were still entitled to due process and a fair trial.

So why doesn't Kronos appear shocked or stunned by this turn of events?

A glance at his father and Tedrick confirmed they, too, didn't seem fazed in the least by what was happening.

"I thank the Conclave for your swift and decisive handling of House Wuras's unfortunate indiscretions, and for your tremendous generosity towards my House and me," Kronos said in a firm but deferent voice.

Seeming pleased by his response, Elder Ozra smiled, displaying a softer side of her I'd never seen before.

"It is well-deserved, Warden Aramon. You have done your House proud and proven your moral fortitude by taking a strong stance for justice, at great cost to yourself. We honor you."

Kronos pressed a palm to his chest and bowed his head in gratitude.

"You are excused, Warden."

Kronos nodded then headed towards the benches where his father and Tedrick sat, giving me a tender smile as he walked past me. I tried to smile back, but in my confusion, my face felt stiff.

"Convict Malaya Velasco," Elder Ozra called, reclaiming my attention. "You are standing before us to have your case and condemnation re-examined. In light of former Judge Daran Wuras's confirmed corruption and the evidence gathered both before and after your trial, this Conclave recognizes that you have been framed for a crime you didn't commit. Therefore, we have overturned your sentence, and your criminal record will be expunged."

I exhaled a shuddering breath. This nightmare was finally over. Although it still didn't make sense that it was happening so quickly, I welcomed regaining my freedom.

"For this illegal incarceration, for your pain and suffering, as well as exemplary damages, House Wuras has been condemned to pay you a sum of sixty-eight million credits, one million for each day you had to endure this ordeal since the murder you were falsely accused of."

I felt faint. Granted, I had expected some kind of damages, but this was obscene. What in the world did they want me to do with this many credits? But the Elder continuing to talk interrupted the plethora of questions battling each other in my confused mind.

"The sum will be transferred to your account by end-of-day, the amount deducted from the seized accounts from both Daran Wuras and Brenor Wuras," she concluded with a smile.

"While I am stunned and grateful for both having that wrongful condemnation revoked, and the extremely generous damages award you are granting me, I am quite confused," I said carefully.

"What are you confused about, Ms. Velasco?" Elder Ozra asked.

Although I noted how she had switched from calling me *Convict* Velasco to *Ms.* Velasco, it was the way her smile didn't reach her eyes that retained my attention. I instinctively understood that she didn't want me asking questions or making waves, which naturally made me even more curious. You could call that an occupational hazard.

"Damages are only awarded after the accused has been found guilty and sentenced. But the Wuras haven't been tried yet."

"Daran and Brenor Wuras have both been tried and condemned," Elder Ozra said in a much cooler tone. "As we speak, they are on their way to Warden Dakon Kothor's playground—which is what I believe they had intended for you."

"What? But... When? How?" I asked, reeling.

"Here and this morning," Elder Ozra said, visibly annoyed by the topic. "Considering the overwhelming evidence presented, they knew better than to bother any attempt at denying their culpability. Therefore, they confessed, sparing this body unnecessary wastes of time."

I opened and closed my mouth a few times, before casting a bewildered look at Kronos, his father, and Tedrick. All three men had the same unreadable expression plastered on their faces.

"How come it hasn't been announced? A case of this magnitude—"

"It will not be," Elder Ozra said in a tone that brooked no argument, interrupting me. The hard glint in her eyes sent a shiver down my spine. "Justice has been served. It does not require to be turned into a spectacle."

"What? But his crimes need to be exposed! The public needs to know what kind of—"

"Ms. Velasco," Elder Ozra interrupted in a frosty tone, "this is Vargos. You are married to an Obosian. Assuming you preserve that union—now that your conviction has been lifted— you will need to adapt to our ways."

"Which is what? Hiding the truth? Protecting criminals *if* they're Obosians?" I hissed.

"Daughter!" Lord Aramon interfered, a stern warning in his voice.

The tense looks on all three men at the bench doused my growing anger. I normally had better self-control, but this Conclave always got a rise out of me. Kronos shook his head in a subtle fashion to tell me not to make waves.

But this is such bullshit.

"Well, I guess it is your people's prerogative to handle things however you see fit," I said in a controlled voice.

"I'm glad you understand that," Elder Ozra said in a friend- lier tone—just barely. "Some things are better left untold."

"For Obosians, maybe. I'll just make sure to advise my publisher not to distribute my article and book on Vargos," I said with a shrug.

Elder Ozra narrowed her eyes at me while a few other Elders audibly gasped as they stared at me with outrage.

"The Conclave—and the Conclave *alone*—will be very interested to read your writings on this incident and other issues related to Obosian law and justice system."

"The Conclave *alone*?" I echoed, disbelief seeping into my voice. "I must be misunderstanding your meaning. Surely, you're not implying that I am *forbidden* from exercising my *legal* right to publish factual writings based on my research and experiences, as I have done throughout my investigative journalism career?"

"Elder Ozra!" Tedrick intervened before the Conclave leader could respond. "If I may be so bold, I request the permission to discuss this specific matter with Ms. Velasco, as well as the other topics we broached."

What the fuck is going on?!

To my shock, Elder Ozra seemed relieved by that request. "We appreciate your offer, Mr. Wilson. I am certain you are better suited to navigate cultural barriers that can impede communication. This will also allow us to turn our attention to the other serious matters on our docket."

"Thank you, Elder. I will make sure to follow-up with you and the Conclave," Tedrick said with a friendly smile.

"We look forward to it, Mr. Wilson," she said with as warm a tone before turning her glowing eyes towards me with a mysterious expression. "We're also looking forward to reading your writings, Ms. Velasco. So say we all."

"So say we all," the others replied before getting up and leaving, like they had done the first time.

Feeling like I'd just gotten bamboozled, I gaped at Tedrick with a 'what-the-fuck!' expression. He narrowed his eyes while taking a speculative expression as I marched towards them. They stepped away from the benches, meeting me halfway.

"It seems you have forgotten my *suggestion* that you

shouldn't be too arrogant with the Conclave, Daughter," Lord Aramon said before I could speak a single word.

Under different circumstances, I would have been touched by him referring to me as 'Daughter' for the second time. But I was too pissed.

"It would have been easier to remember if I'd not just gotten rolled in a big fat pile of bullshit," I ground through my teeth before casting a betrayed look at Kronos. "Did you know this was going to happen?"

"No," he said.

But the expression on his face screamed dishonesty.

"Did you just lie to me?!" I exclaimed, flabbergasted.

This time, his face hardened, and he gave me a stern look while holding my gaze unwaveringly.

"I don't lie. I did not *know* they were going to do this. But I cannot deny that I suspected something along those lines *could* happen," he added.

"Why? What the fuck happened to Obosians being all about the law and justice?!" I exclaimed.

"The law and justice were upheld," Lord Aramon replied in his son's stead. "The criminals were tried and convicted, and the victims compensated, were you not?"

"Okay, fine, but they are burying the story, sweeping it under the rug!" I exclaimed. "If I hadn't lucked out into being your son's soulmate, and had he not decided to give me a chance to prove I was indeed innocent, I'd be dead right now. Reporting these kinds of stories isn't about sensationalism—at least not for some of us—but it's about establishing a precedent. It's about making sure other people in a situation like the one I just faced know they can fight back. It's so that the next time an Obosian judge goes rogue, instead of systematically assuming the victim is lying, everyone will *know* there might be truth to it!"

"And that's where you come in," Tedrick said matter-of-factly.

"Yeah, by writing a fucking article, that they have *no right* to forbid me from publishing outside of Vargos," I exclaimed.

"From a legal standpoint, you are correct," Tedrick said. "But from a practical and realistic standpoint, should you try to release that article or book, it will be buried."

"They can't do that!"

"*They* won't be doing it," he said, his gaze boring into mine, making his underlying meaning clear.

"Oh, my God! *You...* the Enforcers would do it!" I whispered, stunned.

Tedrick nodded, his expression serious but not unfriendly. "Yes, we would."

"But why?" I asked with genuine confusion.

"Stability and trust," he said in a self-evident tone. He smiled at my baffled expression. "When it comes to the enforcement of law and justice, the Obosians are the standard of the galaxy. Their court system *and* Molvi are intergalactically revered institutions. Judge Wuras presided over some of the biggest criminal trials of this era. What do you think will happen if you publish this story? People aren't going to rise up against Wuras, but against both these institutions as a whole and *all* the sentences ever rendered by that court. We cannot allow that."

That hit a nerve. While I'd always considered myself a rational and analytical person, my own experience with this mess had severely damaged the image I once had of the Obosians as the embodiment of Justice. Easily influenced masses and conspiracy theorists would turn this into a circus of epic proportions.

"Trust me, Daughter, I share your frustration. My House's name, my son's name, and yours—my new daughter—were dragged through feces," Lord Aramon said. "Our business severely suffered from this, and it damaged many long-time friendships. I want nothing more than to repay House Wuras in kind. But in the greater scheme of things, personal grievances must take a backseat to stability and the greater good. And no, my son knew nothing of this. As the Patriarch of this House, such discussions are held with me. As my daughter-in-law, conversations involving you would also be handled with me first."

I remained quiet for a moment, weighing their words. As much as this burned my gut, I already knew myself defeated. As an investigative journalist, I'd encountered similar situations, usually scandals involving high-ranking political officials where part or all of the story had been buried to avoid popular revolt, civil wars, or the government getting toppled. While it had sucked not to be able to tell the tale, I'd understood the ramifications and actually agreed it was the best course of action.

So why am I so angry this time? It's no different.

Because it was *my* story. Because, this time, it was directly affecting me instead of me just being on the outside looking in.

"So, we sweep it under the rug," I said bitterly.

"No, actually, we don't," Tedrick said with a smug grin. "Notice how Elder Ozra said twice that the Conclave was looking forward to reading the 'article' you were planning to write?"

"Yeah. But that was to placate me," I replied dismissively.

"No. They genuinely want to read it," Tedrick said.

"Why?"

"Probably because you forced them to open their eyes, just like meeting you forced me to open mine," Kronos said in a soft voice. "Tedrick is right about the power of institutions. It's not just off-worlders who have raised my people on a pedestal when it comes to upholding justice. We have come to blindly believe in our own innate moral superiority. Last time we were here, when you asked the Conclave whatever happened to innocent until proven guilty, it struck a nerve—for them and for me."

"And me," Lord Aramon said. "You bring a perspective that all of us have lost. We are too biased by our own self-importance and self-worth to see our own flaws. Your moral values match ours, but you have the sufficient distance required to call out the shortcomings we've grown blind to. That Wuras was able to act unpunished for so long proves we've failed on multiple levels."

I licked my lips nervously and shifted on my feet, wondering if I was reading correctly what they were saying. "Okay… But… Concretely, what are we talking about?"

"That book you were thinking about?" Tedrick said. "The Conclave wants its equivalent, not in a novel format but as a detailed report. They want everything, from how it started, who was involved, who was victimized, and where the fail-safes should have been. They want you to investigate the fuck out of their criminal system *and* prison system, and to point out its weaknesses and shortcomings. As an officially sanctioned representative of the Conclave, you will have full access to any document, file, and account you deem relevant. Anyone you wish to speak to will *have* to grant you an honest audience."

By the smirk stretching Kronos's sexy lips, I was failing miserably at hiding the insane excitement bubbling inside me. Beyond the fact this was an incredible mandate, having free access to everything without being forced to bend over backwards and beg people for the slightest crumb was fucking orgasmic.

"Assuming I was interested in taking on that monumental task, why are you here? Why are the Enforcers involved?" I asked, trying to sound blasé about it all.

"*When* you take on this monumental task, you will have an insane amount of data to juggle, some extensive research that might be difficult for a civilian to access, even with a mandate from the Conclave. That's where we come in," he said with a cockiness that made me snort.

"Maeve?" I asked, giving myself away by the eagerness in my tone.

He smiled. "She was quite impressed with your work, and it

takes a lot to achieve that. Her status with the Enforcers has… evolved. Expect to receive a similar contract in the upcoming days."

"Wait, what?! I'm not an Enforcer!" I exclaimed, while Kronos narrowed his eyes at Tedrick.

"Neither is Maeve," Tedrick deadpanned.

"What? But…"

"She's a former Enforcer turned Bounty Hunter," Tedrick said, his gaze holding mine unwaveringly.

"Who just happens to… unofficially help out old friends," I said with sudden understanding.

An approving smile settled on his lips. "I like you, Malaya Velasco. That raid on Komoro never would have been possible without you turning the right stone, however improbable it was. I look forward to future collaborations with you."

Before I could respond, he turned to look at Kronos and his father.

"Lord Aramon, Warden," Tedrick said, nodding at each male in turn before walking out of the room.

I gaped at his receding back, my mind still reeling from what had just happened.

"An Enforcer and official reporter for the Conclave. You're not faring too badly, Daughter. We'll just need to work on that arrogance," Lord Aramon said with his usual grumpy and borderline haughty tone.

Before I could come up with some smart response, he gently caressed my cheek in a paternal fashion, his icy-blue eyes softening in a way I didn't think possible, giving me whiplash. He then turned to look at Kronos.

"Five hundred grams, huh?"

Kronos gave him a shit-eating grin. "Five hundred… I'm catching up to you."

Lord Aramon huffed, slapped the back of his son's shoulder, then also walked out of the room. Despite the billion thoughts battling for dominance in my mind, my dumb mouth latched onto that last comment.

"You're getting new piercings with all that algarium?" I asked, already picturing places he could fit a few more.

"*We* are," he said, his face taking on that lascivious expression that always had me weak in the knees.

"WE?!"

"Mmhmm," he said in a suggestive fashion, his gaze settling in an unequivocal fashion on my breasts. He chuckled when I gasped and grabbed my hand. "Let's go home, Enforcer."

CHAPTER 17
KRONOS

I landed in the square of Dakon's playground seconds after Zolran set down his shuttle. Each of my senses remained on high alert as my eyes flicked this way and that to assess any potential threat. I'd heard how savage his Sector was, but my own Dark Quadrant looked like a kindergarten in comparison. These prisoners were beyond foul.

As soon as my feet touched the ground, I summoned my *lumiak*, allowing its electric tendrils to coil over my hands to discourage any of the inmates lurking nearby from getting any weird ideas.

Unlike my Sector, there were no ranked Quadrants here. The entire Sector was merged into a single Quadrant. Therefore, there wasn't one Quadrant leader, but various gangs with their own leader fighting for dominance. A few free agents switched between gangs depending on the situation. And then you had pariahs and punching bags who either got killed early on, or barely survived at the edge. Daran and Brenor Wuras were such pariahs.

When the Conclave had condemned them to Dakon's Sector, I had assumed it would be an instant death sentence. But a week later, they were both still alive. Seeing them bruised and battered didn't stir the slightest sympathy or compassion in me. With Q4 inmates, they either quickly put you out of your misery, or made sure you suffered for a very long time. Considering many of the prisoners here had been sentenced by Judge Wuras, they would make sure to make him rue every day he survived this ordeal.

Thankfully, the reason for my visit to this wretched place came to me without me having to track him down.

"Warden Aramon!" Cilaug exclaimed with the type of enthusiasm one shows a long-lost friend. "I thought you had forgotten about me while you indulge in all that fancy wine your House inherited."

"I am a man of my word, Raithean," I said, mockingly.

"So, what deal have you obtained for me?" Cilaug asked. Although he tried to sound nonchalant, I didn't miss the hopeful spark in his eyes. "Since I figure the reduced sentence isn't happening, I'm assuming some nice little comfort item?"

"No sentence reduction and no comfort item either," I said in the same taunting tone.

His face fell, confusion setting in. "Then what's the deal?" he asked, a sliver of aggression seeping into his voice.

"I'm taking you on a short trip," I deadpanned.

He did that double blink with his nictitating membrane, his confusion deepening.

"Morgir misses you, and Warden Dakon has no particular use for you. So I guess you're moving to my Dark Quadrant," I said, trying to sound bored.

Shock, disbelief, then joy fleeted over his features in quick succession before he emitted a victorious shout that had me chuckling.

"Go fetch your belongings. You have five minutes," I said while Zolran got out of the shuttle with a pair of shackles.

"Anything of value, I keep on my person in this *mazzath* infested swamp," Cilaug said, making sure to make eye contact with a few of the other inmates nearby as he spat the word *mazzath*—which vaguely translated as son of a whore.

I gestured with my head for Zolran to shackle him to avoid any misbehavior during transport.

"I won't miss any of you bastards," Cilaug taunted, before turning his gaze to Daran and Brenor Wuras. "Well, except messing with you two rats. Remember that I helped get you here."

Brenor flapped his wings to approach us, only to hiss in pain and land in a less-than-elegant fashion moments later. While a few winged inmates got their wings clipped, the majority of them received an implant that sent electric discharges to their wing muscles the minute they attempted to fly at a height higher than two meters. The voltage increased with the distance above the limit and multiplied exponentially if they attempted to get past a specific threshold in the forest.

His pain and clumsy landing stirred mocking laughter from the other convicts.

"Take us as well, Warden," Brenor commanded, heedless of the mockery.

"Why in Tharmok's name would I take the likes of you?" I snarled, my voice dripping with contempt.

"We are Obosians and nobles like you," Brenor said.

"You are *nothing* like me, Wuras. You are a criminal, and a murderer. This is what you had planned for my wife, an innocent and righteous woman whose presence you're not even worthy to be in," I said. "It pleases me to no end to know that you will rot here and taste all that you had wished upon her."

Brenor continued to move towards me.

"That's far enough," I warned him.

Zolran, who had just finished clasping the shackles on Cilaug, cast a questioning look my way. I made a discreet gesture for him not to get involved.

"Take us or fucking kill us," Brenor demanded.

"I'll do neither," I said in an icy voice.

With an enraged war cry, Brenor charged me. The old fool didn't get farther than a couple of steps before my *lumiak* had him writhing on the floor. Did he truly think I couldn't control my powers enough not to give him a fatal discharge? But then, there was a reason House Wuras didn't possess a Sector despite being—formerly—a noble house and one of the wealthiest on Vargos. They didn't have Warriors in their bloodline and only Warriors could summon *lumiak*.

I gestured with my head for Zolran to take Cilaug aboard the shuttle, while observing Daran run to his father's side. He glared at me with hatred burning in his eyes.

"You call yourself just, then grant him peace! He could be your grand-sire and doesn't deserve to end his days in this pit of despair," Daran Wuras hissed.

"That vermin is nothing like my grand-sire. I am just, and therefore I uphold the law. And it requires both of you to serve the sentence you deserve. I will not help you get off easy with a quick death. But hey, if you want to put him out of his misery, go right ahead. When you stand before the gods, you'll be judged again. But this time, for patricide. Enjoy your stay, *Judge* Wuras. I'll give my wife your regards."

I took flight under his curses and the laughter of the other inmates. I raced Zolran's shuttle to my Dark Quadrant, reveling in the feel of the wind beneath my wings, against my skin, and flowing through my hair. A part of me almost empathized with the Wuras. I couldn't imagine having my wings clipped by an implant. They couldn't even try to remove it without killing themselves as the device was surgically inserted deeply inside the body near vital organs.

As I soared through the air and marveled at the beauty of this savage world, a single face kept flashing before my mind's eye. Soon, I'd be flying through Molvi's night sky with my mate in my arms, our bodies joined as one as I finalized the bond that would truly merge our souls. As much contempt as I felt for the Wuras, I owed them for bringing my heart to me.

I needed to get today's chores out of the way so that I could return to my Malaya.

Even before I began my descent in my Dark Quadrant's square, I could see the emotional surge from Morgir. Considering it had been a week since both Wuras males had been condemned, my silence had undoubtedly unnerved him. But it had taken a bit longer than expected to negotiate with Dakon as well as sorting out the crystal upgrade I would grant Morgir.

"Warden Aramon, I was starting to think you had reneged on our agreement," Morgir said in greeting, his displeasure audible.

A sliver of guilt coursed through me to the extent that the other inmates had likely given him a hard time once they started believing I'd conned him.

"I am a man of my word, Raithean. But certain things take a little longer to sort out than others," I said nonchalantly.

"Certain things like what?" he asked, his gaze shifting to Zoltan's shuttle landing near us before shifting back to me. "Since this isn't collection day, are we to understand you're bringing us some extra comforts?"

I shook my head. "I'm merely returning a little favor. You gave me a bonus. I'm giving you one back."

This time, his eyes widened with understanding and hesitant hope. When Zoltan lowered the ramp and opened the doors of the shuttle, the expression on the convict's face struck me hard. Morgir and Cilaug had no blood bonds, and yet they looked at each other like blood brothers who thought they'd never see each other again in this life. It disturbed me to see this… loving side of people I'd been trained my whole life to be considered as worthless, as less than rabid animals.

As soon as Zoltan freed Cilaug from his shackle, the Raithean ran down the ramp with his strange gait on his makeshift tentacle legs. Morgir met him halfway. They gave each other a manly hug, the tentacle-like appendages that served as hair intertwining with each other's in an embrace reserved between close friends and relatives among Raithean people.

"Well, looks like you got a little banged up," Morgir told Cilaug after releasing him.

Although he spoke the words mockingly, I didn't miss the underlying emotion in his voice.

"I just have the fearsome look that matches my intimidating personality now," Cilaug deadpanned with a smirk.

I snorted and shook my head. "You can rekindle your friendship later. For now, let us wrap our business."

"Indeed, Warden. I believe you're about to tell us how much energy we're entitled to," Morgir said, glancing smugly at the other inmates.

This, more than anything else, confirmed they had given him a hard time when I failed to make good on my promise in the first few days following Wuras's condemnation.

"I am. As your information proved invaluable, I am bonifying the initial offer, as promised. You're getting one free large crystal, completely filled," I said nonchalantly.

His eyes widened ever-so-slightly upon hearing I'd bumped the crystal from a small to a large, when he'd likely barely hoped for a medium.

"For how long?" Morgir asked, tension audible in his voice. "At least two years, right? I mean, a large crystal is a nice upgrade from the small one of your initial offer. But considering the magnitude of the raid we helped you achieve, two years seem fair."

I smiled, the sadist side of me enjoying watching him squirm with anticipation. "I've weighed the helpfulness of the information you provided and decided it warranted… five years."

"Five years?! You will give us a full large crystal for five years?" Morgir exclaimed, his voice buzzing with excitement.

I nodded. "Five years… each."

Both Raithean males froze, a similar shocked expression plastered on their faces while my words sank in.

"Five years, each?" Morgir said at last, pointing in turn at Cilaug then at himself. "Meaning you will fill our crystal for ten years?"

"You know how to count. There's hope for you yet," I said tauntingly. "Enjoy!"

I flapped my wings to return to my mate as the inmates roared with joy.

"WARDEN!" Morgir called out before I could get more than a few meters away.

Hovering in place, I turned to look at him questioningly.

"Any other trouble you got yourself into that might warrant… another little trade?" the Raithean asked.

I snorted. "My mate is always open to reliable tips that could lead to another worthy investigation. If you ever 'think' of something, make sure it's good."

"Then we'll talk again soon, Warden. We could use an extra ten years to get us covered until the end of my sentence," he said.

I laughed and flew back home.

EPILOGUE
MALAYA

Official Reporter of the Conclave *and* of the Enforcers… Of all the ways this adventure could have ended, I never would have guessed this one. What should have been a simple, cute story of second chances regarding Rihanna and her minotaur resulted in the biggest drug bust and cartel takedowns in history.

And got me a sexy husband and three new piercings…

I couldn't believe I'd allowed Kronos to sweet talk me into getting my nipples pierced on top of getting a helix ring in my right ear.

Now I wanted one in the left ear, too.

In the three months following my case getting expunged, my life had become quite a whirlwind of excitement. I loved my new jobs. My main focus was the thorough investigation and assessment of the Obosian justice and prison systems. However, I also discovered quite a few connecting dots between some of the cases I reviewed, which provided the Enforcers with new trails to follow to take down more criminal organizations. None of my tips had led to as massive a bust as the one against Komoro, but a victory remained a victory. And I had no doubt that there would be more spectacular arrests in the future.

While Vargos and Molvi would likely hog my entire time for the next couple of years, I intended to cast my net farther as my investigative focus had never just been murder and trafficking. I had won prizes for documentaries and articles about outrageous environmental abuse, the exploitation of vulnerable communities, violations of the Prime Directive, and other important topics that needed to be exposed. And now, with my access to Enforcer tools, the sky was the limit.

Having a supportive husband and in-laws made it all the greater. Hearing my grumpy father-in-law brag about his 'little human daughter' gave me all kinds of warm fuzzies. I still had yet to see him smile if only once, but I'd grown to recognize his 'happy' moods through the scowling. In direct contrast, his wife Valla was a little ray of sunshine. Whenever he would start recriminating about something, Valla would just pinch his lips shut between her thumb and index finger and say her piece.

The first time I witnessed it, I nearly had a stroke. Considering she was petite and rather delicate-looking compared to his massive size of mature Obosian Warrior, it felt like watching a mouse challenging a mammoth… who simply caved. He would glare and pout, but then melt like so much snow under the sun when she snuggled against him.

The couple had really grown on me. And I seized every opportunity to visit them whenever I traveled back to Vargos either as part of my investigative work, or to meet with the Conclave for an update. Heck, even Elder Ozra had grown on me.

Behind her stiff and sometimes haughty mannerisms, a profoundly righteous woman hid. She truly embodied the blind pursuit of justice. She took as a personal failure all the flaws I would point out in their system, even though none of it was her direct fault. But the swiftness and decisiveness with which she sought solutions for each of them—no looking for excuses or casting blame around—truly commanded respect. She certainly earned mine.

But that required a lot of traveling, which had been made a billion times easier thanks to my Enforcer Reporter status. Upon officially joining the force, Tedrick had given me a box of shadow stones, which opened portals to direct destinations as far away as the other end of the galaxy. Apparently, the husband of Maeve's best friend was a Shadow Lord, a draconic male with the power to bend space to his will and travel across dimensions.

Considering the ridiculous wealth I'd received as settlement, I'd bought tons of the super expensive shadow stones for personal use, allowing instant travel between here and Vargos. While the shopping malls and entertainment centers of Molvi mostly sufficed to sate my need for socializing, the shadow stones also provided more exotic romantic escapes for Kronos and me.

I'd fallen madly in love with my incubus.

Even though he was more of an introvert, he always made time for me and made sure I had everything I needed to thrive. Although he'd never said it in so many words, I believed he had fallen in love with me, too. He showed it in every way. It was completely silly of me, but I needed to hear those magical three little words. More importantly, I wanted him to officialize our union by bonding with me. I didn't really know all that it entitled, aside from him biting me with his fangs. It bothered me to no end that he hadn't brought it up again in months.

Granted, when he'd been asked the question by the Conclave, Kronos said he would wait until our trial period was over and that my condemnation had been overturned so that I would make that choice freely, not just to save my life. While the former was still five weeks away, the latter—and more important factor in my humble opinion—had long been resolved. Was he delaying because he wasn't quite ready for a lifetime commitment? Did he doubt my feelings for him?

Maybe I should make the first move instead of waiting for him to do so.

The sound of music outside startled me out of my musings. My stomach fluttered while a silly grin settled on my face. I pushed away from my computer desk and raced to my ridiculously huge walk-in closet. I stripped out of my clothes and donned an off-white crop tube top and matching swim skirt.

Kronos and I regularly enjoyed midnight swims—even though they took place when the sun had only just begun to set on the horizon—in the insane pool that circled around half the house. They usually ended in some naughty action right in the water and often finished in our bedroom. Technically, it was *his* bedroom, but I had yet to sleep once in my own. And the sound of music emanating from the main terrace was my cue to join him there.

I hurried down the hall to the main entrance. My mouth instantly watered at the scrumptious sight of my husband. Standing by the table a couple of meters from the pool, Kronos was pouring wine into two glasses. He was fully naked but for that short toga skirt draped around his waist. His long, silver-white hair swayed in the soft evening breeze, and his icy-blue eyes slightly glowed behind his thick eyelashes.

Fuck, my man looked fine!

His scales and horns gleamed under the dying light of the sun and the dancing flames of the braziers strategically placed around the pool. My gaze lowered to the navel piercing he'd gotten out of that algarium he'd received from the Conclave. While I had requested he get one there after he got me to get three extra piercings of my own, it didn't take me long to realize it hadn't been much of a concession on his part. Apparently, the very day we met, as soon as I walked out of the hygiene room in my wedding gown with my pierced navel exposed, he'd been itching to get one there as well.

As silly as it sounded, getting the piercings he had asked for and him getting the one I had requested had felt like exchanging engagement rings.

Kronos lifted his head as soon as the giant glass doors parted before me. The way he looked at me fucked with my head big time. There was no way he wasn't in love with me. Judging by the awe in his eyes as he peered at me, you'd think one of the Obosian goddesses had just appeared before him.

I sauntered towards him, regretting I'd put my crop tube top on. Kronos loooved my piercings. Every time I strutted my stuff in front of him, he'd get that lascivious look that got my girly bits perking up, and then he'd stick out that insane tongue of his and lick the tip of his upper lip in that way that had me instantly wet.

When I got closer, he extended a hand towards me. I took it and let him draw me into his embrace. God, it felt so good in his arms! His body was warm, his skin soft over the hard muscles beneath. And his wild scent always sufficed to get me hot and bothered. Although he'd never said as much, I was starting to think he possessed some kind of natural pheromones that acted as aphrodisiacs. He was a 'sex demon' after all.

Kronos immediately began to sway to the slow music. I slipped my arms around his neck and followed his lead. Obosian music had a tribal feel to it mixed with Latin flavors that I truly enjoyed. But I especially liked the way my husband's hips gyrated to the rhythm, rubbing his pelvis against mine in the most sinful fashion. Kronos was a fabulous dancer. After his amazing performance dancing Singkil with me, I'd started suspecting as much. But then, he seemed to have natural abilities with everything that involved physical skills.

"You are breathtaking, my mate," he whispered while leaning down to capture my lips in a kiss.

It was slow, tender, and possessive, making my toes curl. His slightly calloused hands roamed over my exposed skin as we continued to rock to the music. Before long, they slipped under my top and lifted it up. I didn't resist and raised my arms to let him rid me of it.

He didn't fondle my breast or even get frisky, content to embrace me again. I chuckled at the approving purr that rose from his throat in response to my bare chest against his. He reclaimed my mouth, his kiss taking on a more passionate edge, and his hands getting a little bolder.

My girly bits were definitely taking notice and complaining about his teasing. Kronos would caress my waist, his hand gliding up to the side of my breasts and his thumbs teasing their curves without ever getting close enough to my nipples or to even give each breast a proper fondling. Just when I was about to grab his hands and cover my breasts with his palms, the wretched man pulled away from me.

I gaped at him in outrage, ready to give him hell for teasing me. But whatever words I'd meant to say died in my throat. Kronos was staring at my pierced nipples with *that* look. Right on cue, his wicked tongue poked out, and he rubbed the tip on his upper lip twice, his gaze still locked on my left breast. I could have sworn I felt his tongue on my nipple. My inner walls contracted while my essence instantly drenched the slip of my swim skirt.

Kronos's tail rubbed against the side of my right ankle, then trailed a path up my leg in a gentle caress. Simultaneously, he raised a hand towards my left breast. But he held his hand sideways, half-closed, the way someone would in order to lift someone else's chin with their index finger. Except, he didn't lift anything. Instead, half a second before he reached my nipple, the electric tendrils of his *lumiak* sparked around his finger.

The energy barely brushed against the piercing in my nipple, and yet you'd think a nuclear bomb had gone off inside me.

Lightning coursed through me and ended its journey directly in my clit. I cried out, my knees giving under me while more of my essence gushed out. I would have collapsed if Kronos hadn't caught me.

I clung to him while trying to regain my bearings and to ignore the savage throbbing between my thighs. When applied at a very low level in specific erogenous places, *lumiak* could literally give you an almost instant orgasm. For this reason, Kronos had tried to convince me to get either a vertical or horizontal clitoral hood piercing, but I'd put my foot down on that one. While I'd read intriguing things about how either of those options could increase sexual pleasure, I wasn't ready to mess with that part of my anatomy, especially not before I'd had a few kids.

"Sorry. I couldn't help myself," Kronos said sheepishly, although his sincerity remained questionable. "You're just too tempting. Come, a sip of wine will help."

He led me on wobbly legs to the table a short distance from us and reached for a glass of wine. He handed it to me before taking the second one for himself. I squeezed my legs shut, rubbing them discreetly together to silence the achiness my wretched husband had deliberately provoked.

"You know I'm going to make you pay for this later, right?" I asked, still glaring at him.

He chuckled, his handsome face taking on a provocative expression. "As you like to say, my love, don't threaten me with a good time. I'll take that as an invitation to do it again."

My love?!

I couldn't recall him ever saying that before. He usually called me his mate. Occasionally my darling, and sometimes sweetling, but never my love. We also never just drank wine, unless it was with a meal.

I scrunched my face at him. "Instead of torturing me, how

about you tell me what's the special occasion? Why break out the fancy wine?"

His taunting smile faded, and the oddest expression flitted over his handsome features. It had been too brief for me to interpret, but I could almost have sworn it had been sadness or disappointment.

What the heck is going on?

"It's our anniversary, of course," Kronos said, matter-of-factly.

"Our anniversary?" I echoed, baffled.

"Today is the fourteenth. We married exactly five months ago, right over here," Kronos said, gesturing at the spot by the pool where Priestess Biondi married us.

My stomach dropped, and my cheeks burned. How the fuck did *he* remember that, and *I* didn't?

"Right! It's crazy how time flies," I exclaimed, feeling mortified.

"It does," he said, his expression unreadable.

"Happy anniversary to us, then!" I said with forced enthusiasm while raising my glass.

Kronos also raised his glass. We each took a sip, his intense gaze locked with mine the whole time, making me want to squirm.

"So, I guess only one month left before you're rid of me," I said with a nervous laugh in a clumsy effort to ease the odd tension that had surfaced out of nowhere.

Instead of the snort or huff I expected, Kronos's face closed off. He dropped his arm still wrapped around my waist, took a step back, and placed his still full glass on the table. My blood turned to ice at the sudden change of demeanor.

"Is that your plan, Malaya? You intend to divorce me as soon as our contractual obligations have been met?" he asked, his voice cold.

I recoiled. "No! Not at all!"

To my shock, his eyes went out of focus as he gazed at my soul to verify the veracity of my words. That stung.

"What happens at the end of our trial is entirely up to you," I said, my voice slightly clipped.

Kronos seemed genuinely taken aback. "Why entirely up to me? Either of us can request a dissolution at the end of the contract."

"A Prime Mating Agency marriage can be dissolved at any time, by either party," I corrected. "The compulsory six months are just meant to force the couple to give it a fair try. But if it really doesn't work, they can call it quits. The only penalty will be refunding the PMA and the UPO for whatever expenses they incurred to organize the wedding and relocate one of the two spouses to their new home."

"Yes, I'm aware of that," Kronos replied, sounding a bit confused as to what point I was trying to make.

"The only reason I *needed* to stay married to you was to avoid getting thrown in some Dark Quadrant. That stopped being the case months ago," I said as if it was self-evident. "With the crazy damages awarded to me, repaying the PMA and the UPO for getting me here to you is chump change. If I wanted to leave you, I would have done so months ago."

His eyes went out of focus again, and I growled in aggravation. I took a deep gulp from my wine and put the glass down on the table with a bit more force than necessary.

"You know, it's quite offensive that you keep checking if I'm lying," I snapped.

Of all the reactions he could have had, his skin darkening with embarrassment and his gorgeous face taking on a guilty and vulnerable expression was not what I had expected.

"I'm sorry. You're right. I didn't mean to offend you. It's just… I just need to be certain," he said in a hesitant voice.

"Certain of what?" I asked, confused, although my voice softened a little.

"That you want me. That you want us…"

That struck me like a boulder to the head. He blinked a few times quickly with embarrassment, then averted his eyes, as if he feared what he might see on my face in response to this admission. How the fuck did such a strong, confident, and cocky man suddenly become so insecure? How could he not see that he owned me?

"Of course, I want us," I said, flabbergasted. "Why else would I still be here? I don't need to be with you to work for the Conclave or the Enforcers. I'm here because I'm head over heels in love with your silly ass. I'm here because Kayog is always right. You're my soulmate. I can never love anyone else the way I love you."

Kronos gaped at me, then his eyes went out of focus again. Even though I suspected he'd done it instinctively, I still rolled my eyes.

"Seriously?!"

He visibly flinched, confirming my suspicions it hadn't been deliberate.

"You know what, if you need to play peeping Tom to get reassured, then have at it. Knock yourself out. Ogle away!" I said, throwing my hands up in annoyance.

"No, forgive me. It's just that I'm in love with you, too. And I've been aching to bond with you for weeks, but first I needed to be sure you felt the same about me," he said, with that same timid and vulnerable expression, while rubbing his nape.

I wanted to shake him to knock some sense into him, but I was too busy melting from the inside out. "You silly man. I can't see souls, and yet *I* believe *you*."

His face darkened some more with embarrassment. "You're right. But here is proof of the depth of my feelings for you. Obosians can only bond once in their lifetime. There is no divorce for us. Even death will not allow the survivor to form a new bond with someone else's soul. I want you to be the one and only for me. Bond with me, Malaya. Be mine and let me be yours forever."

Whatever annoyance I may have felt melted away as I took a couple of steps towards him and raised a hand to his chest. His palms immediately settled on my hips as he carefully drew me to him.

"I don't know," I said with a playful pout, while teasing his left nipple with my index finger. "There are undeniable upsides to spending the rest of my days with a sex demon. But do I really want to be stuck with all the strings attached to an official marriage?"

His hands tightened their grip on my hips and pressed my pelvis against his... and his quickly hardening shaft. "Beyond the fact that no other male will ever make you scream like I do—even without physically touching you—some of the perks of bonding with me will be getting your human life span doubled and retaining your youthful appearance for at least half a century more."

My eyes widened in surprise. "Really?!"

"Mmhmm," he said, leaning forward to rub his nose against mine.

"Well, when you put it that way, it does sound like there's more upsides than downsides to being shackled to you," I said teasingly.

He snorted.

I gave him a playful tap on the chest. "Of course, I want to bond with you, horny head. I love you... including that new piercing in your cock."

He burst out laughing. "So romantic, my love. You sure have a way with words."

I lifted my chin smugly and gave him a mischievous smile while caressing his shoulders. "I'm glad you noticed. It's not for nothing that I'm an award-winning journalist."

"Well, Award-Winning Lady Aramon, prepare to be bitten and to have that new piercing do a number on you."

"First, you need to catch me," I said, flicking his nipple piercing then tearing myself out of his embrace.

I ran the short distance to the pool and dove in, the sound of his laughter reaching me right before the water submerged me. He could have caught me long before I even moved a single step away from him. But Kronos had undeniable predator instincts. He loved a good chase. And I loved being hunted by him.

I swam a short distance underwater before coming up for air, surprised I hadn't heard the usual splash of him diving in after me, as we'd often done in the past. As soon as my head emerged, the sound of flapping wings explained it all. Before I could turn around, I felt his tail graze a path along my spine. I gasped, expecting him to yank me right out of the water, but Kronos kept flying past me, the strong wind created by the movement of his wings spraying water into my face.

Heart pounding with excitement, I watched him glide so close to the water, the hem of his short skirt hung barely a centimeter above it. The wretched garment sat just low enough and created just the right amount of shadows to keep me from getting a proper look at my husband's naughty bits. About fifteen meters away, Kronos straightened and turned around. He flapped his wings, hovering in place over the water, his pointed feet breaking the surface, and arms spread wide while *lumiak* crackled and sparked around his palms. He looked like Zeus himself, descended from Olympus come to ravish a foolish mortal.

And I was mesmerized.

I should be terrified by the electric energy swirling around his hands with my sorry butt deep in water. But I knew no harm would ever come to me from him. Even if Kronos used his *lumiak* on the water—which I doubted he would—it wouldn't be with anywhere near enough voltage to hurt me.

Seeing him flap his wings as he charged forward—his toes still disturbing the surface of the water—finally snapped me out of my dazed trance. With a yelp, I turned around, dove underwater and swam. I barely covered more than a meter or two before Kronos scooped me up this time. He slammed my back against his broad chest, and his left arm wrapped around my front, just below my chest, holding me in place. His other hand fisted my hair at the nape, yanking my head back.

My yelp turned into a loud scream as his *bakaan* blasted through me. Kronos hadn't attempted to ease me into it or give me one of the strong waves that usually just had me mad with lust. He slapped me with the nuclear option of instant-orgasm. As I shook against him, I felt a sharp sting in the crook of my neck—and realized he had bitten me. Seconds later, a far-from-pleasant burning sensation spread in my shoulder, down my arm and through my chest.

If not for the waves of bliss still coursing through me, I might be crying out in pain. It quickly became obvious that was exactly Kronos's plan—keeping me distracted from any discomfort whatever his fangs had injected into me would cause.

As my climax began to ebb, I felt my swim skirt slide down my legs and fall off, then Kronos's fingers settled on my clit. He frantically massaged it, making my inner walls clench with need to be filled after that first contactless orgasm. As if in response to that unspoken wish, his tail caressed a path up my leg, grazing my inner thigh before probing my opening. It, too, had received a barbell piercing from the algarium awarded by the Conclave. With Kronos getting me madly wet already, his tail slipped inside me effortlessly, grazing my sweet spot with supernatural accuracy with each stroke, the sensations enhanced by the piercing.

I was holding onto his forearms, my nails digging into his skin while Kronos continued to fly over the terrace. The cool feel of the wind against my damp skin contrasted sharply with the searing heat of my husband's chest against my back. His *bakaan*, still seeping into me—although at a much lower intensity—kept me on the edge, while his fingers and tail making love to me steadily brought me closer to inevitably toppling over. This maelstrom of blissful sensations buried the pain of the 'acid' coursing through my veins from his bite.

Through it all, Kronos covered me with kisses alongside my face, neck, and shoulder, interspersed with words of encouragement and love. My legs began to shake. Sensing my imminent climax, my man gave me one last push with a mild jolt of his *lumiak* directly on my clit. I cried out, and my eyes rolled to the back of my head while waves upon waves of bliss coursed through me.

Eyes closed as I gave myself over to pleasure, I felt us tumbling through the skies, gravity tugging then pushing at us, the wind singing in my ears as it whipped past us, its bite chilling against my feverish skin.

I vaguely felt Kronos's tail pull out of me and then him turning me around in his embrace so we would be chest to chest. His mouth reclaimed mine in a voracious, almost desperate kiss. I wrapped my arms around his neck, my fingers sinking into the softness of his long hair. On instinct, my legs also wrapped around his waist. Despite the lingering high of my second orgasm, I instantly felt hollow when my man's erect cock pressed against my stomach.

But Kronos was in no hurry.

Even as we continued to soar through the sky, so did he continue to kiss and caress me, as if he feared he might have missed a single inch of my skin. He bent me backward, his lips abandoning mine to trace a blazing trail down my neck and to my chest to indulge in one of his favorite treats: sucking my tits. Each lick and nip echoed directly in my clit, making me ache to have all of him inside me.

The wind carried away the sound of my sighs of delight and

needy moans. With a will of their own, my hands buried in his hair found their way to his lower set of horns. I latched onto them as I pressed my chest further against Kronos's mouth.

As with every time I grabbed his horns during sex, Kronos went berserk. It hadn't been planned or premeditated—this time. He jerked his head up. Fangs bared, his irises so constricted, the dark sclera appeared to fill his eyes, Kronos snarled at me. His menacing, almost feral expression sent a bolt of lust directly to my nether region while moisture all but gushed between my thighs.

Moving at lightning speed like a snake, Kronos buried his fangs in my neck again. At the same time, he impaled me on his cock with one powerful thrust. I cried out from the simultaneous burns. But where his first bite had felt like acid rushing through my vein, this one flooded me with liquid bliss. My skin tingled, and my blood boiled, pleasure almost impossible to bear crushing me. His thick cock, the soft spikes along its edges, and its three piercings as he pounded into me sent micro-orgasms coursing through each of my nerve endings.

My stomach lurched with that elevator feeling as we seemed to drop from the sky. But we could crash on the stone terrace, and I wouldn't care. All that mattered was my husband's hard body wrapped around me, his bonding fluids coursing through me, his fat cock wrecking me, and his lips devouring mine in a kiss filled with all the love and devotion he felt for me.

A blinding light exploded before my eyes in a climax like no other. Impossible pleasure swept me away as Kronos joined his voice to mine and his seed erupted inside me in burning spurts. But something was different. I could feel my pleasure *and* his. His love for me had become a physical entity that both filled me from within and wrapped around my body like a warm blanket on a cold winter night.

I embraced it.

In that instant, we weren't a male and a female coming

together in a moment of love and passion. We were truly the two halves of one soul reunited at last.

For the next eternity, Kronos flew us around Molvi's night sky, our bodies still intimately intertwined. Eyes closed, my face buried in his neck, I reveled in this deep communion with my husband. A part of me wished this moment would never end.

But it had to…

As Kronos began his descent, slowly gliding down in a spiraling pattern towards the main terrace, I tightened my embrace around him and snuggled deeper. His chest vibrated against mine as he tenderly chuckled.

When I finally felt him land, I lifted my head with much reluctance to look at him. I blinked, surprised by a blinding light similar to the one that heralded my ultimate climax. At first, now that darkness had fully claimed the night, I thought the glow-stones illuminating our terrace were the cause. Considering how long I'd kept my eyes closed, any source of light could be temporarily blinding. But then, I realized that this wonderful light didn't come from the side, but the source stood directly in front of me.

"You're glowing!" I whispered in awe. "You have a halo. It's… mesmerizing."

"It is my soul, my mate. A light that only you have ever seen and will ever see. My light is yours. *I* am yours until my last breath. I love you, Malaya."

"And all that I am, and ever will be, is yours, Kronos. I love you."

THE END

FAERNYCH

NUNDAR

NEVIANAAR

KRONOS & MALAYA

ALSO BY REGINE ABEL

THE VEREDIAN CHRONICLES
Escaping Fate
Blind Fate
Raising Amalia
Twist of Fate
Hands of Fate
Defying Fate

BRAXIANS
Anton's Grace
Ravik's Mercy
Krygor's Hope
Keran's Dawn

XIAN WARRIORS
Doom
Legion
Raven
Bane
Chaos
Varnog
Reaper
Wrath
Xenon
Nevrik
Rogue

PRIME MATING AGENCY
I Married A Lizardman
I Married A Naga
I Married A Birdman

ABOUT REGINE

USA Today bestselling author Regine Abel is a fantasy, paranormal and sci-fi junkie. Anything with a bit of magic, a touch of the unusual, and a lot of romance will have her jumping for joy. She loves creating hot alien warriors and no-nonsense, kick-ass heroines that evolve in fantastic new worlds while embarking on action-packed adventures filled with mystery and the twists you never saw coming.

Before devoting herself as a full-time writer, Regine had surrendered to her other passions: music and video games! After a decade working as a Sound Engineer in movie dubbing and live concerts, Regine became a professional Game Designer and Creative Director, a career that has led her from her home in Canada to the US and various countries in Europe and Asia.

Facebook

https://www.facebook.com/regine.abel.author/

Website

https://regineabel.com

Regine's Rebels Reader Group

https://www.facebook.com/groups/ReginesRebels/

Newsletter

http://smarturl.it/RA_Newsletter

Goodreads

http://smarturl.it/RA_Goodreads

Bookbub

https://www.bookbub.com/profile/regine-abel

Amazon

http://smarturl.it/AuthorAMS